Egypt and the Game of Terror

Other books by this author:

At the Heart of Terror, Rowman and Littlefield Publishers, Inc., 2004

The Politics of the Middle East, Thomson Wadsworth, 2007

Islamic Extremism, Rowman and Littlefield Publishers, Inc., 2008

Egypt and the Game of Terror

A Novel

Monte Palmer

iUniverse, Inc.
New York Lincoln Shanghai

Egypt and the Game of Terror

Copyright © 2007 by Monte Palmer

All rights reserved. No part of this book may be used or reproduced by any means, graphic, electronic, or mechanical, including photocopying, recording, taping or by any information storage retrieval system without the written permission of the publisher except in the case of brief quotations embodied in critical articles and reviews.

iUniverse books may be ordered through booksellers or by contacting:

iUniverse
2021 Pine Lake Road, Suite 100
Lincoln, NE 68512
www.iuniverse.com
1-800-Authors (1-800-288-4677)

Because of the dynamic nature of the Internet, any Web addresses or links contained in this book may have changed since publication and may no longer be valid.

This is a work of fiction. All of the characters, names, incidents, organizations, and dialogue in this novel are either the products of the author's imagination or are used fictitiously.

ISBN: 978-0-595-47538-4 (pbk)
ISBN: 978-0-595-91807-2 (ebk)

Printed in the United States of America

Preface

Egypt and the Game of Terror reflects more than thirty years of experience in working with culture and politics of the Middle East. It also reflects a desire to help others enjoy this most fascinating of regions and better understand the human failings of those who would play this most deadly of games. Perhaps it is also an effort to answer some nagging "what if" questions and to escape from the irritants of academia, not the least of which are useless jargon, interminable footnotes, and impenetrable prose. *Egypt and the Game of Terror* possesses neither footnotes nor academic jargon. You will have to be the judge of the prose.

More detailed insights on the game of terror can be found in *Islamic Extremism* (2008, Rowman and Littlefield) and the *Politics f the Middle East* (2007, Thomson/Wadsworth). Periodic updates on the Middle East and the game of terror and information on forthcoming novels in the Game of Terror series are provided on my website at www.monte.palmer.middle.east.googlepages.com. Comments and suggestions are appreciated.

Acknowledgments

I would like to express my special thanks to Princess Palmer, my wife, editor, and co-author of thirty years, for her indulgence and assistance in the preparation of this book. Needless to say, the book could not have been written without the goodwill and inspiration of friends and former colleagues of various countries and diverse persuasions. Discretion dictates that I avoid listing their names, but I thank them all. This said, I must stress that all characters in this novel are fictional. Any resemblance to individuals living or dead is purely coincidental.

Chapter 1

Life at the Embassy

The Jeep strained to reach the crest of the mountain rise, navigated a hairpin turn at its summit, and then prepared for the harrowing descent into the valley below. The road was little more that a rocky trail hewn in the side of a mountain in Egypt's Sinai Peninsula. A single crevice in its surface would be enough to send the vehicle careening to the desolate wastes below.

The driver, an Egyptian intelligence officer, paused for a moment surveying the stark panorama that unfolded before him. He then turned to his passengers, an Israeli and an American, and pointed to a crumbling monastery on an adjacent summit. "The monastery is a deserted shell," he said without emotion. "The jihadists use what's left of it as a communication center. They have a training base in the badlands beyond. We will destroy it when the time comes."

The American and the Israeli, also intelligence officers, noted the information. Neither understood the delay in destroying the jihadist base, but that was Egypt's call. The Minister of Interior, Egypt's strong man, was running the show. The visit had been arranged to convince his American and Israeli counterparts that he had the situation well under control.

The Jeep began its descent into the valley, made another hairpin turn, and then dissolved into flames. Its charred carcass disappeared into the ravine some 4,000 feet below. The wreckage was spotted by an Egyptian helicopter, but it would be days before the remains of the intelligence officers could be recovered.

The attack was known only to those persons privy to the most secret of intelligence reports.

*   *   *   *

When the report of the Sinai attack reached the desk of Jake Dryfield, the American Ambassador in Cairo, he summoned his senior political officers to his most elegant of offices. "I told you that the jihadists were rearming," he thundered, throwing the report of the attack on the table in front of them. He was angry, and well he should be. America's war on terror was going nowhere and had been quietly renamed the "long war." It would only be a matter of time before another major attack struck the United States. To make matters worse, America's allies in the Arab world were jumping ship, but none more so than the Egyptians. For reasons that Jake found difficult to grasp, they had declared a truce with the local jihadists.

"The President is mad as hell," Jake continued his tirade, "and all you people do is talk. I'm tired of all this diplomatic crap. I want action!" Jake Dryfield was a political appointee and made no effort to control either his anger or his profanity. A Texas oil man and former football player, he believed in straight talk and had little use for diplomatic niceties.

The Deputy Chief of Mission or DCM, the second in command at the American Embassy in Cairo, sat silently, avoiding eye contact with the Ambassador. "No need for another confrontation," the DCM mumbled to himself. "Things are bad enough as it is." It was his typical response to the Ambassador's tirades. This was his last tour of duty and his will to fight had given way to dreams of retirement.

Clark Smith, the senior political officer after the DCM, was less docile. A cultured and studious man in his mid-forties, he knew that an ambassadorship beckoned if he could make his mark in Egypt. "We are meeting with the Egyptians on a daily basis," Smith stood his ground. "The Minister of Interior has assured us that he has everything under control. He is just waiting for the right moment to strike. As you know sir, the situation is tense."

The Ambassador glowered at Smith with undisguised hostility. Words were unnecessary, but he spoke anyway. "It would seem that you are a more patient man than I, Mr. Smith. The Minister of Interior has been waiting for the right moment ever since I have been here, and that is more than a year now. In the meantime, the Egyptian President twiddles his thumbs while he sucks up money from Washington. When, precisely, do you expect the right moment to arrive?"

The Ambassador's voice was as soft as it was menacing. Smith would have preferred a barrage of profanity to the Ambassador's sarcasm. Anger explodes in tense situations, but soon passes. The Ambassador's sarcasm was laced with contempt and poisoned any hope of reconciliation. Smith didn't expect the Ambassador's friendship, but he did want his respect. It would be the Ambassador's evaluation that determined Smith's future, if there were to be a future.

"Your answer, Mr. Smith. We are waiting for your answer." The Ambassador's words jarred him from his thoughts and for a second he felt the same anguish that he had felt as a student when the headmaster had slammed the palm of his hand on Smith's desk and glowered, "Are you with us, Mr. Smith?"

"Yes, Mr. Ambassador," Smith responded tersely. "The Minister of Interior assured me yesterday that his men are taking up positions. Believe me, Mr. Ambassador, they fear the jihadists more than we do. It's the Arabs that are bearing the brunt of the terror."

"Then why don't the Egyptians cooperate with us if they are so damned scared?" stormed the Ambassador. "We could crush those bastards in a heartbeat if the Minister of Interior got off of his dead ass. If Egypt goes, the whole damn Middle East will blow up. It will make Iraq seem like child's play."

"They are nervous, Mr. Ambassador," responded Smith, choosing his words with care in the vain hope of keeping Jake's anger under control. "As you know, the Muslim extremists come in different varieties. The jihadists are crazed madmen who kill and maim in the name of Islam, but their numbers are few. At least for the moment, they are licking their wounds. The Muslim Brothers, by contrast, are more subtle. They have seen the masses recoil from the violence of the jihadists so they beguile them with illusions that an Islamic paradise that can be achieved by piety and prayer. It is their clinics and schools who care for the needs of the poor. One fair election and the Muslim Brotherhood will be the rulers of Egypt. The Minister of Interior is convinced that he can control the jihadists, but he needs more time to deal with the Muslim Brotherhood. The regime is fighting for its life, and the Minister of Interior has made a truce with the jihadists to give him some slack in dealing with the Muslim Brotherhood. When the time is ripe, he will crush them both in one massive assault. Blood will flow. In the meantime he takes our money and makes promises. I don't like it, but that is his plan. It's fragile, but Egypt is a fragile kind of place."

Smith had picked his words with care, but to no avail. The barrage of profanity had come anyway. "That's a bunch of bullshit," roared the Ambassador. "An Islamic state is an Islamic state. I don't give a damn how they get there. You and the rest of the assholes in this place are a bunch of liberal defeatists. You've been in the Middle East so long that you've fallen in love with the Arabs. It's you friggin' defeatists who are responsible for Iraq, Iran and the rest of the mess in the region. I'll tell you what we need. We need a military coup. Can't have another 9/11. Yes, by God," glowered the Ambassador, "that's the only solution. We need somebody who can kick ass. Send in the Military Attaché on your way out," he dismissed the DCM and Smith. "We'll get started on this right away."

Now in his mid-60's, the Ambassador prided himself on his personal friendship with the President. The President might have quibbled over the word friendship, but the Ambassador was a major fund raiser. The asking price for his service in the last election had been the State Department or a cushy ambassadorship in London or Paris, but the President had asked him to come to Egypt as a personal favor.

"I need you in Egypt," the President had said in a confidential tone. "Things are getting out of hand with the jihadists and I need somebody who can kick ass. Straighten out the 'Rabs and you will be in line for the top spot."

A wry smile played across the Ambassador's lips as he recalled the conversation. "I don't know shit about the Middle East," he thought to himself, "but I do know how to kick ass. These damn Arabs don't understand anything but force."

That, however, was more than a year ago, a long and tedious year of futile negotiations with the Egyptian government that had produced nothing but nods of understanding and assurances that things were getting better. But things hadn't gotten better, and the Ambassador had the sinking feeling that he was being played for a fool. He was but the last in a long line of foreigners to have that feeling, but that was little consolation. "Things are moving," he had written to the President a few months after his arrival. "They know that we mean business."

But that was months ago. Long months of "soon *ya kawaga*" (foreign master), "*insha'allah*" (if God wills) and bland smiles of syrupy politeness and nothing had moved. The Egyptian government had continued its truce with the jihadists and seemed oblivious to CIA reports that these most deadly of religious extremists were using the truce to rearm. Even more frightening were CIA reports of increased contacts between the Egyptian jihadists and the global jihadist networks in Europe and North America. It was just a matter of time until the global jihadists were ready to launch their final battle against the United States and its allies. What was a better starting place than Egypt with its thousands of unprotected Americans?

"No one plays Jake Dryfield for a fool and survives," the Ambassador had vowed at the time, but to no avail. He had screamed at the Minister of Interior and threatened the Egyptian President with a cut in foreign aid. He had even hinted that a change of regime might be in order although that far exceed his instructions. "Screw the instructions," Jake had said to himself, "I raise the money and I can say what I damn well please." More than a year had passed, and Jake had not kicked ass.

"That's the ticket," the Ambassador congratulated himself as he buzzed his secretary. "We'll put the military back in power. Enough of this pussy-footing around. Enough of this democracy crap. It's all a sham anyway."

"Get me the Secretary of State," he barked into the intercom. "Tell'em it's urgent. Get the asshole off the golf course if you have to." Everyone who Jake despised was an asshole, and that comprised most of humanity. Smith and the DCM headed the list.

The Secretary of State received the Ambassador's call with sympathy, explaining that Washington already maintained a list of friendly generals to be placed in power if the regime faltered. "Then why in the hell don't you act?" asked the Ambassador bluntly. "Are you waiting for hell to freeze over?" Unlike career ambassadors, Jake Dryfield was not afraid of the Secretary of State. In his mind, he should have been the Secretary of State. Then he would have kicked ass.

"Be patient, Jake," said the Secretary, anxious not to offend a major fund raiser. "We are monitoring the situation, but it is not as easy as it seems. The regime has been in power for so long that all of its generals are clones of the Egyptian president. The army is still running the country, and a new general would not change that much. The army is also laced with Muslim extremists. The Minister of Interior has tried to weed them out, but things remain dicey. We are not quite sure what the results of a coup would be. It could blow up in our faces, and we can't afford that. The liberals in Congress are also screaming for democracy. They would have a field day if we pulled a coup in Egypt. Don't forget, Jake," he added sarcastically, "Egypt is one of our democratic success stories."

"You sound like the liberals have gotten to your head," said Jake dryly, slamming down the receiver and returning to his desk more despondent than usual. "That s.o.b. is setting me up to take the rap for this mess," he muttered out loud. "He's afraid that they will bounce him if I kick ass. Self-serving s.o.b. He doesn't care what happens to his country."

*　　*　　*　　*

The one member of Jake's political staff that didn't fall in the asshole category was Mandy Brown who was just beginning her second tour in the Middle East.

The very attractive daughter of a long line of ambassadors, she navigated this most masculine of worlds with ease. She flirted without flirting and promised without promising, showing just enough skin to keep life interesting but never enough to question her professionalism. It was a game she enjoyed and it was a game that pleased the Ambassador.

A born-again Christian and too proud to take Viagra, he looked forward to their "little game" as he called it, and found himself consulting her far more often than the other political officers. He even suggested that she call him Jake, but she declined saying that her respect for him would not allow it. "I think of her as my daughter," he explained to his wife, who had her doubts about the matter but saw little cause for worry. "Unfortunately," she lamented in her lighter moments, "there had been little cause for worry for some time. He was still a handsome man with his sparkling blue eyes, mane of white hair and a massive frame that disguised too many Texas steaks, but the passions of old were no more. The thrill of sex had given way to the thrill of politics."

*   *   *   *

Smith walked the two blocks to Tahrir Square and squeezed aboard the train to Maadi, a plush Cairo suburb favored by foreigners. The Embassy viewed the metro as a security risk and warned its personnel to avoid it if at all possible. Crowds of any type were dangerous and the metro was very crowded. With the truce, however, there had been no attacks on the metro, and Smith found it far less dangerous than Cairo's chaotic traffic. In his heart of hearts, he also felt that American diplomats should show their human side to the Egyptians and not go careening through Cairo's chaotic traffic in convoys of white Chevy SUVs, the lead and rear cars stuffed with armed marines. The Ambassador and DCM had no choice in the matter, but others did. Smith, however, was in the minority, and convoys for lesser figures had become the norm, snarling traffic and bringing shouts of anger from Egyptian motorists doomed to yet another delay in the thick haze of dust and carbon monoxide that enveloped Cairo's main arteries. On bad days it enveloped Cairo itself, forcing residents to seek refuge behind closed doors. The Americans, of course, were air conditioned as was Egypt's middle class, perhaps 20% of the population. The rest struggled to survive. It was they who came to the clinics and schools of the Muslim Brotherhood.

Smith walked the few blocks from the Maadi station to his villa replete with marble steps, a tailored lawn, servants, and a swimming pool. The shops in the station area offered the latest in American goods and the aroma of the local Pizza

Hut competed with those of every other US fast-food chain. All were packed with American teenagers, as were the ice cream parlors and video outlets. With a little luck, Americans could almost forget that they were in Egypt. Most bowed to that temptation, centering their lives around the American community church and Cairo American College, an elite prep-school for Americans and rich Egyptians. Neither offered much competition to Maadi's endless series of cocktail parties. For the more adventurous, there were the posh seaside resorts of Herghada and Sharm-el-Sheikh. The latter was particularly appealing, for it was the preferred location of international confabs devoted to the weighty problems of peace and terror. Solutions were few, but the scenery dazzled. The truly adventurous plotted their scuba-diving expeditions to the Red Sea.

In contrast to most of the American community, Smith liked Egypt and relished the excitement of serving in the premiere post in the Middle East. A good tour in Cairo could make his career. The next step would be DCM or even ambassador. Smith's fondness for Egypt didn't prevent him from seeking refuge in his palatial villa or his daily swim in CAC's mammoth pool. "The best of both worlds," he would smile to himself, "with all the comforts of home and Egypt, too."

"It's going to be tough duty going back to a middle class lifestyle," he confessed to his wife from time to time, "three bedrooms, a Ford, and no servants."

"We still have the cabin in Vermont," she would console him, but she, too, enjoyed the diplomatic life, with its elegant lifestyle and endless parties. "Besides," she would add with encouragement, "you'll get the big bucks when you make ambassador." That line had faded from their conversation as tension mounted between Smith and the Ambassador.

The servant opened the door and Smith walked into the study where his wife was waiting with a scotch. That, too, had become routine following his sessions with the Ambassador. "At the very least," she comforted him, "we have the evening free."

Free evenings were as cherished as they were rare. Days of writing dreaded reports about the deteriorating situation in Egypt gave way to the endless parade of diplomatic receptions. Last night it was the British Embassy, the night before the French Ambassador's residence, and the night before that the Egyptian Foreign Office. Tomorrow night was their turn and then the Italian's and Saudi's. The venue changed, but the content was the same. Tables were laden with shrimp, sweets, and finger sandwiches, all from Cairo's best caterers, such as they were. Roving waiters plied the guests with champagne, scotch, wine, juice, and water. The latter were for Muslim diplomats, most of whom refrained from drinking in public. The Saudis offered only water and juice, but the stronger stuff was available in an ante-room off the main hall. All in all, the Saudis had the best food and the Italians the best booze. The Egyptians had the worst of both. The caterers tried to be French, but it was a tough go. "Strange," Smith thought to himself, "the Moroccans and the Lebanese have world class cuisine. The closer to Egypt you get, the worse it becomes. For the poor, it was *foul madammes* (fava beans), *falafel* (deep fried chick peas), and *khousary*, (lentils, rice, noodles, and fried onions).

Even the people at the receptions were the same: the ambassadors or DCMs, a smattering of political officers, the usual Egyptian intellectuals, some generals and business leaders, a few turbaned religious sheikhs, a handful of visiting dignitaries, and a smattering of secret agents masquerading as Embassy staff.

It was at the receptions, black tie required, where Smith exchanged gossip and tips with his counterparts at other embassies, each of whom had their own sources of information. Some were accurate, others fabrications. Most attendees were attempting to get a better read on American policy. The Americans, after all, were the movers and shakers in the Middle East, the big kahuna, the hegemon. It was their voice that counted and everyone listened. The Egyptian intellectuals cursed the regime and offered bits of inside information in hope of getting a study grant to the US or a visa for a relative.

"If things are really that bad," Smith taunted them in frustration, "why don't you do something about it?"

One Egyptian had laughed, saying, "It's our fate, my friend. You can't change it. The regime is too strong. They let us talk, but one false move and we are in prison. Brutal, my friend, brutal. No regard for human rights or democracy. Everything is a sham."

Another had blamed the United States. "You keep them in power," he said. "How do you expect us to change anything? You're the big kid on the block. You get what you want and don't give a damn who you crush."

A third was more philosophical. "It's like the Nile," he had confided to Smith. "You can see it and touch it, but you can't stop it. It goes on forever." It was always the same story. The regime was corrupt and oppressive, but too powerful to buck.

The stories had been the same in Iran before the collapse of the Shah. An endless array of curses were tempered with testimony to the Shah's invincibility. The political officers of the era had duly noted the complaints, but filled their reports with the testimonies of the Shah's invincibility. Washington didn't give two damns about the Shah's human rights record. All they cared about was his power.

Like a well choreographed chorus of magpies, the Iranian intellectuals had painted a picture of an all powerful tyrant who was driving his people to ruin. "All powerful," the reports to Washington had glowed. "All of our sources paint the same picture."

It was all a grand lie. The Shah's regime was collapsing of its own weight while his family (brothers, uncles and cousins to the fifth degree) smuggled billions of dollars to Europe. When the light suddenly dawned, it was too late and the Ayatollah Khomeini and his Islamic Revolution were at the gates of Tehran. The political officers had paid the price. A few, like the DCM, had survived, but they didn't make ambassador. Most were now selling shoes. The marble palaces, servants, screaming convoys, and endless cocktail parties had all become memories of the past.

The field reports, including those of Smith and his colleagues, were now different. Occasional hints of optimism were sandwiched between layers of gloom and despair. "It's not what Washington wants to hear," Smith consoled himself, "but at least it's honest." All they want are painless solutions that win elections and send opinion polls soaring; impossible solutions that pretend that Islam can be crushed and that the Arabs will accept Israeli domination of the region. No wonder Iraq turned into another Vietnam. If you tell the truth, you are a defeatist. If you attempt to explain the complexities of the region, you are written off as an Arabist, the Israeli epithet for Arab lovers.

Jake didn't like defeatists, he didn't like Arabists, he didn't like romantics, and he didn't like bleeding heart liberals. They were all assholes who didn't understand power politics.

*   *   *   *

Smith accepted the drink from his wife, sank in the closest arm chair, and looked at his mate with fondness. "My head, my eyes, my heart," he murmured in mock recitation of Arab greetings. "I couldn't survive without you."

The passions of youth had mellowed with exhaustion and too much alcohol, but in its place had emerged a deep and abiding friendship. His wife lived the drama of the Foreign Service through his eyes, never flinching at last minute demands for a party or remote postings in the middle of Africa. Invariably she taught at the local American school, as she did now, playing the diplomat's wife at night. Deepening friendship had seen her become his confidant and the sounding board for his ideas. Always positive, she was also honest, chiding him when need be, for his romanticism.

"What's the latest community gossip?" sighed Smith, not wanting to relive the scene at the Embassy. His wife was his window on the American community, and rare was the day that she didn't regale him with news of a new scandal. "You have the most exciting of lives," he would tease her, knowing that she would give her right arm to be in the Corps.

Tonight, however, it was news of a new teacher rather than a scandal that she brought to his attention as she settled into a chair beside him with a glass of white wine. She didn't have his stomach for booze, but found the wine soothing. "She's a bit too prissy for my blood," she lamented, "but she said that her husband speaks Arabic and works for the Institute, whatever that is. From what I can judge, he's in hog heaven and she would rather be back in Nebraska."

"Strange," murmured Smith, "The Institute, if it is *the* Institute, shuns Americans. They're a bright bunch, but are afraid that Americans will steal their data and use it against them. Even the spooks can't get close to them. Having an American on the inside is too good to be true, but we'd better have a closer look. Why don't you organize a Sunday tea for the new teachers and their spouses? That won't scare him and we don't have to commit ourselves."

"I thought you were going scuba diving?" questioned his wife with compassion. "This will be the fifth time in a row that you have put it off."

"If I don't get the Ambassador off my back, we'll be scuba diving in Vermont," replied Smith with resignation. "Maybe this guy knows something. What names should I be looking for?

"Parker," responded his wife, "Scott and Constance Parker."

Chapter 2

Two for Tea

It was a typical afternoon reception. Two hours of formality served with finger sandwiches, sweets and a choice of tea, coffee, coke, or white wine. Smith and Mandy circulated among a dozen or so new teachers, welcoming them to Egypt and making small talk. A particularly nubile young lady from Mississippi confessed to Smith that she felt secure just knowing that the American Embassy was watching over her. Smith nearly choked on his drink. The American Embassy in Cairo had been transformed into an armed bunker guarded by Egyptian troops. It issued warnings of impending danger, but had no way to track the thousands of Americans milling around Cairo.

Smith's wife rushed to the rescue before he recovered and began to take his responsibilities seriously. "His passions may have cooled," she said to herself, "but not to the point that they couldn't be revived by little Miss Southern Geniality.

Then turning to the nubile young lady she cooed with thinly veiled sarcasm. "I'm sure you won't be lonely, my dear. The men in Egypt are very attentive." She wanted to add, "All thirty million of them," but diplomats' wives don't say those things in public.

Constance Parker was in less danger. Beautiful in a severe sort of way, she smiled rarely and then with a coolness that froze the most ardent of males in their tracks. "It's rape or nothing," an Egyptian colleague had quipped to a friend following an ill advised attempt to waylay her in a deserted corridor. "I don't think she likes men."

Mandy had come away with the same impression following an abortive effort to make conversation with Constance Parker. Her main interests, as far as Mandy could tell, were the community church and the feminist movement in Egypt. She didn't like Egypt and she wasn't overly pleased with her husband. "I don't know why he found a place in Zamalek when all of the Americans are in Maadi," Constance had complained. "Zamalek is in the middle of the city and I either have to ride that infernal school bus for an hour or risk my life in a taxi for almost as long."

"Or more," added Mandy in sympathy. She would be less sympathetic after she met Parker.

"So, Parker," said Smith with studied warmth, "what brings you to Cairo?" He knew the answer, but decided to go slow. No sense revealing that he had ordered a background check on the guest of honor.

"Some friends at the Institute had a research grant from the United Nations and asked me to join them," replied Parker, looking at his glass of tepid white wine as if it were hemlock. "It's publish or perish, so here I am."

"Then, this isn't your first trip to Cairo," Smith continued the charade, relieved that he hadn't given up a Sunday in vein. "Perhaps you would enjoy something stronger than wine," and not sensing the need for an answer, led Parker to a wet bar on the spacious porch overlooking the dry swimming pool. "They can't seem to fix the cracks," he commented with resignation, as he handed Parker a glass of rare single malt scotch.

"Diplomats live better than academics," laughed Parker, accepting the glass with appreciation. "I usually save this stuff for special occasions, if then."

"Ten bucks at the commissary," laughed Smith. "No taxes and no transportation charges. They smuggle it here in the pouch."

It is hard to say precisely when the friendship between the two men began, but it was probably over that glass of scotch. Nothing happened in particular, just a cautious game of show and tell between two people curious about the world of the other.

"So," said Smith, returning to his unanswered question, "you're an old Egyptian hand."

"That's probably too strong," cautioned Parker. "I've lived here off and on, but it still baffles. Every time I think I have things figured out, they throw me a curve and I come up empty handed. I guess that's why I keep coming back. That and I like the place."

"We all have empty hands," acknowledged Smith, adding his bit of honesty to the kitty. "At least you have an advantage. They trust you and you come and go as you please. With us everything is formal. You walk into a room and the conversation stops. When they do talk, it's to sell you something, usually a pile of crap. If not that, they need a favor."

"Strange," said Parker, raising the stakes, "I thought you people knew everything. You deal with presidents and prime ministers and the CIA has a thousand spies, or so it seems. Besides, I don't think the Egyptians trust anyone, even themselves."

"Different worlds," laughed Smith, draining his glass. "Each thinks the other has the world by the tail." He wanted to suggest that they join forces, but that was premature and probably out of the question. Academics distrusted the Embassy as much as the Egyptians. "But at least," Smith thought to himself, "Parker isn't afraid of us. He also seems to enjoy the game."

"What a lovely wife your have Mr. Parker, or is it doctor?" asked Mandy with professional warmth as she cornered Parker on his way out of the porch.

"Either will do," replied Parker in his relaxed mid-Western style. Most people just call me Scott. It cuts down on the formality." And, to dispel hints of flirtation, he added, "Thank you for the compliment. My wife is anxious to make friends in the American community and it was very gracious of the Smiths to invite us to their home."

"Very gracious," acknowledged Mandy having received the thumbs up from Smith. "I'm sure you will see more of them. It's good for us to break out of the official community. All we do is talk to ourselves. It's always the same, and I can write the script in advance. "Are you are from Nebraska, too?" she changed the topic, initiating the inevitable game of where are you from that Americans find so irresistible.

"No," laughed Parker, "Wisconsin, not to far from Chicago. We are more liberal and have a better sense of humor. And you?"

"Rhode Island, not far from Boston. You could probably tell from the accent." So much for the rituals, Mandy mused as she relinquished her prey to Miss Southern Geniality.

"Doesn't it just make you feel so happy that the Embassy is here to take care of us?" she gushed, striking a pose that accentuated her obvious charms.

"Yes, it does," Parker had smiled, some how hoping that her tits would compensate for his nausea. It was not to be. He preferred intelligent women. Sex, like everything else in his life, was a game. He was good, very good, and demanded the same from his partner. There was also the problem of afterwards. What do you do after? The reception over, Parker bid farewell to his hosts and a cast a lingering glance at Miss Southern Geniality. He was, after all, human.

Chapter 3

The Bliss That Wasn't

Perhaps it was Parker's love of games that sustained his relationship with his wife. Sex was rare, but when she was good, she was very good. They had fallen in love in the heady environment of the University of Wisconsin, that most liberal of universities. Parker was a graduate student; she an undergraduate of charm and intellect who wept for the poor and looked to him for enlightenment, sexual and otherwise. She denied him nothing and displayed a curiosity not often associated with rural Nebraska. Their life was a whirlwind of plays, lectures, intellectual debates, and sexual fulfillment, the former filling the gaps between the latter. Even in public, his hand would find its way under the coat that covered her lap on cool days, and that was most of them. She protested, but to no avail. They dreamed of saving the world and bringing peace to the Middle East. Parker proposed and she accepted. In her mind, she had accepted on their first date. Together they had found a joy and a sense of fulfillment that was the stuff of romance novels.

How had this lanky graduate student succeeded where others had failed? He was handsome to be sure, with his wavy brown hair and sparkling blue eyes, but looks were not important to her. There had been lots of handsome youth in her life, and some had achieved more success than others. She had welcomed their attention, but recoiled from the frenzied assaults in hay lofts and pick up trucks. Fear had become the ally of morality.

Parker had not hurried her. There had been no need to. His nonchalant manner had eased her fears and his kisses had washed away the stern admonitions of her mother. It was as if Parker had liberated a long suppressed diablerie gene inherited from her father. Parker had even taunted her. "Why rush?" he teased. "Let's enjoy the game while we get to know each other. We are very different people. Perhaps I'm not what you are looking for." The very expression implied marriage, and she hadn't demanded more.

He was what she was looking for. She felt it in her heart and she felt it in her loins. She had, to use her father's favorite poker expression, "gone all in."

"You can't stay on the sidelines forever, my princess," he had cautioned her. If you've got a good hand, play it." Her mother had cast him a withering glance, and he took his leave. It was poker night, and a welcome reprieve from this most Christian of ladies.

Alas, like all new comers to the game of poker, Constance had begun to question the wisdom of her bet. Had she gone all in too soon? Did he share her love, or was their romance just a game like everything else in his life? What would happen if she lost?

Who could blame her? She had little experience with games. Her father had attempted to teach his daughter the joy of games, but her mother would have none of it. "Frivolous and a waste of time," she had warned this most obedient of young ladies. "They begin as an amusement and then lead to gambling, drink, and other things." Other things, remained undefined, but it was clear to the young Constance that her father was in the dog house. There would be no harsh words, merely a deep chill that withered all that it touched. Sometimes it would pass in hours; others in days.

Yet, her parents loved each other and had worked out a reasonable co-existence. He ran his bank, played poker twice a week, golfed on the weekend, and fished when the weather permitted, which was most of the time. Even ice fishing was preferable to long winter nights at the mercy of his wife. Her mother ran the house, attended to the moral upbringing of their only child, helped at the church, and fussed at her husband for being a poor influence on the child.

"Little boys never really grow up," her mother had warned Constance in confidence, "at least not the interesting ones." Then, allowing herself a rare bit of humor, she added, "A few nights with the boys keeps them out of your hair and other places."

Constance had blushed, but her mother merely smiled and went about her business. It was time for her daughter to grow up.

Her father seldom interfered in his wife's affairs, but when he did, he got his way. It was he who had encouraged Constance to accept the scholarship at Wisconsin despite its liberal reputation.

"You've got to spread your wings," he had told her as they talked over breakfast. "You will never learn to fly if you stay too close to home. We will miss you more than you know, but we'll never be that far away."

Her mother, listening from the kitchen, had wept, but said nothing. She knew that her husband was right. There was no future for her daughter in the village. A few boys inherited the family farm and married their childhood sweetheart. The rest left. Even the family farm was becoming a thing of the past. Her daughter had no childhood sweetheart and knew nothing of the rigors of farm life. She had done for her everything that she could do. Now it was up to her. There would be no frost in the house, only a profound sadness.

* * * *

It was in the throes of self-doubt that Constance sought out the friend who had introduced her to Parker. She obviously knew him well, but had remained vague about their relationship.

"Charming, isn't he?" teased the friend who had brought them together. "He is every girl's dream: handsome, witty, confident, and cool. A bit selfish, perhaps, but all men are. Don't be fooled. Scott is going to get what he wants. He disarms with his humor and uses charm as a weapon. His wit can destroy as quickly as it delights. If you want what he wants, you will live a wonderful life."

"What does he want?" ventured Constance, not sure that she wanted to hear the answer.

"He wants to succeed. He wants to do some good in the world. He wants a good wife. He wants to play games and enjoy life. As far as I can tell, they are all wrapped up in one. If he does his bit to make the world a better place, God will forget the rest. And," she continued after a pause, "he wants you. He thinks that you will make the perfect partner: friend, wife, and editor. He has proposed, hasn't he?"

"Not that I recall," replied Constance dourly, her mind equating proposals with diamond rings.

"Maybe not formally," comforted her friend. "That's not his style. He begins with ambiguous statements that leave room for maneuver, and then moves in for the kill. It's the gambler's instinct, I guess."

"He gambles?" questioned Constance with alarm.

"I'm not sure that I would call it gambling," replied her friend. "He only bets when the odds are in his favor and he wins far more than he loses. He also knows when to quit. He got that from his father, a local preacher. The old man would temp him to greed and then make a fool out of him. When Scott pouted, his father mocked him and told him to grow up and be a man Sniveling was not allowed in the preacher's family."

"We've got it too good for you to be bellyaching boy," he admonished his young son. "Look at all of the misery in the world. Get off your butt and go do something about it."

It took a while, but Scott learned patience and got over his dreams of easy money. He never got over his love of games and played them all: poker, chess, cribbage, bridge and anything else you could think of. It sharpened his mind and eased the tedium of a restless person who found school boring. He could not live without a challenge and found it in outsmarting others. He was hell bent on beating his father at poker and studied the odds with the passion of a mathematician. He also read books on strategy, learned how to read his opponents, and became a master at disguising his emotions. When he could play his father even up, the old man stopped playing for money. Scott was livid, but the old man merely laughed and said that playing with less than a six to four advantage was against his religion. Scott got the message. Games weren't about, money. They were about winning and life. Small games were training for bigger games, and bigger games for the biggest games of all. Money was merely a symbol of victory.

"I'm not sure I like his father," cringed Constance, overcome with a sudden wave of sympathy Parker. "He seems so cold and impersonal."

"Not so," corrected her friend. "No child had felt more certain of his parent's affection or more stifled by their efforts to mold him into a preacher's son. The old man didn't believe in sparing the rod and Parker had little interest in becoming a martyr. He dressed well, had impeccable manners, stood up straight, shook hands with firmness, looked people squarely in the eye and seduced their daughters. He made it a game. If appearances were everything, so be it."

"His father is a psychologist at heart, and so is Scott," she continued. "He uses mind games to unnerve his opponents and he is not averse to bluffing if it suits his purposes. Not too often, mind you, but he likes the drama." Then she added with a wicked smile, "I've seen him bluff people out of their clothes." She didn't elaborate. There was no need. Constance had gotten the point.

"I hope that he is not bluffing with me," uttered Constance, irritated that Parker had transformed their courtship into a poker game.

"No," smiled her friend. "He loves you. You have a pristine quality that he finds irresistible. There aren't too many like you around any more. It must be your rural Nebraska background."

"Then why all the ambiguity?" snapped Constance in exasperation. "If he intends to marry me, why doesn't he say so? He knows that I am looking at wedding dresses."

"It's part of the game. He likes the cards that he can see, but is still pondering those that he can't. But, don't worry," she teased her friend, "he must have seen enough. He has asked my advice about rings."

Constance blushed, but returned to the issue at hand. "What if I don't want what he wants?"

"Then he will lose interest in you like he has lost interest in the others." Tears formed in her friend's eyes as she spoke. "We were classmates and lovers. My parents attended his father's church and I had always assumed that we would marry and that I would be a preacher's wife. But it was not to be. He had no interest in the church and less in marriage. We began to quarrel over little things and eventually started dating other people. It was my fault, of course. He was too young and restless to contemplate marriage, however distant. That would come when he had conquered his worlds. He is still my best friend, but romance is no longer and option."

"Was he religious as a youth?" probed Constance, elated by Parker's interest in rings and more concerned about Parker's religious views than warnings of doom. She did want what he wanted. Achievement and doing good were the essence of her upbringing, and she rejoiced in his desire for a wife who would be something more than the mother of his children. She found his love of games frustrating, but was willing to manage it the way her mother had adjusted to her father's mania for poker. Morality was the issued that rankled. Religion was part of her life and it had to be part of their marriage."

"Religious?" smiled her friend. "To be sure, but in the broad sense of the word. He finds churches to be hypocritical, but has a deep faith in God, Christ, and his own ability to succeed. He believes that it is his religious duty to leave the world a better place, but sees nothing wrong enjoying earthly pleasures as he goes along. One is the reward for the other. He idolizes his father, but his real hero is Ben Franklin. Strive for self-improvement, avoid extremes, do well by doing good, understand that a spoon full of honey catches more flies than a barrel of vinegar, don't be disturbed by trifles and accidents common and unavoidable, be loyal to your friends, enjoy the ladies, fight your excesses if you can, and don't be dumb. Scott had a little trouble with his excesses, but the seeds of morality and hard work had been planted. His father wasn't convinced so he urged him to take a job in a factory to get a taste of reality. He stuck it out for a month or two and then joined the army. It was time to see the world."

Constance promised herself that she would nurture Parker's moral instincts with love and caring. It would be her love that helped him rediscover the church. Her conscience appeased, she flew to his arms in search of her ring. At least for the moment, she was still her father's daughter. She had gone all in and won.

"Easy tiger," he had whispered, "save some for tomorrow."

*   *   *   *

Parker's father had not resisted his son's enlistment in the army. Things had come too easy for the boy and he needed a dose of reality more than he did the university. That would come when the boy had his head together.

Army life honed Parker's poker skills and toned down his brashness. The army was a serious place and Parker developed the persona of a thoughtful person. It played well, and he was given office duties while others dug ditches. In lonelier moments he ventured to church in hope of finding the inspiration of his father. Instead, he encountered an enterprising preacher who recognized his charismatic qualities and persuaded him to sell heirloom Bibles on the base. He was a natural, and it was to be his first venture in doing well by doing good. It wasn't the pious who bought his Bibles, but reprobates fearing for their souls. "Ah, my friend," Parker intoned, when he stumbled upon a heathen craving redemption, "you seem to be down in the dumps. Spent all of your money on drink, whores and gambling? I've been there myself. Why not set aside a few dollars for God? You can have this most beautiful of Bibles for no money down and only ten dollars a month. Your mother will be proud and there is special section to inscribe the names of your children and grand children."

Parker leafed through the elegant pictures of these most elegant of Bibles with the skill of magician as his voice resonated with the zeal of a repentant sinner. Most bought and many wept. Some even sought him out to confess their mid-deeds. It was like taking candy from babies. The company passed on his commissions, about 20%, and handled all of the collections. His college fund was assured. It was a proud Scott Parker who regaled his father with stories of his enterprise and good works. To his consternation, he received only a sharp rebuke for his efforts. "Still chasing easy money, huh, boy?"

Parker gave up selling Bibles and channeled his energy into off duty classes at a nearby college. God rewarded him with an intellectual awakening and a tempting array of coeds and ladies of lesser distinction. His father applauded Parker's academic reformation, but retained his skepticism about the boy's moral fortitude.

In reality, he had wronged his son. Parker, like generations of youth before him, had used his military service as an interlude of adventure, maturation, experimentation, and self-discovery. A tour of duty in the Middle East had deepened his fascination with this most ancient of regions. While others clung to the base in fear or disinterest, Parker probed it's casbahs and palaces, his imagination fired by the *Arabian Nights* and its tales of seduction, mysticism and court intrigue. How else could one understand how a region that had given birth to world civilization now threatened its doom? By the end of his tour of duty, the Middle East had become his obsession.

In a curious way, the frivolity of Parker's youth had been a blessing. His adolescent fantasies fulfilled, he threw himself into his studies with a zeal that would have made Ben Franklin proud. Most focused on the Middle East in one way or another. He studied its history, religions, culture, psychology, economics and politics, and he studied the Arabic language. The more he studied the region, the more he became convinced of its uniqueness and the need to immerse himself in its culture. There was no other way to get inside a Middle Eastern mind and see the world as Middle Easterner's saw it. American logic and Middle Eastern logic were simply different. You didn't have to like what you saw, but at least you knew where they were coming from. Terror just didn't happen; it happened for a reason.

Parker's grades soared and he was offered a full scholarship to grad school, a notion unthinkable only a few years earlier. His father's indoctrination had not been in vain. Morality and achievement had been implanted, but Parker's world had little in common with that of his father. There were few absolutes, just varying shades of gray. How like the Middle East itself, where everything was appearances and nothing was what it seemed.

Intellectual maturity had given way boredom with the game of sexual conquest. He began to yearn for a mature sexual experience that could only be achieved by the love of an intelligent and innovative lady. Like all good games, it would have to be more psychological than physical. It would be a game of mutual growth and mutual fulfillment. He needed a mature woman who knew how to challenge; who kept inventing new games, who knew how to win by surrender, total surrender.

It was time to marry. When a high school sweetheart had introduced him to Constance, he knew instinctively that he had found his mate.

✳   ✳   ✳   ✳

In Parker's mind, the whirlwind of their courtship would continue forever. Not so for a young lady honed on the harsh plains of Nebraska. For every season there was a reason. Life was serious business and the business of marriage was rearing a family and serving God. Redemption for her Wisconsin years, as she called them, had come with marriage. She had married a worthy man and her intentions were to rule him much as her mother ruled her father. The metamorphous had been alarmingly sudden and taken Parker by surprise. It was as if she had awoken after the wedding and pondered the nature of wifedom. Her models were her mother and her aunts, all studies in American gothic. The diablerie gene inherited from her father had served its purpose and receded into her unconscious from whence it had come.

Invariably, they had grown apart. He blamed her for changing. She blamed him for not changing and suggested that it was time that he grew up. Both had begun to worry over the wisdom of children, and a series of miscarriages had deepened their despair. Yet, neither was willing to forsake a love that had been so profound. He treated her with kindness and respect and often discussed his projects with her. Her keen intelligence also made her an adept editor and critic. They had become friends rather than lovers, each with a separate private life. Hers revolved around the church and charity work, his around a circle of friends that she found abhorrent.

"Be glad that he works hard and is ambitious," her father had written in response to her plea for advice. "Be a good soldier and do your part." The lecture was not new, and perhaps she knew that it was coming. She had always been a good soldier, excelling at school and doing whatever her parents expected of her. She also knew that her parents approved of Parker and were reluctant to see a divorce. "The man looks you squarely in the eye and has a firm handshake," her father had commented upon meeting Parker, as if those were the only values in life that mattered. "He will go far."

"You don't know him," she had teased, which, of course, was true. He knew nothing of her Wisconsin years other than that she had made the honor roll and was preparing to marry well. When she called her mother in search of sympathy, she received a dour, "We all have our crosses to bear, and now you have yours. Don't whine."

Chapter 4

▼

The Noises of Cairo

Parker had done well. The ten years that had passed since his marriage to Constance had seen him mature into a leading scholar in the study of the Arab psyche. His works were quoted by Arabs as authoritative, and he was consulted frequently by international organizations. This, after all, had been the basis for his invitation to spend a year at the Institute, the first American to be so honored. The director of the Institute, better known as the Boss, wanted Parker's expertise to jump start a moribund bureaucracy that consumed a lion's share of Egypt's wealth while producing nothing but frustration and despair. For Parker, the project promised the opportunity to interview people in depth, probing their fears and motives without being accused of espionage. At long last, he would be able to achieve his life's dream: discovering the soul of Egypt.

Who could not be excited about probing the soul of Egypt, the cradle of world civilization and the very heart of the jihadist movement? There were so many Egypts to explore. Pharaonic Egypt with its towering pyramids gave way to the Egypt of the Ethiopians, Persians, Greeks, Romans, Byzantines, Arabs, Abbasids, Mamlukes, Crusaders, Turks, French, and British. Parker had only to close his eyes to imagine the glories of each.

When at long last Egypt had regained its independence after five thousand years of foreign occupation, a new pharaoh had appeared in the guise of a young military officer. His name was Abdul Nasser and it was he and his band of military officers who drove the foreign princes from their palaces and liberated Egypt from the British. He vowed to transform Egypt into an industrial power by building a massive dam to capture the energy of the Nile. The unity of the Arabs would follow and with it an end to western domination of the Arab world. When the *kawaga* schemed against him, Nasser nationalized the Suez Canal and used its revenues to finance his great dam, his new pyramid. War followed, but it was Nasser who reigned supreme over the combined forces of the British, French and Israelis. It had been the United States that had forced the conspirators to withdraw from the lands of Egypt, but that was merely testimony to Nasser's genius. What the Egyptians could not accomplish by force they had accomplished by wile.

Heads, long bowed, raised in pride as Egyptians vowed to never again kowtow to the *kawaga*. There had been a new beginning, a new dawn. The road would be long, but the Arabs would regain the glories of yore and Egypt would be at the helm. The *kawaga* would be humbled and Israel would be swept into the sea. The soul of Egypt, or so it seemed, had been revived.

Alas, it was not to be. The executioners of sultans past gave way to Nasser's secret police and their tax collectors to a rapacious bureaucracy that sucked the blood of the poor in the name of socialism. Nasser, the new Saladin, remained a hero, but his heirs were no better than the sultans of old, perhaps worse. They, like the other petty kings and dictators of the Arab world, lived in fear of revolt and begged the *kawaga* to protect them from their own people. They licked his boots and they licked the boots of the Israelis, groveling before a country no larger than a postage stamp.

If Parker marveled at the glories of the past, it was the misery of the present that had become his preoccupation. It was there that he would search for the soul of Egypt.

* * * *

Constance endured Parker's trips to the Middle East stoically, teaching at the local American school and working with the local community church. This latest trip was no exception. Like most Americans stationed in Cairo, she cared little for the glories of its storied past. She sweltered in its heat, choked on its dust, cringed at its noise and feared its surging crowds. Oh, how she feared the surging crowds. They made way for her with great politeness, but never mind. Terrorists lurked in her dreams and more than one overly aggressive male had groped her as a crowd surged by.

Her apartment sheltered her from the heat, the dust, and the surging crowds, but nothing could shelter her from the incessant noise. It robbed her of sleep and jangled her nerves. And noisy it was. Cairo, the city of a thousand mosques, was also the city of a thousand noises. Minarets blared the call to prayer, buses backfired as they belched volcanoes of exhaust into the putrid air, pile drivers pounded incessantly, water buses and river barges plied the Nile with broken mufflers, sirens screamed, trains rattled across the nearby bridge, horns honked in protest to traffic that stalled for hours, children screamed, street vendors hawked their wares, televisions blared from coffee houses as soccer games vied with the Koran for the attention of the masses, and Egyptians shouted to be heard over the din.

Cairo was even noisy in the middle of the night. If the air conditioner didn't work, which was often, they slept with the windows open and the sounds of Cairo invaded into their bedroom. Constance, exhausted by hours of screaming kids, complained, but was soon transported by dream to the serenity of rural Nebraska. Parker envied her. He was not so graced. The night sounds enthralled him and sleep became impossible. Perhaps they held the key to the soul of Egypt. They were softer than the sounds of the day, mysterious, seductive, and sinister. It could not be otherwise, for the night belonged to revelers, thieves, dope dealers, foolish lovers, and death squads. From time to time a shriek pierced the air. Was it a man beating his wife? Who knew? Who cared? Decent folk were locked in their flats, doors triple bolted and windows barred.

There were even touches of humor as the guard stationed in front of a neighboring building attempted in vain to wake his replacement asleep on the roof. Parker felt sorry for the poor soul, for a general lived in the building and the guard could not leave his post. "Ahmed, Ahmed," he called in a plaintive voice calculated to stir his replacement without waking the general, an invitation to a sure thrashing. It was futile, but he persisted only to be drowned out by a marine guard at the Embassy bringing pleasure to the secretary who lived in the neighboring flat. Their window, too, was open and her obvious pleasure moved Parker to caress his wife. That, too, was futile and he abandoned the venture when the Marine guard, his mission accomplished, asked the lady if she had ever seen anything quite so big. She giggled, but said nothing and he was pleased. Parker could see her rolling her eyes, for she had many guests, but he was a young man and was inexperienced in such matters. Perhaps he planned to marry her and take her back to rural Nebraska.

The first ray of dawn brought the morning prayer and a new set of noises. The boat people began beating the sides of their wooden skiffs in the hope of attracting fish to their nets. They were followed by the first buses and they by taxies and the relentless blast of car horns. A new day had dawned.

How long could she continue to bear her cross, Constance wondered? The question troubled her, for her beauty was finite. If she were to find a new husband, it would have to be soon. She loved Parker and lived in the hope that they could find a new foundation for their marriage. They would have to change together much as they had grown together during the Wisconsin years. But could they change?

Her faith was immutable, but not inflexible. It certainly left room for a vigorous sex life in a Christian environment. That was where the problem lie. Parker's religious views shared none of the fire and brimstone of Bible belt preaching. His was an intellectual Christianity devoted to bettering mankind rather than saving souls.

Could she change him the way her mother had presumably changed her father? She doubted it, but continued to bear her cross. So, she suffered the agonizing round trip from Zamalek to Maadi on the CAC school bus surrounded by screaming kids.

Parker had pondered divorce, but found the thought painful. It meant defeat and the loss of the dream. Remarriage was assured, but to whom and at what cost? He loved his wife in a curious sort of way, and was unburdened by a cross of guilt or anything else. He did, however, take friendship very seriously, and she had been his best friend. He didn't want to hurt her. His memories of the Wisconsin years remained strong. If only he could rekindle the spark of the past. If only the humanism of her father could reassert itself. As for his presumed infidelities, why should a man have to bear the burden of his wife's guilt?

Thus they co-existed. The more Parker's spirits soared, the more her's crumbled and the heavier her cross became.

Chapter 5

Boulaq–A Hell of a Place

Once a desolate village separated from Cairo by the Ismailiya Canal, Boulaq would become Cairo's main river port and the site of its steel foundry, printing press and rail yards. Then as now, it had been a refuge for rural migrants attracted by the lure of jobs in the city. The city had few jobs, yet they came, squatting where they found relatives and bringing with them the *fallah's* (peasant's) loathing of the government. They also brought their clan feuds and their devout faith in Allah, the one God. A vast labyrinth of narrow allies and collapsing buildings, Boulaq had also become a haven for crime and drugs. One had to survive and there were no jobs for the youth.

The Ismailiya Canal had long disappeared, its putrid waters giving way to Galal Street, a dusty thoroughfare choked with carbon spewing buses and gaudy Mercedes. To its right, coming from the river, is the tram, its filth littered tracks shaded from the sun by a fly-over easing passage to Cairo's elegant suburbs. Beyond the tram is a narrow row of factories. Beyond the factories is downtown Cairo, a mélange of glass and steel shamed by the elegant buildings of an earlier era. To the left of the tram is residential Boulaq, an occasional pockmarked ally spewing motor bikes, donkey carts, and vintage cars wired together with coat hangers into the chaotic traffic of Galal Street. There are exceptions, of course, for the gang lords drive nothing but the best. It is their persona and the symbol of their power.

*   *   *   *

Sheikh Yassin made his way along Galal Street, dodging pot holes, chatting with the faithful, and tasting the wares of its vendors: a dish of rice and lentils from Ahmed, a falafel from Mohammed, a piece of hard candy from Hamdi, and a cup of freshly ground Turkish coffee from Aristotle, the Greek. The Sheikh was not hungry, but he knew that his presence was a sign of *baraka*, God's blessing. He insisted on paying for them all, for the vendors were poor, but he could not. It was an honor to serve Sheikh Yassin. Was not the Sheikh with his simple robes and flowing white beard the holiest man in Cairo?

Sheikh Yassin turned into a muddy alley littered with cars and push carts that marked the entrance to Boulaq, perhaps the most wretched of Cairo's slums. That, of course, was a matter of dispute, for Cairo had many wretched slums. Some, like Boulaq, stretched to eternity and were part of Cairo's soul. Others, tabbed random settlements by the press, seemed to spring up overnight. They were little more than huts cobbled together from mud bricks, packing cartons and whatever else came to hand. Slabs of metal hammered from discarded oil tins served as roofs and leaned against each other in mutual sympathy, choking the narrow alleyways that passed for roads. Most were bereft of running water and electricity, such as it was, came from generators or wires linked to an adjacent mosque. The police seldom penetrated this area, the garbage men less so. Sewage was ad hoc.

Sheikh Yassin made his way through the labyrinth of ever narrower allies until he reached a cluster of buildings that constituted his mosque compound. There were many mosques in Boulaq, but Sheikh Yassin's mosque was the largest. Its school and clinic provided services to the poor long ignored by the government. Even if the government had provided services, it would not have mattered. They still would have come to Sheikh Yassin's mosque. The services he provided were far superior to those found in the government's clinics. Doctors and dentists provided their services free of charge as a religious obligation. Legal aid was also available and, in case of emergency, a small loan was to be had. More importantly, the Sheikh had *wasta* (connections); he could fix things. One does not survive in Egypt without *wasta*, for little happens in this most ancient of countries without a bribe or connections.

The journey had been slow, for Sheikh Yassin, an imposing figure with a towering frame and belly to match, was stopped by all who knew him. It was the polite thing to do. In Egypt one does not pass on the street with a nod of the head or the wave of the hand. To do so would imply indifference or contempt, and no one in Boulaq was indifferent to Sheikh Yassin.

He was a gentle man. It was rumored that he knew everyone in Boulaq by the first name, and many considered him a saint. Even his enemies viewed him with respect, for he was a well educated man who bore the scars of Egypt's feared prisons. He was also a member of the ruling council of the Muslim Brotherhood, the largest and most powerful of Muslim organizations. If fair elections were held in Egypt, it would the Brotherhood who won, transforming the corrupt remnant of a once glorious socialist revolution into an Islamic government.

"Be patient," the Sheik preached to the throng of believers who crowded into his mosque and overflowed into its court yard and the alleys beyond. "Be patient with your troubles," he quoted the Glorious Koran. "This most corrupt and venal of governments is collapsing before our faith. It is but a matter of time before the righteous shall rule Egypt and the lands beyond. There is no need for violence. Lo, God Almighty has decreed that Muslim's shall not kill Muslims. That is what the Americans want. They want us to kill each other so that we do not kill the Israelis. They want us to kill each other so they can enslave us. They want us to kill each other so they can rape our lands and steal our oil. They want us to kill each other so they can destroy Islam. Verily I say to unto you, God Almighty will smite the United States much as he will smite Arab leaders who serve the great Satan."

"Be smart," the Sheikh continued, now in a soft and conspiratorial tone. "Parliamentary elections are approaching and you must vote against the ruling party even as they beat you with clubs and throw you into prison. What do have you to lose but you misery? Your place in heaven is assured. Is that not what matters? God is great. Each election swells our ranks and brings us closer to salvation. Oh, how the Almighty toys with them, foretelling their doom, for they are doomed to an eternity in hell. Feel them quake. They know their fate and yet they do not repent, groveling at the feet of the Americans as if mortals could stand in the way of God. How silly they are! How pathetic! Do they not know that the Americans have been warned? Have they not seen America humiliated in Iraq? You have seen the results of the last elections. We are almost there. They can no longer stop us."

His verses became a refrains repeated over and over, time after time, for the Arabic language, the language of the Glorious Koran, is a most passionate of languages and inflames with repetition and exaggeration. With each new refrain the crowd grew louder and more excited, for no one was more adept at mesmerizing the faithful than Sheikh Yassin. His sermons were recorded on tapes and disks that were passed from hand to hand to be replayed by the faithful.

It wasn't merely the content of the Sheikh's sermons that had stoked his audience to a frenzy of passion, but the deep resonance of his voice and the poetic beauty of the Koran. For many, it was as if the Prophet Mohammed was speaking to them through his chosen interpreter, for no one could recite the Koran with greater power, emotion and eloquence than Sheikh Yassin. Hardened criminals wept, vowing repentance and pledging themselves to the cause of Allah.

In reality, the Sheikh's sermon was quite moderate. He had decried violence against Muslims and he had not called for the killing of Americans, some ten thousand of whom resided in Cairo, most with minimal security. He had also been careful not to criticize the President directly, maintaining the fiction that Egypt's seemingly honest leader was absolved from the sins of his subordinates.

The Sheikh's sermon expressed the core of the Brotherhood's strategy: strike a moderate Islamic middle ground between a decadent and corrupt government on one side and the nihilist jihadists on the other. Egyptians despised their government and they feared the jihadist who rained death upon them in the name of Allah. It was innocent Egyptians who had been the primary victims of jihadist terror and it was innocent Egyptians who had lost their jobs when jihadist violence had driven the tourists from Egypt. The Brotherhood would play the government and the jihadists against each the other, tempting them to mutual destruction.

Sheikh Yassin had been one of the authors of the Brotherhood's strategy of non-violence, arguing that its earlier strategy of assassination and mayhem was counter-productive. The military was too powerful to fight in the trenches. They had to be subverted from within, their ranks infiltrated by Brothers. "Let the government spout their empty slogans of welfare and Arab nationalism," he had urged the Supreme Guide of the Brotherhood. "Our people know them for the thieves that they are. We will not be deceived and Islam will win in the long run."

The Sheikh's logic had proven sound. The government had careened from socialism to capitalism as robber barons, most former socialists, enriched themselves and the expense of the poor. Many had even married the daughters of old aristocrats and even more had forged marriage alliances with the nouveau-riche spawned by Egypt's halting transition to capitalism. It was their Mercedes that raced down Galal Street, weaving between the stinking busses and dodging pedestrians to the best of their ability. Preachers paid by the government praised

God in the elegant mosques constructed by the heirs of Nasser as a show of piety, their graceful minarets reaching toward heaven. Cynics suggested that their sermons had been written by the government, but that was hardly necessary. The government clergy were servile employees of the ruling party, anticipating its every need. They were appointed by the government and bribed by the government to extol its virtues. Life in Egypt is difficult. One has to survive.

The masses seethed and demanded violence, but Sheikh Yassin continued to urge patience. It was a tough sell, and the ranks of the jihadist swelled. In the end, Sheikh Yassin had been vindicated. The masses had recoiled from jihadist violence and the jihadists and the Egyptian government had battled each other to a standstill. More than ever, the Brotherhood claimed the middle ground, offering development and democracy in an Islamic guise.

Alas, good news seldom lasts long in Egypt, and the war between the government and the jihadists had stopped as suddenly as it had started. A truce was declared and over the next few years the government released thousands of jihadists from prison, even those accused of assassinating President Sadat. Former jihadists issued public statements denouncing violence and apologizing to the Egyptian people for past mistakes. Their pictures appeared in pro-government magazines accompanied by hints of forgiveness in the name of Islam. The government claimed victory much as it had claimed victory in each previous lull in the fighting.

The truce had been discouraged by the Americans who viewed it as folly.

"This may be a ploy to rearm," the former U.S. Ambassador had warned the Minister of Interior, but he was not unduly worried. He knew that the Egyptian security forces had maintained their surveillance of the jihadists.

"Things are under control," the Minister of Interior had assured him at the time. "Amnesty was the condition of their surrender. It was better to let them go free than force them to fight forever. Besides," the Minister of Interior assured him with a quiet nod, "this will give us time to deal with the Muslim Brotherhood. They had used the jihadists against us. Now we will use the jihadists against them. They hate each other more than they hate us, and jihadists know the Brotherhood better than we do. They have their spies, willing spies, for many in the Brotherhood are secret sympathizers of the jihadists."

"Do you really find the Brotherhood to be that great of a threat?" the former Ambassador had asked. "There has been no violence since the attempted assassination of Nasser, and that was decades ago. Besides, they are old and venal. The Supreme Guide is in his 80's and still thinks that he is fighting the British. Most are on the take and have no real interest in revolution. All of the fire went out of the organization when the jihadists split away during the 1970's. It has been all down hill for the Muslim Brotherhood since that time."

"Don't be fooled, my friend," replied the Minister of Interior with a hint of arrogance that came naturally to him when he talked to the *kawagas* (foreign masters). They know so little about Egypt, and yet they think that they know much. They will never understand the soul of Egypt. "It's all a game," continued the Minister of Interior. "The Brotherhood trains its people in the use of weapons and can turn out a fully armed militia at the drop of a hat. For the moment, they think that they can win by elections and internal subversion, but that is all a facade. Believe me, my friend, I know the Brotherhood well.

"My grandfather, may God rest his soul, was among those who plotted the assassination of Nasser. All but my grandfather, may God have mercy on his soul, were killed by Nasser's police. Only he survived. The reasons, my friend, and I thank God that you are my friend, because my grand-uncle, was a member of Nasser's Free Officers, the heroes of the Great Revolution. My grand-uncle, may God rest his soul, begged Nasser for mercy, and the great leader agreed, but on one condition."

Again he paused, wetting the former Ambassador's curiosity. "He agreed on the condition that my family, and it is the most powerful of families, would pledge their undying support for the Revolution. It was a terrible price, for my family was among the most powerful of families under the monarchy. We owned huge tracts of the best land and we owned the peasants who dwelled in its villages. They were our children and our militia. One grand uncle was a large merchant, the second a banker, the third a member of parliament, and the youngest an officer in the military. My grandfather had been a lawyer, but devoted his energies to the Brotherhood. There was no sector of Egyptian society that was beyond our reach. There was much to lose, but their father called them all together and made them swear on the Glorious Koran to accept Nasser's terms. They swore, and they saw their wealth swept before them as Nasser embraced socialism and confiscated our property."

The former Ambassador had allowed the Minister of Interior his petty arrogance. It cost him nothing and he knew that the Minister of Interior, like most Arab officials, hungered for the respect of the Anglos and the French. Such were the scars of British colonialism. Generations of Egyptians had been forced to memorize the history of Britain, but knew little of their own heritage other than the glories of their beloved Islam. Indeed, there were few glories beyond Islam. It was their ego as well as their history. Because they had been taught that they were inferior, the slightest praise from a Western official became front page news. It was a sign of approval from the gods on high. Cooperation and good will followed. Henry Kissinger, that most clever of US officials, had paved the way for peace between Egypt and Israel by putting his arm around Anwar Sadat, Nasser's successor as the President of Egypt, and saying "Anwar, you and I are world statesmen. It is up to us to save the region." That, at least, was how Parker's friends at the Institute explained Egypt's betrayal of the Arab cause.

But woe to the American official who affronted this most fragile of egos. All hope of cooperation vanished and the routine became the exception. Simple matters took months rather than weeks and only then when they were in the interest of Egypt or its venal officials.

"But you have survived quite well," commented the former Ambassador with a note of irony. "You are the Minister of Interior, your oldest brother is in charge of the Central Bank, and a third brother is once again an industrialist. Rather than vast tracts of land you now own hotels and office buildings."

"Quite right, my friend," glowed the Minister of Interior with pride. "My family was clever and knew how to exploit the revolution. Socialism has collapsed and we have regained our heritage. But, my friend, we cannot survive an Islamic revolution. It makes no difference whether it is the jihadists or the Brotherhood. The leaders will differ, but the result will be the same. Secularists will flee or be killed. Our property will be stolen and used to support terror throughout the world. It will become Iran and Iraq all over again."

"The jihadists failed because they were all emotion and violence. They killed a president and a minister or two and thought that the masses would swell up in revolt. For a while it was touch and go, and if the Brotherhood had joined in, I'm not sure what would have happened. There might have been civil war. But the Muslim Brotherhood didn't join in. They waited for the government and the jihadists to destroy each other. The jihadists played into their hands by killing anyone that disagreed with their crazed views. Killing became an end in itself. The masses recoiled and the fate of the jihadists was sealed. They couldn't survive without mass support. The Brotherhood applauded and bided their time."

"But now, my friend," sneered the Minister of Interior with obvious delight, "the Muslim Brotherhood will pay for its folly. The jihadists have surrendered, and we have turned our cannons on the Brotherhood. While the old men pontificate, we are nabbing their younger leaders. That's where the Brotherhood's strength lies, and soon they will all be dead or in jail. Then, my friend, we will strike the final blow and the show will be over. The Brotherhood will be destroyed, and we will mop up the jihadists at our leisure."

The former American Ambassador had listened intently and in the end, nodded his approval. He was an experienced diplomat who had worked his way up through the ranks and respected the cunning of the Minister of Interior. The former Ambassador also knew the limits of his own power. The Egyptian regime was in a desperate struggle for its survival and was going to do what it had to do regardless of what the Americans said. "It is better to play along and keep in touch," he had said to the Secretary of State. "At least the violence has stopped, and it won't hurt us to keep the Brotherhood under wraps." The Secretary of State, who knew little of the region, agreed.

*   *   *   *

At sixty, Sheikh Yassin was one of the younger leaders to whom the Minister of Interior had referred, for even the younger leaders in the Brotherhood were now in their fifties and sixties. Age is venerated in Egypt, and young men are expected to be patient. The Minister of Interior had thrown Sheikh Yassin into prison shortly after the truce with the jihadists, but soon realized the errors of his ways. The Sheikh had smuggled his sermons from prison and turned the courtroom into a circus.

"There is no in point creating a saint," the Minister of Interior had grumbled to the chief judge. "Release him on a technicality. Let the press portray it as a victory for democracy." The chief judge was obliging. He, too, was a member of the ruling party.

In a perverse sort way, Sheikh Yassin had welcomed imprisonment. He was too prominent to be given a military trial, the Minister of Interior's preferred method of dealing with his adversaries. Nor, did he fear the brutality and torture of his earlier imprisonments. His faith, much like that of Parker's wife, was unshakable. Civil right groups, mostly American, had packed the courtroom and flashed their stories around the globe. The American civil rights groups had influence in Washington and could not be bullied by the police.

"Stupid Americans," the Minister of Interior had hissed to his adjutant. "They scream at us to curb the fundamentalists and then have a fit when we try to put them in jail. They can't have it both ways. Any more democracy and we'll all be wearing turbans."

"Those of us who are alive," noted the adjutant with a touch realism. There was little doubt about the fate of Egypt's ruling class should power slip from their grasp, and power was slipping from their grasp. Gone were the days when they could kill with impunity.

Sheikh Yassin had not been surprised by the news of the truce. His informants were everywhere and had kept him abreast of the negotiations between the two sides. He had he not been particularly worried. The truce was an aberration, a frantic grasping at straws by two irreconcilable foes. It could not last. It had also been an incomplete truce, younger firebrands refusing to go along and fighting a rear guard action from their hovels in Boulaq, Upper Egypt and the Delta. "Besides," he had laughed to the Supreme Guide, a relative by marriage, the jihadists will lose what little popular support they retain if they denounce violence. Without violence, they are lost. Nothing else distinguishes them from the Brotherhood and they will return to the fold with their tails between their legs." Things, however, were not well. Sheikh Yassin had been released from prison, but the truce had held. The government continued to arrest mid-level Brotherhood leaders, and the jihadists were rearming. The Brotherhood was in danger. Something had to be done to shatter the truce between the jihadists and the Minister of Interior. But what?

Chapter 6

American Hospitality

The motorcade of the Minister of Interior approached the U.S. Embassy with the sirens blaring and the surrounding security guards snapping to attention. The gates of the Embassy swung open as marines descended on the three vehicles, alert for an ambush. The Minister of Interior bristled at the insinuation that there were terrorists in his ranks. It was the first of several insults that the second most powerful man in Egypt would suffer that day. It wouldn't have happened under the reign of the former Ambassador. He should have been welcomed by Jake in person, but wasn't. The DCM had done the honors. Jake was on the telephone pleading his case for a military coup with the Secretary of State.

"Thank you for coming, Your Excellency," said Jake, as the Minister of Interior was ushered into his office. Jake looked the Minister squarely in the eye as he greeted him with a crushing handshake that bruised the Minister's arthritic fingers and sent waves of pain streaking up his arm. Arabs seldom shake hands firmly and prefer to avoid eye contact. Cultural sensitivities were not Jake's strong suit, and he had given short shrift to the DCM's preaching on the topic. A ritual embrace would have been more appropriate, but Jake wasn't into embracing other men. It was bad enough that he had to refer to the Minister as Excellency. "If mister was good enough for the President of the United States," Jake murmured to himself, "it should be good enough for an Egyptian."

Jake's demeanor reflected his unsatisfactory discussion with the Secretary of State. Unlike his predecessor, he had no intention of softening his message with the diplomatic vagaries that the Egyptians were so adept at misunderstanding. "America is locked in a war on terror, and the Egyptians damn better understand that," he had thundered at the DCM during their latest go-round of cultural indoctrination. "They started all of this crap and I don't have time to pussy-foot around."

The DCM did not argue. He had given up attempting to school Jake in the niceties of diplomatic culture. Besides, Jake was right. It was Egypt that had spawned the jihadist movement and it was exiled Egyptians who were in its forefront. There was a truce in Egypt, but not beyond.

Never one to mince words, Jake came right to the point. "The President has asked me to share the latest CIA data on the resurgence of Egyptian jihadist groups with you, Your Excellency. The CIA has clear evidence that they are rearming and that they are in constant contact with Al-Qaeda and other international terrorist organizations. He fears that it is only a matter of time before they begin attacking Americans in Egypt much as they are attacking foreigners in Saudi Arabia. This, as you well understand, Your Excellency, would be a disaster for both Egypt and the United States. He was hoping that we could cooperate more fully on the matter."

"But you have our fullest cooperation, Mr. Ambassador," replied the Minister of Interior in a reproachful voice. "The jihadists have been defeated in Egypt. They begged for mercy and have become objects of scorn. We could have kept them in jail, but to what avail? They would have become martyrs and played their silly games with the government. Now they wander free, objects of scorn and futility. Egyptians have no respect for losers. Believe me, Mr. Ambassador, it is the Muslim Brothers and not the jihadists who pose the greatest threat to both of our countries, yours and mine. The jihadists are a handful of criminals and maniacs, nothing more. They strike and run, hoping that the government will collapse, but they have no army. They can't occupy territory or consolidate their gains. Look at the attacks on the United States. They couldn't capitalize on their victory. The United States shook off the attack and bin-Laden became a hunted animal."

Jake was not impressed and had the poor taste to recall the recent murder of the three intelligence agents in the Sinai. Then, with a malicious smile, he reached for the file on the corner of his desk and extracted the morning's intelligence report from the CIA. Affixed to its front page was a gruesome picture of five Egyptian men, their throats slit and *Allah Akbar* carved on the chests. He slid the picture to the Minister of Interior, noting with gravity, "They were American agents in the war against terror." Sensing the Minister's discomfort, he added with a touch of irony, "Perhaps they were your agents as well."

"Regrettable," acknowledged the Minister of Interior with a shrug of his shoulders. "It was the work of criminals and thugs, nothing more. We can't allow ourselves to be distracted from the danger of the Muslim Brotherhood, Mr. Ambassador. They are the true enemy. They number in the millions. If you include their supporters, the number grows to hundreds of millions. They claim to be peaceful, Mr. Ambassador, but don't be fooled. They can field an army in minutes. They have a government in waiting. They hate the jihadists because jihadist violence scares people away from Islam and inflames the West. Perhaps you should thank the jihadists for the wake-up call."

"Don't forget, Mr. Ambassador," the Minister of Interior hammered home his point, "there are a billion and a half Muslims in the world. Our figures suggest that no less than 20% of them are sympathetic to the Muslim Brotherhood and its allies, perhaps more. That is 300 million Muslims dedicated to the creation of an Islamic state, Mr. Ambassador, an Islamic state in Egypt and an Islamic state in the United States of America. Don't forget, Mr. Ambassador, Egypt is the headquarters and heartland of the Muslim Brotherhood. They cannot be defeated unless you defeat them here."

Despite his contempt for Egyptians, Jake was alarmed by the image of 300 million Muslim Brothers. That was a lot of ass to kick. It wasn't in Jake's nature to back down, and so he did the next best thing. He raised the ante in hopes of forcing the Minister of Interior's hand.

"Speaking only for myself, Your Excellency," said Jake in a conspiratorial tone, "I would welcome a greater involvement of the military in controlling both the Brotherhood and the jihadists. You people know how to get things done better that the civilians."

"But we cannot do that," responded the Minister of Interior with a reproachful smile that masked his loathing for Jake. "Egypt, as you know, is a democracy. Even the President of the United States has praised us for our progress in the area of human rights."

The Minister of Interior had already planned a silent coup should the coming elections prove problematic, but that was not a matter to be discussed with the Ambassador, and especially this ambassador. If the time came, there would be quiet words with the director of the CIA. For the moment, however, the Minister of Interior was content to torment his adversary. "Democracy is such a fragile flower in this part of the world, Mr. Ambassador," he gushed. "We must all do our best to make sure that it survives. That is my primary responsibility as the head of Egypt's security services. Democracy, Mr. Ambassador, is the ultimate guarantee against the Muslim extremists."

Jake bristled, knowing that he was being played for a fool, but said nothing. Others had underestimated him to their detriment, and Jake's eyes now narrowed as he studied the Minister of Interior's facial expressions and body language. Suddenly, a smile played across Jake's lips and he felt at ease, a feeling that had escaped him since his arrival in Cairo. He had made no claim to understand diplomacy and found its subtly demeaning and debilitating. "A study in irreality," he confided to close friends, coining a new word for the English language. "Pathetic countries with no more than a handful of people become equals of the United States. Idiots become excellencies."

Jake didn't like people, but he seldom underestimated them. The more he studied the Minister of Interior the less he liked him and the more he respected him. By his very nature, Jake was inclined to respect a man who had killed thousands and tortured many times that number. But it was not merely the Minister's storied past that impressed Jake. Aside from a hint of arrogance, the Minister had revealed no emotion. Even the suggestion of a coup had not fazed him. Jake had no inkling of the cards that he was holding. It was this thought that had brought the smile to Jake's lips. He was in a poker game. Not merely a poker game, but a no limit poker game that could determine the fate of the world.

Jake may not have understood diplomacy, but he did understand poker. It was his passion. The higher the stakes, the better he liked it. It wasn't the money that mattered, but the destruction of a lesser opponent. More than one adversary had left Jake's table bankrupt, and others had been forced into unspeakable humiliations. Jake seldom lost, but the pain of losing had made him shrewd and cunning. In his heart of hearts he worried that he was not as intelligent as some people, and especially those with fancy degrees and effete manners. Money and winning reassured him that he was the best. "Don't take it so hard," a friend had consoled him after one of his rare losses. "It's only money, and you have so much more than the rest of us."

"You're right," said Jake with a forced smile. To admit a weakness would be the kiss of death.

The image of 300,000,000 Muslim Brothers descending on the United States with drawn swords had terrified Jake at the time, but no more. Everything had fallen into place once Jake realized that he was in a poker game. There can be no bluff without a credible threat, and the Minister of Interior was using the Muslim Brotherhood as a bluff to force him into accepting his truce with the jihadists. "Good show," Jake smiled to himself, giving credit where credit was due. "This slimy bastard has trumped my CIA card with his threat of 300 million Muslim Brothers. Damn good show." But Jake was not fooled. More than ever he was convinced that the Minister of Interior was on the side of the jihadists.

Jake looked the Minister of Interior squarely in the eye, rubbing his chin in contemplation, and said in a thoughtful voice, "You are right, Your Excellency. Democracy is the only way to solve the Muslim problem. Please count on my support in every way possible. In the mean time, we will have to work together to destroy the extremists, all of the extremists."

The Minister of Interior left the Embassy with a deep sense of unease. He missed the former Ambassador with his wit and charm. Had he allowed himself to be flattered by this most elegant of ambassadors? Perhaps, but so be it. Things got done, and both sides were happy. Cooperation and flattery had now given way to humiliation and intimidation.

It was not the humiliation, however, that preoccupied the Minister of Interior as Jake bid him farewell at his office door. Rather, it was Jake's direct assault on his truce with the jihadists. The Ambassador had bluntly opened their discussion with the CIA's accusation that the jihadists were rearming. This had been followed by his suggestion that he would welcome a coup. Ambassadors didn't speak for themselves and Jake, according to sources, was close to the President. Why else would they have sent him to Egypt? Equally threatening were Jake's comments about democracy. Something was in the works, but what?

Chapter 7

▼

Curious Dances

Much to Parker's delight, he found that they had been placed on the guest list for Embassy receptions. He loved the strangely choreographed affairs with their lavish food and abundant drink. "Grand balls becoming of the world's monarchs," he thought to himself, "with masked couples changing partners at each pause in the music." There was, of course, no music, and there were no masks, per se. The dances were mind games between diplomats, their emotionless smiles hiding their thoughts far better than masks of porcelain. Parker loved games, and mind games in particular. His appearance and demeanor differed little from those of the diplomats, and he might well have joined the Foreign Service if an overly inquisitive mind had not led in other directions. "You look so normal," one of his professors had cautioned, "but you have too much imagination for a diplomatic career. I don't think that you can take orders that well."

The dances were slow dances, painfully slow. Jake found them infuriating. He watched in anger as the diplomats of the world, his own included, exchanged polite niceties while terrorists stalked the United States. This was not the way that one kicked ass.

Parker's virtual dances with Mandy had been pleasant mind games that hinted, ever so subtly, at the possibility of other games. Or, was that part of her mind game? They had danced twice that first evening, decorum and the presence of his wife prohibiting a greater show of interest. It was also her job to work the crowd. She suggested meeting for tea by the Nile. Probably just professional, he cautioned himself, but the vibes had been good.

Smith passed by from time to time during the reception, lamenting that, as one of the hosts, he didn't have time to chat. Then, as if a light had flashed in his mind, he suggested a nightcap at his villa. "These damn receptions don't last too long," he sighed in obvious relief, "and I still don't have the foggiest idea of what you are doing at the Institute of Social Analysis. We can't get near the place and they won't come here. You can ride with me and I will have my driver take you back to Zamalek."

Friendships come easy for those working abroad, and the friendship between Smith and Parker came easier than most. Both relished mind games and found sanity through humor. They shared a mutual admiration for the position of the other and a common search for the soul of Egypt. Each, in his own way, had become preoccupied with the Islamic revival and its impact on the region. Barriers, however, had to be overcome. Smith could not risk a slip of the tongue that might find its way, however inadvertently, to the Minister of Interior or worse, to the Egyptian press. By the same token, Parker was unwilling to betray the confidences of his friends at the Institute. That trust had been the product of years of mutual collaboration. It was not to be squandered by overzealous diplomats or their colleagues on the "other side of the house," a subtle reference to the CIA.

Their night caps had become a ritual of confidence building. Parker regaled Smith with portraits of his colleagues at the Institute and the caravan of visitors to the Boss's office. His message was clear: I tread where you cannot go. Smith reciprocated with stories of Jake, his frustration with being a travel guide for congressmen, and the difficulty of dealing with the Israelis. "Whatever weapons we give them," he lamented, "they always want more. I've never seen such an insecure people. They can destroy the Arabs ten times over and they still don't feel secure."

"Perhaps with cause," Parker responded. "The Arabs can lose a thousand battles and still survive. The Israelis can't afford to lose one. They are also having a tough time with the terrorists."

"As are we," nodded Smith. "But, the Egyptians don't seem to understand that. They have made peace with the jihadists, the most vicious of all terrorists. It's insane."

"Quite," said Parker.

The topic had been broached and then immediately put aside. Neither Parker nor Smith was ready to commit further at this point. Both felt a sense of exhilaration at the conclusion of the evening. For the first time in his life, Parker felt that he could have an impact on the real world. Rather than merely studying politics from a safe and sanitized distance, he had suddenly become part of the political process.

Smith, for his part, chaffed under the isolation of the Embassy and the sterile rigidity of diplomatic protocol. Talking to Parker he felt as if it were he who was sitting in the Boss's office sipping endless cups of tea and eavesdropping on the endless pageant of officers, bureaucrats and clergy passing through its portals. Each night-cap with Parker had become a flying carpet that enabled him to change places with his alter-ego.

If Parker had found the Embassy reception stimulating, his wife had not. Parker, as a curiosity and source of inside information, was much sought after. Everyone wanted to dance with him. She, however, had nothing to say and was soon abandoned by her suitors. Neither did she enjoy the night-caps which followed. Indeed, the first would be her last. Taken aside by Smith's wife, they had chatted about school in a desperate attempt at friendship. They failed miserably.

"What a bitch," Smith's wife had hissed once the driver had whisked the Parkers back to Zamalek. "You know that I love you, but I'm not going through that again. I've never met anyone quite so bitter and quite so self-righteous."

Parker's wife was equally disenchanted, finding her hostess to be a pompous sot. "She thinks she's a goddess because she's a diplomat's wife," Constance had complained to Parker on the return trip to Zamalek. I don't know what you see in those people, anyway. They are godless alcoholics living in marble palaces at taxpayers' expense." Then, feeling a particular annoyance at a husband who had enjoyed himself far too much, she turned to Parker and asked with bitterness, "What game are you playing now?"

"Jihad," whispered Parker beneath the hearing of the Egyptian driver as he sunk his fingers into his wife's thigh.

"God, I wish you'd be serious," she lashed out at him, recoiling to the far side of the back seat. "I don't know how much longer I can take this filthy city and your filthy friends at the Embassy."

"I am serious," he responded, not bothering to pursue her thigh to the far side of the car. "God will provide."

She knew that she wouldn't leave. She also knew that she was done with the Embassy and Parker's odious friends. The church became her excuse for avoiding the Embassy receptions and the night caps that followed. It also became her social outlet and her link to sanity. She became the church's secretary, a time consuming job of little interest to a reluctant congregation. Her only competition for the job had come from Miss Southern Geniality. The pastor inclined toward the latter, but was easily outvoted by a congregation that consisted largely of the plump wives of American executives.

* * * *

Parker's tea with Mandy had gotten off to a slow start. Far from meeting at a secluded hideaway, they had met at one of the tourist casinos (drinks, no gambling) that stretch along the Nile as it wends it's way through the heart of Cairo, separating the city proper from its Giza suburbs. Security guards were as numerous as tourists, for the murder of even a single tourist could send foreigners fleeing in panic. Parker had walked from the Institute and arriving first, was escorted by the maitre'd to a preferred table adjacent to the river. Parker often stopped at the casino on his trek back to Zamalek and was known to be a generous tipper, at least by Egyptian standards. Mandy arrived a few moments later, being deposited by an Embassy car that waited discreetly at a distance. He rose to greet her, flashing an engaging smile of one sincerely pleased to see his guest. She smiled in return and leaned forward to receive the ritual hug so common among casual acquaintances. To her surprise, the embrace had been stiff, awkward and totally at odds with his character.

"You're not a hugger!" she laughed, recovering quickly to avoid embarrassment.

"Never on a first date," chided Parker, enjoying the humor of the situation. His choice of words was unfortunate, for the thought of them having a "date" implied far more intimacy than she was willing to accept from a married man who she barely knew.

"What luck," she grimaced internally. "He's yet another male seeking refuge from a dull marriage." She had hoped for more than that from Parker. She wasn't sure of precisely what she had hoped for, but it wasn't this. Her thoughts, however, mellowed as she reflected on her futile efforts to strike a responsive chord with Parker's wife. The woman was clearly a bitch.

"I don't date married men," she smiled kindly, in a practiced maneuver to keep an important relationship alive while holding the predator at bay. She was an attractive woman, and men found it difficult to separate business from pleasure, especially oriental men inured to the charms of their dark haired sisters.

"Merely poetic license," Parker brushed aside her comment as if it were irrelevant. "I seldom introduce my wife to ladies whom I intend to date."

"It might not be a bad tactic," Mandy thought to herself, but pulled in her claws, and made do with, "Sorry, but you don't know how many jerks there are in the world. Your wife is a charming lady and I don't blame you for being in love with her."

"Charming and beyond," smiled Parker with his unique talent for adding a hint of ambiguity to otherwise mundane sentences. "We have been together for a long time."

Mandy had not wanted an assault, but neither had she wanted his affirmation of love for a female that she found obnoxious. There was no way that he could be in love with that woman, but he had defended her with a nonchalant ease that conveyed sincerity. Finding it hard to read Parker, she retreated to safer ground.

"So, Professor, what precisely do you do? Or do you prefer Doctor?"

"I prefer Scott, but if you leave me no choice, I prefer Professor. Hospitals seem so dismal."

"So what do you do?" she repeated her question.

"I guess you would say that I'm a political psychologist with a passion for the Middle East and the Arabic language. A childhood affliction. I read the *Arabian Nights* too many times as a kid. You know, flying carpets, genies in a bottle, daring thieves wielding massive daggers, four wives, a harem full of concubines, and dark-eyed houris around every corner. The trouble is," he lamented with feigned sadness, "I haven't found any of them."

"*Miskeen*," said Mandy, using the Arabic word for poor bastard. "No flying carpets, no concubines in the harem, and no dark-eyed houris. Only dull bureaucrats and thieves."

"Not so," responded Parker. "I can conduct the most amazing interviews as long as they seem bureaucratic. Don't forget, almost everyone in Egypt is either a thief or works for the government."

"That also includes the jihadists," Mandy had wanted to say, but didn't. "Don't startle your prey," she cautioned her self. There would be time for that when they had become better friends. Suddenly, she realized that she wanted to become better friends, wife or no wife.

"Thank you for the tea," said Mandy as Parker handed the maitre'd a bill and motioned for him to keep the change. Perhaps a penny or two would reach the waiter. "I hope we can do this again."

"You mean a second date," laughed Parker. *"Insha'allah"* (if God wills), he added with a teasing smile. No phrase is more common in the Islamic world or is better suited to making vague advances without fear of rejection. He, too, wanted to become better friends.

"Touché," smiled Mandy and entered the waiting car, the driver at attention.

Chapter 8

▼

The Goddess of the Nile

Parker passed by Boulaq several times a week, dodging the pot holes that Sheikh Yassin had dodged, moving from the sidewalk to the gutter to avoid a convoy of chattering women in *hijab* (religious dress), most with offspring in tow. Like most convoys, they claimed the right of way. Returning to the sidewalk to avoid a swerving motor bike, Parker skirted a stack of used tires, jumped over a trickle of raw sewage, and found himself humming a few bars of "Over the garbage and through the sewage to Grandmother's house we go." Parker was a clever man, perhaps too clever.

Coming to the entrance of Boulaq, he stepped carefully off the elevated sidewalk, dodging as best he could the pool of dubious liquid that awaited below. Most sidewalks in Cairo, if they exist at all, are about a foot high to keep cars from using them as parking lots. Those lining Galal Street were beaten into submission, and the few that remained were pitted with gaping holes once destined for trees to hide the slum that lay beyond. With little choice, the residents of Boulaq crowded the sides of Galal Street, seemingly unmindful of the onslaught of speeding Mercedes.

For all of its chaos, Parker loved Cairo: the noise, the swirling dust of a desert city, the endless stream of traffic, the jostling crowds, the ever changing pageant of color, the Nile, the pyramids, the dazzling beauty of its elegant mosques, the gazelle-eyed beauties with immense breasts peering down from garish theater posters with promises that would go unfulfilled, the book stores with their wares sprawled across the sidewalk, the humor of a people who laughed to ease their despair, the intrigue, the pulse of a city that never slept, and the riverside cafes that were as buoyant at four in the morning as they were in early evening.

Parker peered down the narrow road leading into Boulaq, resisting the temptation to wander its putrid alleys. One did not love Boulaq. But, for those in search of Egypt's soul, its lurid appeal was irresistible. It could not be otherwise, for the majority of Egypt's 70 million plus residents lived in its vast slums or equally putrid villages, many still without running water. Residents of the latter had to make do with primitive wells. A few preferred the water of Nile because of its reputed powers of fertility and sexual prowess.

It was not the broad thoroughfares of Heliopolis, the glitzy villas and high rises of Maadi, or the tree lined streets of Zamalek and Garden City that captured the soul of Egypt. Their residents were its rulers, the wielders of the Mercedes that careened down Galal Street. They should have been happy with their wealth and power, but they were not. Both were fleeting. Jihadist assassinations had eased only to be replaced by the ominous prospect of a Muslim Brotherhood victory in the approaching parliamentary elections. Even the walls of middle class neighborhoods were smeared with that most frightening of slogans, "God is the solution."

Parker made his way past the shops that had hosted Sheikh Yassin, but resisted the temptation to stop. He paused to have his shoes shined by Ahmed the crippled bootblack, passed the Children's Hospital and the Al Ahram towers, and then made his way to one of the gleaming new office buildings that were squeezing the residents of Boulaq ever deeper into despair. He didn't have to glance at his shoes to know that Ahmed's efforts had been in vain, but passing a few minutes with the cripple had become part of his routine. Like all those who give to beggars, he felt uplifted by his charity, as small as it was. He had thought to ask the bootblack about the cause of his deformity, but found it difficult to understand the cripple's guttural accent. The temptation, however, was great, for no character in Neguib Mafouz's novels of life among Egypt's poor had made a greater impression upon Parker than that of the cripple maker.

Parker showed his pass to the guard at the door and showed it again to the security guards lounging behind a table just beyond the entrance. Parker was known and the inspection was cursory. He mounted the elevator to the third floor, the first of several floors occupied by the Institute, and dropped his briefcase in his office. He then knocked on door of the Boss. Receiving no response, he made his way to the secretary's office and received the inevitable *lissa ma gash* (he'll be here in a little while). He refused the invariable offer of tea and climbed the stairs to the fourth floor, entering the bull pen where researchers were more or less engrossed in their various projects. Most arrived at ten and left at two, but the hours between were flexible and allowances were made for necessary errands. The wife of a retired general read novels and chatted with friends. A giant of Nubian heritage held court for an endless series of supplicants. A wispy youth scarred by small pox scribbled furiously in a notebook. Others came and went as the spirit moved them. All but the Wisp found Parker sympathetic and, barring a rare deadline, were unsparing in their hospitality. Few people in the world are more gracious that the Egyptians, but the Wisp was an exception. He remained sullen and viewed Parker with suspicion.

The Boss arrived, and Parker descended to the office of his long time friend. The Boss greeted him with warmth and Parker sank into one of deep leather chairs that formed a semi-circle around the director's massive desk, its surface stacked high with reports and books. A steady stream of visitors filled the chairs, sipping coffee, tea, or coke, and smoking whatever burned. The Boss preferred a pipe but graciously accepted the Cuban cigars that Parker provided on a daily basis. Visitors came and went. All were duly introduced to Parker, and each shared in the conversations of the others. Many stayed for an hour or more. The Boss headed Parker's project and ran interference for its researchers, but otherwise contented himself with an occasional comment. That was fine with everyone, for without the Boss's support, there would be no project.

Leaving the Institute, Parker wandered along the Nile, stopped to visit friends at the American University, checked the books at Madbouli's, and then sipped tea at Groppies while he read the Arabic papers. Vanity, perhaps, but Arabic was a difficult language and he was proud of his accomplishments. It was true that he couldn't penetrate the secrets of Ahmed the bootblack, but few outside of Boulaq could.

Parker returned to his flat overlooking the Nile and made a few cryptic notes that would be indecipherable to the secret police. "The Minister of Interior is very curious about our project," the Boss had warned him. "Don't give him any unnecessary ammunition." Parker hoped that he would be able to decipher his artful scribbling once he returned to the States. His labors done, Parker joined his wife on the balcony. She was still chaffing from the long school bus ride from Maadi and had little desire for conversation. His thoughts drifted to the Institute, her's to rural Nebraska.

This most glorious of routines repeated itself day after day, for there was little else for Parker to do at the moment. The project had been designed and the interviewers trained. Things would be frantic when the data started coming in, but that was down the road. For the time being, he was free to pursue his search for the soul of Egypt. He had also become fascinated with the psyche of the Islamic extremists, but that was his secret. He had been welcomed as a specialist in motivation, not as a snoop. Curiosity about politics brought stony silence, but none more so than the chill that had followed his off handed joke about the CIA.

Parker had not repeated the mistake, and avoided sensitive topics. He learned by listening and engaging in random chit-chat. He seldom asked questions, for that would arouse suspicions. He was, after all, an American. The Egyptians, by contrast, were curious about everything, including his love life and his contacts with the Embassy. He said nothing of the former and made no secret of the latter. How could he? Nothing he did went unnoticed. Besides, it was his link to the Embassy that made him so interesting to his Egyptian colleagues. It added to his mystique and hinted of influence that might be of use to them. Honesty was the best deception.

Other researchers of lesser rank emerged from obscure portals carrying requested documents or seeking instructions. Their visits were brief and of little interest to Parker. That was, until a tall gazelle clad in Islamic chic peeped through the door, hurried to the general's wife, uttered a few words, snatched a glance at Parker who was sitting with the Nubian, and then fled to from whence she came.

"Lovely, isn't she?" smirked the Nubian, when they were alone. "So stunning in her Islamic finery crafted in Paris to reveal more than it conceals. You know that she came to see you just as no less than ten others have come to see you over the past week or two. Ah, but you didn't notice. You must be more perceptive if you are to discover the soul of Egypt. Surely you don't intend to content yourself with those pallid Western women who flock to the East in the search of romance. *Miskeen* (poor bastard), they will find nothing for they have no soul. Believe me, I have tried them all. Nothing my friend, but nothing, compares to the soul of Egypt. But this one is the queen, the goddess. There are none more beautiful."

After a long pause the Nubian continued with a mournful sigh, "But alas, she is not for mortals. Her grandfather is Sheikh Yassin, a member of the ruling council of the Muslim Brotherhood and one of the most powerful men in Egypt. One word from the Sheikh and Boulaq will erupt in anger. Her smile can be the kiss of death. Those who have come too close to her have disappeared, perhaps abroad, perhaps not. Her reputation is of great importance to the Sheikh, for moral flaws are political flaws. Even I am afraid to pick this plum," continued the Nubian, his eyes gleaming and his massive belly shaking with hilarity.

They laughed until they cried, these two kindred souls from different worlds, but the Nubian had made his point. Hilarity in Egypt is deadly serious. So serious, in fact, that Abdul Nasser, that most powerful of Egyptian dictators, had maintained a special office charged with collecting jokes about the government and crushing the most damaging. His hope had been in vain.

Parker's favorite joke began with Nasser's son waking up hungry in the middle of the night and wending his way to the fridge found it empty. Surprised by approach of his stern father, the youth asked with the deepest respect. "Is it true that you are the father of the country? That is an esteemed honor."

"Yes," replied Nasser, "I am the father of the country,"

"And who is mother?" asked the youth.

"Your mother is the people, my son," replied Nasser.

"And who am I?" asked the son.

"You are the hope of the future," responded Nasser, patting the youth on the head with affection.

Later that evening the boy heard his parents making love in the adjacent bedroom. "My God," thought the boy, "the father of the country is screwing the people while the hope of the future starves to death."

*　　*　　*　　*

"It hardly seems fair to blame the Sheikh for the errors of the granddaughter," said Parker, picking up the thread of the conversation.

The Nubian nodded his head thoughtfully, but sighed. "You know our society. We are tribal. The grandfather is the patriarch, and the indiscretions of his children reflect on his power and his honor. How can the Sheikh hope to rule the country if he can't rule his family? His fault, of course, was spoiling his eldest son and allowing him to live in the United States for a period after completing his studies. He became secular and raised his daughter in the American way, at least to some degree. Ask the Wisp, he is closer to these things than I am. He studies the lady's every move. He stalks her silently on his gum-sole shoes. She is his obsession."

"But he always seems so busy," said Parker evasively, adhering to his policy of not showing excessive interest in Egyptian politics. "He seems to find me suspicious."

"Bah," responded the Nubian, himself curious about the affairs of the Wisp. "He would sell his soul for a fellowship in the States. He has tried repeatedly, but keeps getting turned down. He needs some connections. Use your *wasta* (connections) with the Embassy."

Warning bells flashed in Parkers mind. The conversation had become unaccustomedly direct. Was the Nubian exploring his ties with the Embassy? Or, was he merely trying to help a friend, if the Wisp were, indeed, his friend. "It's not that important," responded Parker. "Anyway, I have no *wasta* at the Embassy."

"But you have the loveliest of *wasta*," persisted the Nubian, replacing his serious demeanor with a leering smile that could only refer to Parker's tea with Mandy along the Nile.

Parker was not surprised that he had been observed with Mandy, for the city that never slept was also a city that never closed its eyes. *Bowabs* (door watchers) peered from every building, gathering scraps of information that might bring a few piasters from an interested party. Much the same was true of waiters, cooks, cleaners, drivers, and the garbage men who scaled the back stairs of his apartment building, its recesses so littered with filth that they had become unpassable. Neighbors spied on neighbors, anxious to uncover a hint of scandal. One family's gain was another family's loss. The Minister of Interior employed thousands of special agents and legions of stringers. The President's Office had its own intelligence network as did the various branches of the military and the ruling party. The Israeli Mosad was there in force, as was the CIA and the Saudi Mukabarat. The Brotherhood had their spies and the jihadists had theirs. All knew that the fate of Egypt would shape the Middle East, and all knew that the regime was too rotten to endure. All were nervous.

Parker was surprised by the news that his meeting with Mandy had reached the Nubian, a mid-level researcher in a scientific research institute. It could, of course, have been a chance event. Perhaps a member of the Institute had wandered by and recognized Parker sitting with a striking blond of interesting proportions, not too much of anything, but just enough of everything. This was interesting news, indeed, for the dark-eyed houris who found unaccustomed excuses to visit the bullpen in search of a glimpse of the handsome *kawaga*.

"Merely a pleasant diversion," smiled Parker, happy to have a secret of interest to his Egyptian friend. "Besides," he continued maliciously, "it's hardly worth the effort if she doesn't have a soul."

"Rumor has it that she does," replied the Nubian softly.

Mercifully, the door opened and the gazelle slipped through, snatched a glance at Parker and rushed to deposit a folder on the desk of the general's wife.

Suddenly a strange sound ushered from the Nubian's throat. It was a hoarse rasping sound of a soul in agony. The gazelle's face flushed a crimson red as she fled from the room.

"It seems that you have yet to find the soul of Egypt," gloated the Nubian, as he savored Parker's bewilderment. "That's the sound that Arab women make when they have an organism."

"I thought you were afraid of the Sheikh," Parker mumbled, acknowledging the Nubian's superiority in things cultural and lamenting his own failings. "What happens if she complains to her grandfather, the Sheikh?"

"She can't complain because she can't admit that she understands these things," responded the Nubian with a broad smirk on his ample face. "Besides, she craves my body."

Chapter 9

How Best to Serve God

Sheikh Yassin was in a forgiving mood as he made his rounds of Boulaq that warm autumn day. A compassionate man, he stopped to pay his respects to Sheikh Hassan, the jihadist leader recently released from prison by the Minister of Interior. They had been comrades in their student days, struggling to keep the Brotherhood alive during the tyranny of the Nasser years. Both bore the scars of that era. The socket of Sheikh Hassan's left eye was covered by a patch and he walked with a heavy limp and then only with the aid of a cane. His eye had been gouged out by an overzealous inquisitor and his right knee cap shattered by the heavy wooden clubs used to beat suspects into confession. He had not confessed and bore his wounds as a living testament to his faith. Sheikh Yassin had been left to rot in a stinking prison cell, but was seldom tortured.

The reasons for Yassin's lighter treatment were obvious to both. Yassin was from a big family that had *wasta* and the means to pay bribes. Thus, his body was not among the starved carcasses whisked from their cells in the dead of night, the only witnesses to their passing being the maggots in their porridge. Sheikh Yassin, too, had stood the test of faith by refusing to purchase his release with a pledge of good conduct and the unspoken obligation of informing on his comrades. As both were students, they fared better than workers and peasants. The government feared students because they were idolized in a society of illiteracy and despair. Their bodies could not be swept away in the midst of night, their fate known only to their God, the God, who now sheltered them in paradise.

It was in the prisons of Egypt that the works of Sayeed Qutb, the maverick Muslim Brotherhood philosopher, were debated. Egyptian society, Sayeed Qutb had preached, was no different than Mecca in the years before God revealed the Holy Koran to the Prophet Mohammed. Countless gods contended for power, each with its own temples and moneylenders, but none more powerful than the gods of greed and whoredom. Just as the forces of the Prophet Mohammed had destroyed the corrupt society of Mecca, Sayeed Qutb had preached, so the jihadists must destroy the corrupt societies of Egypt and the Muslim world. They, too, were ruled by the gods of greed and whoredom, and America had become their high priest. There could be no compromise with the enemies of the true God whatever their superficial piety. Reform was an illusion, a clever trick to lead the faithful from the path of righteousness.

Sheikh Hassan had embraced Sayeed Qutb's philosophy with an all consuming passion. He had wept when Qutb was hung on a trumped up charge of treason and vowed to sweep the secularists from Egypt.

Sheikh Yassin, by contrast, had recoiled from Qutb's views, condemning them as heresy. The Koran spoke of compassion, equality, development and unity among Muslims. It forbade the killing Muslims and innocents. Islam revered women and children. They were to be protected, not slaughtered. Had not the Prophet Mohammed forgiven the people of Mecca and led them to the path of righteousness? Had he not permitted Christians and Jews to live in peace among Muslims? Did Muslims, Jews and Christians not worship the same God and honor the same prophets? To be sure, the Prophet Mohammed had ordered Muslims to protect their faith, but not at the risk of destroying that faith itself.

"Be logical Hassan," Yassin had pleaded. "If you kill all who have sinned, nothing will remain but a mass grave. Did you not fall prey to wine as a youth? Redemption came by the will of God. Allow it to come to others. Our job is to prepare the way. When society has repented, its leaders will follow."

Sheikh Yassin was also a pragmatic man. Nasser's assault on the Brotherhood had convinced him that the government was too powerful to be overthrown by a rag-tag bunch of naive fanatics hopelessly divided into bizarre sects, each headed by a self-proclaimed sheikh jealously guarding his power. Armed conflict was madness, a receipt for the slaughter of what remained of the Brotherhood. To be sure, society was corrupt and rotten, but that was a blessing. It was God's way of paving the way for an Islamic state. The more people recoiled from the oppression and decadence of the government, the more they would flock to the Muslim Brotherhood. Subversion was a surer way to victory than confrontation. There would be a coup, but it would be a peaceful coup. The agents of the devil would order their troops to attack, but the troops would refuse and Islam would reign. Much as in the days of the Prophet, there would be peace and enlightenment.

Sheikh Hassan had bristled at Yassin's logic and screamed, "Muslims who break God's law are no longer Muslims. Innocents who serve the enemies of God are no longer innocents. Is not the mother who suckles the soldier of tomorrow the enemy of God?"

"Read the Glorious Koran, my friend," Sheikh Yassin had responded with infuriating logic. "We are all sinners and God will judge our fate. Are you not a sinner for claiming the right to excommunicate Muslims and deny them their place in paradise? It is for God to judge who is a Muslim and who is not, my emotional friend, not you."

"Death in the service of the God will absolve me," sneered Hassan. "If I am to sin, may it be in the service of God."

So the debate had unfolded. Hassan and other disciples of Sayeed Qutb became jihadists, killing in their mad effort to cleanse the earth of sin. Yassin and the remnants of the Muslim Brotherhood struggled to remain true to the movement's path of good works and proselytization. Rather than killing Muslims, they would lead them to the path of righteousness. That was God's will. The searing wound that divided the jihadists and the Muslim Brothers was so deep that former friends had been become the bitterest of enemies, hating each other more than they hated Nasser and his successors.

One can only speculate on the fate of the Islamic revival if the Israeli blitzkrieg of 1967 had not come to the rescue, smashing Nasser's glorious army, the largest in the Middle East, in less than a week. Cairo had been bombed and soldiers ran, many leaving their heavy Russian boots to rot in the sand. They were the lucky ones. Sunken hulls clogged the Suez Canal and charred tanks, their crews interred, littered the Eastern desert. Egypt's vaunted Mig fighters lay shattered on their runways, their powers untested. They were the hope of Egypt's military and had been the first target of the Israelis.

From the ashes of defeat rose a simple voice, "God is the solution. We have been punished for deserting the way of Islam. Repent and you shall be saved." It began as a whisper, for members of the Brotherhood were still hunted as animals, but soon came to a crescendo. The hunters had lost the taste for blood.

Anwar Sadat, the successor to Nasser, had seized upon this voice to smite his opponents, and they were many. He emptied Egypt's prisons and allowed the Muslim firebrands to crush the Nasserites and communists. The Brotherhood vowed peace and prayer and was encouraged to rebuild its network of mosques and clinics. The jihadists lurked in the shadows, biding their time as their numbers multiplied. Was Sadat unaware of the virulent new strain of Jihadism that had been spawned in Egypt's prisons during the twenty years of Nasser's vengeance, a strain of Islam so extreme that God and violence had become one? Perhaps, but he was a desperate man, and desperate men do desperate things.

Sheikh Yassin was among those released from prison by Sadat as was Sheikh Hassan. Each was convinced of the righteousness of his cause. The gulf between the two men was unbridgeable. While the Brotherhood preached passive resistance and patience, the jihadists unleashed a reign of terror so violent that even its ardent supporters recoiled in horror. Violence had become an end in itself, killing for killing's sake. The jihadists attacked government officials and they attacked foreign tourists. No one was safe, neither Muslims nor non-Muslims.

The army seemed reticent to attack, its ranks having been infested by jihadist cadres. In the end, special police units were created to strike the jihadists, often destroying apartment blocks or whole villages suspected of harboring a single jihadist leader. Sheikh Hassan was among the first to be re-arrested. Inured to pain by his faith, he smuggled orders to his followers via the Islamic lawyers, that infamous fringe of legality who, for reasons only understood by the Egyptians, were allowed entrance to Egypt's prisons in the name of human rights.

Egypt had approached the brink of civil war. Then suddenly, the jihadist tide crested and a truce was declared. The reasons were many. The slaughter of suspected jihadists had taken its toll, but it was not the special police or the mass arrests that had led to the collapse of the jihadists. It was their mutual hatreds, their lack of coordination and their pointless violence. Islam forbad the killing of Muslims and, aside from a few tourists, the jihadists seemed intent on killing any Muslim who rejected the goal of returning Islam to a time warp of the 7th century. The jihadists had become more frightening than the government and their supporters fled.

The government had also been clever, allowing the Muslim Brotherhood just enough success to convey the impression that a moderate Islamic state could be achieved by peaceful means. In retrospect, this had been a mistake. The Brotherhood had flourished, challenging the government at every turn. Even fraudulent elections had become dangerous; the insidious sermons of the Brotherhood mosques even more so. How many mosques did the Muslim Brotherhood control? Thousands, or perhaps tens of thousands. It was now the Brotherhood rather than the jihadists who threatened the survival of the regime. The government had created a monster far more dangerous to its survival than the jihadists. So the government had changed strategies. Guided by the newly crowned Minister of Interior, the jihadist leaders, most rotting in prison, were offered their freedom if they confessed their errors and renounced violence.

The Egyptian President had been hesitant, but the Minister of Interior persisted. "They have become old men," the Minister of Interior had argued. "Our spies have monitored their laments. They long for their families and curse their isolation. They have become forgotten people, relics of the past. The younger leaders no longer listen to them and the exiles sheltered in London and Paris claim the glory for their victories. Confusion reigns. In the meantime, they grow older and weaker, begging their frail bodies to survive for another day. They fear death and know that their relatives will not see their bodies, only the maggots. Give them their freedom, Mr. President, but only at the price of confessing their errors and renouncing violence. Their suffering will have been for naught, and people will despise them for their spiritual weakness. The killing will ebb, and we will be free to deal with the Brotherhood."

The Egyptian president seemed skeptical, but had little choice. His regime couldn't survive the continued violence. "Have you discussed this with the Ambassador," he asked in resignation. It was not necessary to say which ambassador, for there was only one ambassador that mattered.

"Yes, Your Excellency," replied the Minister of Interior. "He agrees."

It is not clear that the former U.S. Ambassador would have agreed with the Minister of Interior's claim, but he had been suitably diplomatic and his response had remained subject to interpretation.

* * * *

Sheikh Hassan had listened with interest as the Islamic lawyer whispered news of a curious conversation between his cousin and the Minister of Interior. "The Minister of Interior," the lawyer's cousin had hinted during one of the massive family gatherings so common in Egypt, "might be willing to consider a truce with the jihadists providing the violence stopped."

The offer was informal and it was clear that the initiative would have to come from the prison sheikhs, as the jihadist leaders in prison were referred to. The government, obviously, could not announce a truce for that would be a confession of failure and prepare the way for a civil war. If the prison sheiks recanted, they would be freed in a grand gesture of Islamic compassion. There would be nothing sudden, mind you. It would take place over the course of years. In the meantime, prison conditions would improve, there would be no more torture, and families would be allowed to visit.

More vague discussions had followed and, with much sadness, Sheikh Hassan and the other prison sheiks had confessed their errors and renounced violence. Their confessions were plastered on the front pages of the Egyptian press. The exiled leaders had denounced the truce, as did many of the younger firebrands, but the violence had largely stopped.

Sheikh Hassan's gamble had been a desperate one. Peace and public humiliation would be traded for the opportunity to free thousands of jihadists from prison. Authority networks and militias would have to be rebuilt and the public would need time to forget the mistakes of the past, a great deal of time. In the meantime, the government would destroy the Brotherhood, leaving the faithful little choice but to embrace the jihadists. There would no longer be a seductive middle ground promising Islam without pain. The more corrupt and oppressive the government became, the greater the power of the jihadists would become. A cruel smile played across Sheikh Hassan's lips as he allowed himself a rare moment of enjoyment as he contemplated the brilliance of his plan. The government had to destroy the Brotherhood to survive, but it could not destroy the Brotherhood without a reign of terror so violent that the excesses of the jihadists would soon be forgotten. It could not be otherwise, for rare was an Egyptian family without a link to the Brotherhood.

Hassan was not a dreamer. He had suffered too much to be deluded by whimsy. He also knew the risks of his plan. He feared humiliation and the shattering of his moral authority more than he feared the terrors of prison. Without violence the jihadists would be less than the Brotherhood; they would have no reason to exist. Hassan also knew that the Minister of Interior would be watching and waiting, biding his time until he had crippled the Brotherhood. Time was of the essence, but how much time did he have? How much time would pass before the government could crush the Brotherhood? How much time before God called him to paradise and judged his actions? Would he be judged for his sacrifices or for his betrayal?

There, in the gloom of his cell, his frail body shivering in the damp and cold, his prayer rug facing Mecca, Sheikh Hassan had prayed to God for a sign that his plan was divinely guided. He also feared that his spirit had been broken, and prayed for forgiveness. Was the truce no more than a fantasy that his mind had concocted to allow an old man to die in the arms of his family?

That was in 1997, and he had whispered the same prayer five times a day as he rededicated himself to God and to the struggle for Islamic purity. He saw signs in the patterns of the stars gleaming through the small window in his cell and he saw signs in the tea leaves that settled prophetically to the bottom of his tin cup.

Huddled in the court yard of the prison, he listened intently as the crazy one read his palm and promised miracles. Rubbish, he rebuked himself, fearing to offend God, but then relented. "Who I am to question the methods of God? *Allah Akbar.*"

Then came the miracle of September 11, 2001. His prayers had been answered. He had received his sign from God. The jihadists had struck at the very heart of America. Bin-Laden had become a saint and the moral authority of the jihadists had been reaffirmed. Violence was vindicated. The jihadists had been shown the true way. Henceforth, they would avoid killing Muslims. It was counter productive and sapped the popular support upon which they were dependent for money, shelter and recruits. Americans and Israelis were the true enemies. Muslim apostates, with the exception of the Saudi royal family, could be dealt with when the Americans had been conquered. In the meantime, Muslims would forget their fear of the jihadists and glory in the death of the infidels. The ranks of the jihadists would swell and the passivity of the Muslim Brotherhood would smack of cowardice and futility.

Sheikh Hassan restrained his euphoria. Everything depended upon the truce holding until the jihadists could rebuild their forces, and that had now become iffy. Egypt was the key country in America's control of the Middle East, and Hassan's forces had to be ready when the Minister of Interior betrayed them. The US wanted jihadist blood, and they wanted it now. The Minister of Interior had held firm, but the time for rebuilding had shortened.

There was also the problem of the street sheikhs, a loathsome group the petty thugs who pillaged and peddled drugs in the name of jihad. They hovered in the ghettos by day and struck at night. They parroted jihadist slogans and issued decrees (*fatwas*) attacking the truce and calling for violence against anyone who bowed to the West. Reporters were attacked, starlets raped, banks robbed, and bars fire bombed. All were pious acts designed to encourage the contributions of the faithful and shake down the merchants that lined the slums of Cairo and Alexandria.

Once again Sheikh Hassan prayed to God for assistance, and once again his God had responded. The US lurched into the quagmire of Iraq and the war against terror had been put on hold. At the very least it had been renamed the "long war." Each American death, and there were thousands, became a jihadist victory. The American public was losing its appetite for foreign adventure. The hunt for bin-Laden titillated the media, but was little more than a sideshow. He had completed his task. Jihadism had been vindicated and it was the thousands of home grown jihadist groups throughout the world that would complete his task.

Their leaders were veterans of Iraq and Afghanistan. No one was free from their reach. Egypt would once again be in the forefront.

Freed from prison, Sheikh Hassan had returned to his headquarters in Boulaq to plot his next move. The scars of humiliation were far deeper than the scars of prison. His sermons were poorly attended and, in the eyes of many, he had become an object of scorn. Little did they know of his strategy. Yet, Sheikh Hassan could say nothing of his plan, for the secret police were everywhere. His truce with the Minister of Interior was a truce of convenience among two foes of the Brotherhood. Scores would be settled once the Brotherhood had been crippled, but who would strike first?

* * * *

Thus it was that Sheikh Yassin paused to pay his regards to the comrade of his youth. Memories of the past remained bitter, yet he held out hope that Hassan was ready to return to the fold of the Brotherhood, bringing an end to the bitter feud that had shattered the Islamic movement for more than three decades. Had Hassan not publicly renounced violence and apologized for the suffering that he had wrecked upon Egyptian society? Sheikh Yassin remained skeptical, but knew his duty.

The sight of Sheikh Hassan moved Yassin to tears. Some twenty-five years of imprisonment had left him a broken and crippled shadow awaiting the angel of death. "Muslims," he whispered to himself, "must forgive Muslims. Errors have been made, but God will decide. We carry out his will, but it is not for us to judge."

Sheikh Yassin's sympathy was short lived. Sheikh Hassan, hobbling to his chair with the aid of his cane, gazed at Sheikh Yassin from his remaining eye with the hatred that one reserves for traitors and cowards. It was Yassin, in Hassan's eye, who was responsible for the Brotherhood's refusal to join the jihadist revolt of the 1990's. It was he who had kept the government in power.

"Peace upon you, my brother," came the unexpectedly strong voice of Sheikh Hassan as he glowered at his guest. "I pray that your peaceful revolution is going well. How well the government has shown its appreciation for your loyalty during its time of need."

The bitterness of Hassan's sarcasm left little room for further discussion, and Sheikh Yassin wished his former friend Godspeed and continued on his way. He knew Hassan well. He also knew that few could match Hassan's fanaticism or his cunning. "Islam allows the oppressed to disguise their faith," Sheikh Yassin mused to himself, "and that is precisely what my friend Hassan is doing. There can be no question that he is intent on destroying the world in the name of Islam."

* * * *

It was a troubled Sheikh Yassin who made his way from Sheikh Hassan's ramshackled complex. Turning a corner, Yassin's gaze fell upon Mizjaji, and his mood turned from disappointment to anger. A gaunt young man with piercing black eyes and scraggly beard, Mizjaji was the dominant street sheikh in Boulaq and the lord of its underworld. His ragged appearance honored the Prophet Mohammed's rejection of personal ostentation and stood in sharp contrast his followers who flaunted gaudy displays of gold and jewelry. Mizjaji wanted it that way. He alone, wore the symbols of faith and his followers were forbidden to do so. He shaved the heads of those who disobeyed his orders, and repeat offenders were rare, very rare. Sheikh Yassin was venerated as a saint; Mizjaji was feared as the angel of death.

Rumors abounded of Mizjaji's ties with Al-Qaeda and his clandestine meetings with a rich Saudis. No one knew the alleys of Boulaq better than Mizjaji or the back stairways of Zamalek. His men accompanied the garbage barges on their nightly rounds. As the children of the garbage tribes sorted through the filth for treasures to be recycled among Cairo's poor, Mizjaji's men studied the residents who dwelled within: the government officials, the wealthy Egyptians and the Americans. All were noted.

"To what do I owe my uncommon good fortune?" asked Sheikh Yassin with disdain. "One seldom sees you in light of day." This, of course was true, for the light of day was dangerous for Mizjaji. He was wanted by the police and his enemies were many, not the least of whom was Sheikh Yassin. In Boulaq, he was safe. The police seldom penetrated the area, and he seldom moved without a band of thugs in accompaniment.

"This is the day I collect the offering (*zakat*) for my poor mission," responded Mizjaji with guarded sarcasm. "We are a poor mosque that does not enjoy the support of the Brotherhood. God sustains us with the meager contributions of the faithful." Sheikh Yassin's glare left Mizjaji's soul as withered as the stump of an arm that dangled from his side. The poor merchants that lined Galal Street gave out of fear rather than faith, as did the wealthy merchants of Zamalek. The hollow shell of Mohammed's pastry shop was all of the encouragement they needed.

"May your day be blessed, my Sheikh," continued Mizjaji, for even he could not disguise his awe of Sheikh Yassin. "May God bless you and your family and may they all walk in the path of God."

"Thank you, my youth," responded the Sheikh with studied coolness, "My family is truly blessed and may God guide you to the true path." Mizjaji bristled at the rebuke, but displayed no emotion.

Sheikh Yassin had also bristled. Mizjaji's reference to his family was a slur on his son, a wealthy banker, and Zahra, his beloved granddaughter. Now a symbol of Islamic piety, her college days had been less devout and rumors of illicit entanglements had abounded. Marriage had proven difficult. She had returned to God, but the reference rankled. It was also threatening, for Mizjaji was the most vicious of the devil's minions.

The poor mosque to which Mizjaji alluded was an abandoned storefront in a remote alley of Boulaq known to only a few people. Attendance was sparse, for it was dangerous to attend Mizjaji's mosque. Mizjaji, himself, entered the mosque only when its blind caretaker signaled that all was well, and then through a labyrinth of tunnels and secret passage ways, some extending as far as Galal Street. Deep in the labyrinth were the weapons cache treasure troves, storage areas for drugs, and the infamous cave of Ali Baba. It was in Ali Baba's cave that Mizjaji and his disciples plotted their next move. It was also to Ali Baba's cave that inductees were led blindfolded after having been paraded in a circular route around the stinking alleys of Boulaq in the wee hours of the morning. It was here the angel of death appeared and described the joys of heaven and the fate that awaited the families of traitors.

"Why does God All Mighty allow thieves and criminals to masquerade as his servants?" Sheikh Yassin asked himself in despair. But then like all persons of true faith, he answered his own question. "Because they have a purpose. But what purpose? What good could come from this man of evil?"

Chapter 10

Smoke Rings

It would be unfair to say that Zahra had dressed imprudently as a college student, for that was not the case. It had never been the case except in the minds of religious extremists who had condemned her Paris fashions. That had not kept them from leering as they hungered for a glimpse of forbidden skin. The Koran had urged females to be prudent, but said nothing of veils or cloistering. These had come later as males sought to justify their insecurities in the name of God. No matter, the point was moot. Paris chic had given way to Islamic chic and, to the great relief of Sheikh Yassin, Zahra's wardrobe now honored the letter of Islamic law if not its spirit. For the chosen few, her eyes promised pleasures beyond description. Parker was one of the chosen few.

Their eyes had crossed for a fleeting second. No more was allowed. No more was necessary. "Careful," the Nubian had chided him. "Arab eyes are not like the squinty eyes of the West, painted but hollow. When all else is covered, the eyes become the messenger of the soul. Such glorious eyes they are, so large and expressive. They are messengers of the soul painted by the devil himself. Arab women, my friend, are God's most spectacular creation."

"So you married a Swede," laughed Parker, struggling to sort out his emotions and unwilling to grant the Nubian a victory.

"Now you see the psychological scars of colonialism, my friend," replied the Nubian with unaccustomed honesty. "My ego demanded it. The British taught us that we were toads, inferior beings born to be subservient to the *kawaga*. Even now we have self doubts, and so we reassure ourselves by conquering your women with our superior weapons."

Cementing his victory, the Nubian returned to Zahra. "This one, my friend, is more than a woman. She is a jinn, a creature of the spirit world that separates humans from God. She is of the world of angels, fairies and witches. But angels and jinn are special. The Glorious Koran speaks of both. Oh, how they tempt us, these jinn. I pray that you have a guardian angel for you are beyond salvation. She has already possessed your soul."

Parker enjoyed the seductive illusions of the Nubian, but gave them little credence. They were merely a game, flights of fancy by two adolescents thrust unwillingly into the world of adults. Zahra's enigmatic smile, too, had been a game, a seductive illusion but nothing more. How many times had his female students initiated sex play with similar smiles, each promising more than the others? They smiled, and finding little encouragement, moved on to greener pastures. Time was too precious to waste. Parker found the parade a pleasant diversion, but nothing more. "When the parade stops," he smiled to himself, "I will know that I am an old man. It would be the same with Zahra," he reassured himself, flattered by the diversion but unwilling to go beyond an innocent flirtation. She, too, would soon go in search of greener pastures. In reality, her visits to the bullpen had begun to taper off.

"You see," Parker teased the Nubian with mock sadness. "Two weeks have passed and already she has lost interest."

"How little you know of the East, my erudite friend," chided the Nubian. "Nothing is what it seems in our world. We talk in circles, fearful of revealing our hand while seducing others to betray a confidence that will destroy them. But never more so than in the world of sex, my friend, for the world of sex is the most dangerous of worlds. Honor killings are common, for there is no greater shame than the shame that a careless woman can bring upon her family. Only her death can remove the stain and prevent a feud. Everyone is watching: relatives to prevent a disaster and neighbors to assure one."

"Yet, the temptations of the devil grow stronger. Marriage has become too expensive. Young men are too poor to support a wife and even if the girl's father could scrape together the money for a dowry, there is no place to live. A nation of child brides is becoming a nation of anxious spinsters. Maybe that is why the less cultured continue to mutilate the clitoris of their daughters, hoping beyond hope that it will quell their passions. Grandmothers insist upon it. Hospitals allow it when requested, even though it is against the law. Better there than at the hand of a mid-wife. You know what sanitary conditions are like in the villages. It is a ghastly affair. Many girls die of infections. But, then, girls are not so important in the village."

The Nubian savored the discomfort in Parkers eyes and laughed maliciously, "Don't worry my friend. Zahra is sound. Her grandfather is too civilized to allow her to be carved on. But hurry, my friend, time is of the essence. We in the East do not have the luxury of protracted love games. It's too dangerous. She has made an offer and you have accepted. Now she will find a way to make it work. That is her responsibility." To himself he whispered, "You have dared to search for the soul of Egypt, my friend, and now we shall see just how clever you really are. Perhaps you shall find it."

"What is my responsibility?" scoffed Parker, not really wanting to know the answer.

"My God," intoned the Nubian in shock dismay, "don't tell me that you are moralist. The pretty diplomat will be pleased." As if he were lecturing a student of doubtful intelligence, he added in exasperation, "Your responsibilities, my friend, are to taste the honey and escape with your life. You don't want to marry her, do you?"

Parker had pooh-poohed the Nubian's comments, condemning himself for losing yet another hand to the Nubian. The Nubian was also right. Not a day passed before Parker found himself alone with Zahra for the first time in their briefest of flirtations. It was not in the bullpen, for tongues had begun to wag, but in the cavernous office of the Boss's secretary, her tiny desk dwarfed by hoards of ever encroaching file cabinets, their drawers bulging, their tops laden with stacks of files waiting the peace of oblivion. Every word scribbled in the Institute found its way into this holiest of sanctuaries, most penned in faded ink no longer legible to the naked eye. It didn't matter, for requests for all but the most recent files were met with the inevitable *insha'allah*, if God wills. As no one wanted to take responsibility for destroying something of potential significance, everything remained, making its way from the over burdened file cabinets to poorly labeled boxes littering the emergency stairs.

It was a brief and inadvertent encounter, or at least as inadvertent as such encounters can be. Leaving the Boss's office, cigar in hand, he had passed by the secretary's office to fill out yet another form doomed to an eternity in a dimly lit corridor. One copy to the Boss's secretary, one to the Minister of Interior, one to the Ministry of Finance, and the remainder elsewhere. The Boss' secretary was a pleasant lady of limited intelligence who found the morass of regulations as puzzling as he. "*Bukra*" (tomorrow), she smiled at Parker's request for a form that she had never heard of and continued doing whatever it was that she was doing. The year would probably end before the matter was resolved. She called her children on the hour, and listened with bated breath for news of a new shipment of subsidized food to the commissary. One had to be alert, for supplies vanished quickly, often to be resold on the black market. Tea breaks were imposed by law and merged imperceptibly with the lunch hour. In the meantime, she helped Parker as best she could, losing her train of thought whenever someone stuck their head through the door asking about the Boss's whereabouts. "*Lissa-magash*," came the inevitable answer if they were lucky enough to find her at her desk. "He hasn't arrived yet. He will be here shortly." In Egyptian time, that meant that the Boss would arrive sometime within the next three hours if not detained by more pressing matters. He was an important person and important people in Egypt were not expected to keep regular hours. But, by and large, the Boss spent a fair amount of the day at his office. It was his throne, the seat of his power.

Parker was patient with the secretary, often bringing her small gifts in appreciation of her efforts. In many ways, she epitomized the essence of his project: discovering why it was that the Egyptians, the brightest people he knew, remained locked in backwardness and poverty. "Perhaps," he murmured to himself half in jest, "it is because the most dazzling of Egypt's intellectuals are plotting its return to Islam."

It was in the midst of Parker's conversation with the secretary, if such it was, that Zahra had entered the office, her arms laden with files and approached the secretary for instructions. She had allowed herself a quick glance at Parker, for that was expected. Failure to do so would have been a confession of interest. Following a brief exchange of pleasantries, the secretary had pointed vaguely to a row of file cabinets somewhere in the rear of her shrinking sanctuary and resumed rearranging the stack of papers on her desk. It was not so much what Egyptian bureaucrats did that was important, but that they were seen doing something.

Parker had not encountered Zahra in the secretary's office before and fought to control a sudden rush of excitement. The moment passed and he chided himself for falling prey to the Nubian's fantasies. How could he have noticed Zahra in the secretary's office before? He seldom ventured there and only then to receive the inevitable *lissa magash*.

The buzzer summoning the secretary to the Boss's office sounded. It was the one command that she obeyed and, grabbing a note pad, she scurried out the door. Zahra smiled as the secretary disappeared, her burden of files having been deposited somewhere in the far reaches of the office. It was less a seductive smile than a smile of triumph. Arriving to where Parker stood, she paused and whispered in a soft voice, "I love the aroma of your cigar. May I taste it?"

"You would probably prefer a new one," responded Parker with ease, taking an elegant cigar from his case and clipping its end. "Would you prefer to light it or should I do light it for you?"

"I know so little of these things," replied Zahra. "It would taste better if you lit it for me."

Parker lit the cigar and passed it to Zahra. She caressed the cigar with a clumsy seductiveness, and then, regaining her composure, moistened its end with a gesture that bordered on the obscene. Their eyes met, locked in final negotiations. Zahra drew deeply on the cigar, and then allowed the fragrant smoke to drift seductively from her mouth, smoke rings, like halos, encircling her deep auburn hair.

"Shit," said Parker when Zahra had disappeared down the hallway, the lingering smoke from her cigar blending with the seductive scent of her perfume. "That damn Nubian was right."

Smoke rings gave way to desperate kisses, and they to a bit more. Hours of passion compressed into thirty seconds.

"I see your romance is going well," taunted the Nubian. "The signs are everywhere. The loved one no longer comes to visit us and your brow has become worried. Her friends have noticed a sparkle of excitement in her eyes that she makes no effort to hide. They can only guess at its cause, but what else do they have to do with their time?"

"I hate to admit it," laughed Parker, "but I have become addicted to your fantasies. Soap operas that I pray will come true. But alas, they don't. Soon she will marry and I will die in despair."

"Be of good cheer, my friend," replied the Nubian, not do be denied yet another victory over the *kawaga*. "She can't marry!"

"Of course she can marry," retorted Parker with contempt. "She is rich and beautiful. What more do you want?"

"Rich, beautiful, and sullied," lamented the Nubian with a tinge of sadness. "I don't know what happened in her youth, perhaps nothing. But that is the rumor. She was too bold during her college years, and no man of standing will touch her." Then, catching his error, he corrected himself. "No one will marry her."

"Half the country will marry her for her money," scoffed Parker.

"Far more," conceded the Nubian, "but that is impossible. She will not be allowed to marry below her class. Ideally, there would be a marriage alliance within the big families. Her father is rich, but needs to strengthen his ties with the generals that run the country. That would also benefit the Sheikh. Either that or an alliance with one of the bankrupt aristocrats of the old regime. The new money yearns for a touch of royalty. Alas, it cannot be. She has been sullied. Besides, her mind has been corrupted by your Western fantasies. She believes in love and she is in love with you."

"Your fantasies, not her's," grumbled Parker.

The Nubian smiled the smile of a jackal on the track of his prey. "Let's see, where do you meet? She comes at ten and leaves at two. It can't be outside of the office because she is watched. Your office would be ideal, but that's too risky. She has no reason to venture there and would be easily spotted. The kiss of death, so to speak," added the Nubian, erupting in a fit of macabre laughter. "It must be the secretary's office. She is also the secretary for your project and Zahra's presence there would attract no attention."

Parker smiled at the thought of the Boss's secretary assisting with the paper work for his project, and seized upon the secretary's incompetence to change the subject. Perhaps she was good for something after all. "Surely you jest," replied Parker with bitterness. "The lady is never there and does nothing when she is."

That's the beauty of it," laughed the Nubian triumphantly. "Everyone knows that *kawagas* expect secretaries to work, and everyone knows that they don't. They don't have to. They work for the government. The only danger to her job is making a serious mistake, and when you do nothing, there is little chance of a mistake. You put pressure on her, and she escapes by going to the Institute's commissary or taking her tea breaks. This frustrates the Boss, and he asks Zahra to fill in. You are there. Zahra is there. The secretary is not there. What more could you ask for?"

"Perhaps more than thirty second sound bites of your supposed passion, my deluded friend," replied Parker, preparing his masterstroke. "You have forgotten to mention the janitors, the other secretaries, the researchers, the endless stream of visitors seeking an appointment with the Boss and, above all, the Wisp. He worships the sight of her. That place is never empty for more than a minute at a time."

"Maddening, isn't it?" responded the Nubian with mock sympathy. "There are too many robes and pins to dispense with in 30 seconds. Ah, the eternal wisdom of the Prophet. But how the tensions build, my friend. Oh, how the tensions build. They cannot be denied forever. And then, my friend, and then ..." The Nubian didn't finish his sentence, choosing instead to run his finger across his throat.

Parker wanted to be angry with the Nubian and his insane laughter, but could not. He was being warned.

* * * *

The next day Parker had looked deeply into Mandy's eyes, blue but hollow as the sun reflected off of her contact lenses. A curious smile drifted across his lips. "Do you find my eyes beautiful," she asked, suddenly anxious for reassurance and praise.

"Lovely beyond description," he smiled mischievously, "but not as lovely as your nipples." She flushed with embarrassment, for this was their first meeting since they had found themselves alone in her flat, the guests of her impromptu party having long departed. She hadn't intended for things to develop as quickly as they had. It was a professional flirtation to maintain his interest, perhaps, but nothing more. But it had become more, so much more. She did not deny that she found the lanky mid-westerner attractive. Tall and powerful, his playful eyes had teased her beyond her studied flirtations.

As they sat side-by-side on her balcony overlooking the Nile, her defenses had crumbled. Each kiss and each touch pushed them toward the inevitable conclusion. She had no regrets. "Blame the Nile," he had whispered, "It is seductive."

Now, enjoying their tea beside the Nile, she squeezed his hand in gratitude, his praise easing fears that he had found her modest breasts disappointing. She was not petite, but found the voluptuousness of Egyptian women intimidating.

* * * *

Even jinn have their bad days. While Parker sat gazing into the eyes of Mandy, Zahra had ventured into the bullpen only to find it empty with the exception of the Wisp. Their eyes crossed briefly, more than enough time for the eyes that had promised so much to Parker to destroy the pock marked researcher. "Your lover is not here," he whispered slowly as his eyes flashed with hatred.

* * * *

As Parker penetrated ever more deeply into the soul of Egypt, his wife found solace in her church work. She organized the chaotic records of itinerant pastors and arranged study groups on Biblical prophesy, feminism, and the plight of Egypt's Christians, the Copts. Nothing, however, fired her zeal more than the outrage of female genital mutilation. Medical professionals preferred the term clitorodectomy. It was less emotional. The study groups filled the hours from the end of the school day until the last school bus whisked the school's students from their cultural enrichment programs to waiting parents in Zamalek. When Parker was home, they ate in silence and then sat on the balcony watching the barges and *falukas* (sail boats) ply their way up the Nile. Invariably, they drifted into their own worlds. He read or watched Egyptian tv and she graded papers or worked on the affairs of the church. If Parker had plans in the evening, which was often, she sat alone in self-imposed exile. He invited her to join him; she declined. Parker had the luxury of sleeping in. She did not. The school bus came early in the morning. Such, at least, was her excuse.

That was before the study groups. Once lonely evenings were now spent probing the intricacies of biblical prophesy and arranging for Egyptian feminists to bear their souls to their American sisters. The injustices of the third world that had fueled her passions as a student flared again, and with them her interest in her husband. She knew little of the region and he knew everything, or so it seemed. Evenings of staring across the Nile in stony silence gave way to intense discussions of the Copts, the maltreatment of Egyptian women and eventually, biblical prophesy. As always, he turned simple truths into complex riddles. They disagreed on most things and, not to be defeated, she probed ever deeper into the mysteries of the Middle East.

Their discussions rekindled her thrill of intellectual discovery and merged imperceptibly with a renewed desire for sexual rediscovery. He obliged. It was awkward, but it was a reprieve. Perhaps they were moving toward a compromise that could save their marriage: a glorious middle-ground somewhere between the austere piety of rural Nebraska and Parker's more humanitarian version of Christianity.

Chapter 11

Spies and Conspiracies

A smile of quiet satisfaction played across the lips of the Wisp as he slipped into a remote door of the Ministry of Interior and made his way to the office of the Minister. He was not often so honored. The Wisp's accounts of Parker's arrival at the Institute, however, had piqued the Minister of Interior's curiosity. This was all the more the case following the Minister's unfortunate meeting with Jake. The Minister of Interior didn't trust the *kawagas*, and he particularly didn't trust Jake. Like most Arabs, he suffered from the *kawaga* complex, the demeaning belief that the *kawagas* were smarter than the Arabs. They despised themselves for it, but how could it be otherwise. It was the legacy of colonialism and had become part of their culture. The *kawagas* ruled the world, orchestrating events in the Middle East much as a grand chess player plotted the destruction of his opponent. Jake's talk of a military coup could not have been accidental. It was too bold, too direct. Jake's guarded references to his friend, the President, had also been worrisome. Anglos didn't share the Arab's love of embellishment and exaggeration. Nothing the *kawaga* did happened without a purpose.

What, then, was the purpose of Parker? There could only be one answer. He was a secret contact between the Embassy and the liberals that dominated the Institute. Trouble makers these liberals. Too weak to threaten the regime, they embarrassed it by leaking stories of torture to Amnesty International and by their incessant calls for democracy and human rights. He had done away with more than one of them, but they persisted. Now, it seemed, they were conspiring with the Embassy.

"But why were the Americans conspiring with the liberals?" the Minister of Interior wondered out loud to his adjutant. "It didn't make sense. The liberals were too weak to help them. Besides, the Americans didn't really want a democratic government in Egypt. The old Ambassador had told him so himself. The Islamic threat was too great. There could only be one explanation. It was Jake's ploy to put pressure on him to cancel his truce with the jihadists." Hopefully, the Wisp's news would clarify the situation.

The Minister of Interior sat behind his massive desk, staring at the Wisp in stony silence as he recalled his spy's much embellished stories of the romance between Parker and Zahra. "Fool," he sneered. "You promised information on the *kawagas'* plan for the Institute, and now you tell me love stories."

"That is his purpose," the Wisp stammered, his face blanched and his body trembling in fear.

"What is his purpose?" roared the Minister of Interior, his deeply circled eyes flashing in anger. It had been a difficult week and he was not in the mood for humor.

"The *kawaga* is the Embassy's link with the Brotherhood," mumbled the Wisp, his body still shaking.

The Minister of Interior's eyes blazed with excitement as he grasped the astuteness of the Wisp's revelation. "That thought had occurred to me," he replied, denying the Wisp the credit for his insight. "Yes, the thought had occurred to me, but the link seemed obscure. Keep your eyes open. Use more people if you have to. Even if there is no link, we may have a surprise for our friend Sheikh Yassin." Then, with an imperceptible movement of the hand, he dismissed the Wisp.

The Wisp was euphoric. Wending his way back to the Institute he analyzed the interview in minute detail from its disastrous beginning to the Minister's confidential allusion that he was preparing a surprise for Sheikh Yassin. Such allusions were a symbol of trust and perhaps, a promotion. Had he not ordered the Wisp to use more people if need be? That, of itself, was a promotion. The Wisp had not expected credit for his work. That was beyond the realm of possibility. The Minister of Interior was infallible: all knowing and beyond reproach. The mere suggestion that a key idea had eluded him was a threat to his power, and the Wisp had come dangerously close to crossing that line. The important thing was that the Minister was pleased. His life depended upon it. That was, of course, unless Parker could arrange for a fellowship to the United States.

The more the Minister of Interior reflected on the Wisp's revelations, the more concerned he became. If the Wisp were right, which now seemed more plausible than his earlier fears of a plot between the Embassy and the liberals, the situation was more serious than he believed. Sheikh Yassin would never allow his granddaughter to flirt in public with a *kawaga* without a good cause. It would destroy him in the eyes of the devout. Perhaps the US was going to accept a moderate Islamic regime as a counter weight to the jihadists. They had done so in Turkey with a blend of Islamic and military rule. Perhaps that was their plan for Egypt. At the very least, they were toying with the idea. Otherwise, there would be no need for negotiations with Sheikh Yassin, however indirect.

More than ever, it was important to prevent a strong Brotherhood showing in the coming parliamentary elections. The more powerful the Muslim Brotherhood emerged from the elections, the more the Americans were likely to consider a religious government. "But they will not do well in the elections," the Minister of Interior smiled to himself. "I swear by God that they will not do well in the elections." He knew that it would be his neck if they did.

Abruptly, the Minister of Interior's thoughts returned to Jake with a mixture of fear and begrudging admiration. Obviously it was he who devised this devilish plan for communicating with the Brotherhood. It was a stroke of genius. Communicate with the Brotherhood through a spy planted in the bastion of liberalism in Egypt. No one would suspect the link. Not the Egyptian government, not the liberals, not the military, not the jihadists and not Sheikh Yassin's own people. No one would suspect a thing until it was too late. There would be no leaks, no time for corrective action. It would be a fait accompli. Retrieving Parker's file from a crowded side table his eyes fell upon the brief entries noting the casual meetings of Parker and Mandy at the riverside casinos. Romance? Perhaps, but the Minister of Interior didn't believe in romance. It was known that Mandy was Jake's favorite, perhaps something more. Obviously it was she who was managing Parker and using their apparent romance as a guise for monitoring the progress of his negotiations.

"Well," smiled the Minister of Interior to his adjutant. "There is time for corrective action. Young love should not be secret. Sheikh Yassin must be congratulated on the good fortune of his granddaughter. The world must rejoice. Perhaps we can implicate the good Sheikh in the disappearance of this American agent. Who knows, Zahra's little romance might be just the spark that we need to destroy the Brotherhood. But first, the elections. We don't want to rile the Brotherhood before the elections. Let them think that all is well and that they are poised for victory. Issue more press releases stating that we guarantee totally fair elections. Lay it on thick. The Brotherhood will bite because Parker hinted that the Embassy wants a fair election. Why else is he talking to Sheikh Yassin? It will also get the international press off our backs. We're living in a damn fish bowl. Everyone is watching our every move. What we need is a distraction, but what?"

"Perhaps God will provide," smiled the adjutant, sarcastically.

"Yes," responded the Minister of Interior, "perhaps God will provide." He had no idea of how prophetic he was.

Chapter 12

Love Brings Worries, It Was Ever Thus

Their timing had become impeccable. The Institute's commissary opened at ten, assuring that the secretary left her office at least ten minutes in advance. Parker slipped into the secretary's office a few seconds after her departure, and Zahra slipped into his arms. It was still an early hour by Egyptian standards, but that was no guarantee of peace. The janitors wore soft-soled shoes and appeared without warning. The Wisp's shoes were softer. Thirty seconds of bliss followed by hours or fear and self-recrimination. Zahra, who was so cautious at first, now seemed oblivious to the danger and urged him to new follies. Parker found the game irresistible. It was the most dangerous game that he had ever played and his adrenalin soared.

Zahra, too, was playing a game. The more she tempted the fates, the more she pelted him with insane questions. "Why don't you love your wife?"

"How do you know that I don't love my wife?" he lashed out with cruelty, perhaps hoping to drive her away.

"Because you are in love with the pretty one at the Embassy."

"Then why are you in my arms?"

"Because when you know me, you will forget the others," she replied with confidence. "But would he?" she worried.

"Too bad that you're not blonde," the Nubian had taunted her." Blondes are better." Then he added with a malicious leer, "Perhaps you are too big." She was accustomed to the crudeness of Egyptian men, but was disturbed by the increasing boldness of the Nubian. He had always been crude, but now he had become personal, daring her to complain.

Zahra also worried about marriage, for there was no life for an Egyptian woman without marriage. Most of all, she worried about wounding her grandfather. The Wisp's biting comment, "Your lover is not here," had shaken her. She understood Egyptian politics and understood the magnitude of catastrophe that threatened her family. What a fool she had been listening to her heart and pretending that marriage to Parker would wipe away the follies of the past. She had told herself that they would live in America and that all would be well. But how could she leave Egypt? Men could leave the womb of the family, but not a woman. There was also the pretty one. Perhaps she was not so big.

It had been Zahra who had informed the Sheikh of Parker's arrival and who had described how his project would find ways to motivate Egypt's civil servants. "He seems very interesting," murmured the Sheikh in his enigmatic style. "I hope the project goes well. God knows that something must be done to breathe life into those parasites that suck the blood of the country. Yet," he continued with skepticism, "it is hard to believe that your liberal friends would allow an American to probe the soul of Egypt without a reason. What he learns about bureaucrats he can apply to the rest of us. We are all bureaucrats at heart. You must keep me up to date."

Zahra had been thrilled by the Sheikh's interest in Parker. He had always doted on her, but only as one dotes on a pretty toy. He had encouraged her education, but had berated her father for her experimentations. As always, her father had averted his eyes, unable to confront the Sheikh. Her appointment to the Institute had also brought little cheer to Sheikh Yassin. He was not opposed to women working before marriage, but the Institute was problematic. It was too liberal, too Western. Besides, the time for marriage had come. Perhaps a suitable alliance could be salvaged before all was lost.

But now there had been a change. The Sheikh had listened with increasing interest as she whispered the latest rumors about Parker, but none more so than her recounting of his affair with the pretty one. With the mention of the pretty diplomat his eyes had sparkled with excitement. "It all seems to fit, doesn't it?" he said to her as one speaks to a confidant. "First the Americans use the Institute to study our soul and then we learn that the *kawaga* is controlled by the Embassy." His words were more than a confidence. They were also a warning.

"Perhaps it is just a romance," suggested Zahra, not wanting to prejudice the Sheikh's view of her future husband. "It is known that he is not pleased with his wife."

"Doubtful," responded the Sheikh. "The story makes a good cover, but the *kawagas* are too clever to allow romance to disrupt their plans, whatever they are." He looked at Zahra carefully, noting the smile that played across her lips. It was not the response he had expected from a co-conspirator.

During the Sheikh's weekly visit to his son's house, it was a troubled Zahra who searched for words that would not come. She knew that there was no higher obligation than loyalty to the family. The state was nothing; the government a gang of corrupt thieves. Your family was your only salvation. You were what your family was. You were nothing without it. That message had been pounded into her mind since birth. And now, she had betrayed her family. Their honor was at risk.

Zahra attempted to stammer the latest rumors, but failed. Words were not necessary. Sheikh Yassin looked at her kindly as they sat in the alcove of a massive living room lined with ornate couches and gilded chairs. Her father was an important man and his guests were many. The furniture reflected the wealth of a banker, for wealth was power and misers despised. "It seems that you are fond of this American," said the Sheikh. A skilled interrogator, he spoke softly and with kindness. She nodded her head in agreement, tears streaming from her eyes.

The Sheikh had not been unprepared. He had sensed her interest in Parker from the beginning and watched with concern as it had deepened. He knew that Arab women were incapable of controlling their emotions. That was their glory and their weakness. God was wise in ordaining that they be restrained by men. He had been lax in allowing his son to raise Zahra in the Western tradition. Now, there would be a disaster. All hope of a suitable marriage was gone. A civilized man, he refused to consider the other option, an option that would be demanded by the zealous fire-brands if he were to retain their respect and loyalty. How could he lead the faithful if he ignored immorality in his own family? He would be no better than the government preachers, urging the faithful to honor an immoral regime in the name of God. People would mock him behind his back, calling him the Imam of hypocrisy.

Yet, in his heart of hearts, he continued to believe that things did not happen without a purpose. Everything was the will of God. The challenge to man was to understand God's will and to facilitate it. Was he being punished for unintended arrogance? If so, he must repent. Or, were Zahra's indiscretions part of a larger plan to restore peace on earth, a plan that would see rightly guided Muslims reclaim their lands in the name of God. To be sure, God could impose his will on Earth with a single sweep of his hand. But that would not suffice. The children of Adam would not have learned their lesson and would soon return to their evil ways.

No, the way to redemption would be tortuous. That was the will of God. If Zahra were to regain her honor and her ability to marry, it would be because she had a role in the victory of enlightened Islam, the Islam of the Muslim Brotherhood. But what was that role to be?

Zahra sat motionless as the Sheikh, his eyes half-closed, struggled to divine the will of God. Too terrified to breathe, she tried in vain to banish the thoughts of Parker that crept into her mind.

"What do you command me, Oh, Lord?" Sheikh Yassin beseeched his Maker. The question was not new, for things were going poorly for the Brotherhood. The truce between the government and the jihadists had held despite American pressure. Each apostasy, the secular and the jihadist, was now marshaling its forces against their common foe.

A vague plan, yet intangible, formed in Sheikh Yassin's mind. It was not a new plan, for every time that he struggled to find a solution to the Brotherhood's dilemma he came up with the same conclusion. The Embassy had to be involved. It could not be otherwise, for the Americans ruled the world. There had to be a realignment of forces, a new game that pitted the Brotherhood and the Embassy against the government and the jihadists. The logic was impeccable. The Embassy feared the jihadists and had lost faith in the government's ability to control the country. The truce had been the last gasp of a failed dictatorship struggling to cling to power by allowing the jihadists to rearm. It was a pact with the devil. The Brotherhood, for its part, needed to convince the US that it was a moderate and responsible organization capable of leading the Muslim world to peace and prosperity. Barring this, victory would be problematic. The Brotherhood could not withstand the combined forces of the government, the jihadists, and the Americans.

Logic was not the problem. The question was how? How could he be sure that the Embassy would play? Direct negotiations were out of the question, and even informal contacts were problematic. They had been tried in the past with disastrous results. The Embassy had sent ambivalent signals, only to leak news of its contacts with the Brotherhood to the Minister of Interior. Repressions had followed and Sheikh Yassin was blamed. His credibility had been called into question. That, however, was before. The truce between the jihadists and the Minister of Interior had changed everything. An alliance with the Embassy was more pressing than ever.

The Embassy had also changed. The betrayal had taken place under the watch of the old Ambassador. The new Ambassador was different. He was more powerful and more dangerous. Great care was needed. Everyone was watching everyone, each waiting for the other to slip. He feared the Minister of Interior and he feared Sheikh Hassan, but he feared the hot-heads within the Brotherhood most of all. They had not suffered the repression of the Nasser years and yearned for a show down with the government. They scoffed at his calls for patience and plotted his downfall. Zahra had provided them with their opportunity. They would demand her death knowing that he could not comply.

"Zahra had provided them with their opportunity." The phrase stuck in his mind as he looked at his beloved granddaughter, choking back his own tears. "Zahra had provided them with their opportunity." The more he repeated the phrase the more his mood lightened.

"I've been a fool," he chastised himself, once again marveling at the infinite complexity of the Maker's genius. The illicit love affair between Zahra and Parker had become his opportunity. It was the perfect channel for communications with the Embassy without alarming the Minister or Interior, the jihadists or, most of all, his more radical colleagues in the Brotherhood. "Perhaps," he allowed himself a brief moment of self-congratulations, "a suitable marriage alignment is still in order. *Allah Akbar.*"

Unsure of what to expect, Zahra bowed her head, avoiding the Sheikh's eyes. She feared for herself and she feared for Parker. As a child she had eavesdropped on the conversations of the Sheikh and his colleagues and knew well the dangers that confronted spies. It was she who had made this beautiful American a spy. Her folly had betrayed them both.

"God will provide, my child," whispered the Sheikh, raising her chin with his hand. "Now tell me the latest news. I must know what our enemies are saying. It is our only salvation."

Zahra was not deceived by the softness of the Sheikh's voice. His effort at compassion merely intensified the severity of his message. That message was brutally clear: "It is our only salvation." He was not addressing the stupidities of a young girl. He was addressing his fate and, perhaps, the fate of the Brotherhood. All had become one, or so it seemed in her feverish mind. Nor, as she acknowledged with bitterness, was she still a young girl. She was an unmarried female, her body tempted by the invasion of the meat and the fat.

It was with a dull and emotionless voice that Zahra recounted her fleeting encounters with Parker in the secretary's office. After a deafening pause, she blurted out the Wisp's accusation, "Your lover is not here."

The details had been sketchy, and the Sheikh asked but one question, "Nothing beyond the secretary's office?"

"Nothing," replied Zahra, relieved, yet finding it difficult to disguise the disappointment in her voice.

"Let this be our secret," he smiled at Zahra. "God will provide. For the moment, do not change things. That will cause more concern than an innocent flirtation." He prayed that it was an innocent flirtation.

"But," mumbled Zahra in disbelief, only to be interrupted by the Sheikh.

"No buts, my little one. Nature must take its course. That is God's will." Then, excusing himself, the Sheikh made his way to his son's study.

The son rose to greet the Sheikh, laughing half in jest, "I bring you sorrow, my father, but Zahra brings you joy."

Zahra, too, had notice the smile that played on Sheikh Yassin's fine lips as he had excused himself. It was not the playful smile of her youth, but the intense smile of a poker player who has just pushed all of his chips into the pot. The smile of no return.

"What is God's will?" wondered Zahra as she sat motionless, watching the Sheikh make his way to the study of her father. "Am I to betray the man I love or become his wife?"

"Now," plotted Sheikh Yassin, "I must spread the word that my informant in the Institute has uncovered an American plot to destroy the Brotherhood by initiating a coup d'etat with the support of the liberals and the military. I will tell them that the Liberals will be placed in office as a facade while the generals rule from behind the scenes. Elections will be delayed until the Brotherhood's leadership has been decimated. The truce with the jihadists will be maintained as a ruse to quiet extremist currents until the Minister of Interior and the Americans have destroyed us. I will admit that the details remain sketchy but that, God willing, we shall learn more soon. There is no need to mention Zahra's name. To point it out would arouse suspicions. One does not reveal the names of their informants. Let the hot heads relish their cleverness. Once they have figured things out, we will invite the *kawaga* to my offices for consultations."

The members of the Sheikh Yassin's council listened enthralled as he revealed the *kawagas'* plot to destroy the Brotherhood, a murmur of collective excitement circulating the room. Worry crossed the faces of the older members. "The situation is dire," acknowledged the Sheikh, "but perhaps it is part of God's plan. We must have faith." The younger members of the assembly, who were few in number and not that young, strained forward in their seats in the hope that the Sheikh would elaborate his plan, but to no avail.

Finally, a hot-head found the courage to speak. "What is God's plan?" he asked nervously. It was a mistake.

"I said perhaps it is part of God's plan, my son," the Sheikh scolded the hot-head. "We do not know yet. We need more information."

"Can your informant get the information?" questioned the hot-head, now swallowing the bait that Sheikh Yassin had dangled in front of him.

"I'm not sure," responded the Sheikh slowly and with unaccustomed hesitation. "One cannot sacrifice the innocent. That is God's will. I have already taken liberties that my conscience cannot justify."

"We all must sacrifice," murmured an older member of the council, hoping to bolster Sheikh Yassin's resolve. "Perhaps the answer will come to you in prayer."

"We all must pray," responded the Sheikh. "As always I need your suggestions."

The sheikh had predicted their reaction in advance, for he knew them well. They had taken the bait and the foundation for Zahra's innocence had been established. He would reveal information slowly, allowing the hot-heads to suggest an alliance with the Embassy in an effort to save the Brotherhood. It would also be they who exonerated Zahra by begging her to continue her sacrifice. That would not be too hard. The real trick would be convincing them to invite Parker to the Mosque complex. There was no other option. Parker must be convinced of the Brotherhood's good intent. Conversations or whatever with Zahra would not suffice. Sooner or later, Parker would have to convince the Embassy that he had spoken directly with Brotherhood's leadership.

Inflamed with a new sense of urgency, the Sheikh's council had met several times that week. While the older members urged caution, the younger members were buoyed by the Sheikh's change of heart. After years of dithering, the time for action had come.

Finally, the hot-head could wait no longer. "We must see this *kawaga* spy in person," he cried, unwilling to allow Sheikh Yassin to dribble out information as he saw fit.

"Too dangerous," replied the Sheikh. "We will be accused of conspiring with the Americans. Besides, why do you want to bring the American spy to our compound? That will only help his mission. It will also alarm our enemies."

The older members nodded in agreement, but the hot-head, now inflamed with dreams of grandeur, was not to be denied. "Precisely, my sheikh," exuded the hot-head. "This is our opportunity to help his mission. Let him see the good works that we do in our clinics and schools. Show him where the jihadists hide their arms and give him tapes of their indoctrination speeches. We know everything they do."

"Alarming our enemies will bring us a thousand woes," cautioned an elderly member of the council now in his mid-eighties. "You were not there during the years of terror when we were hunted like animals."

"The words of youth are sometimes worthy of merit," murmured Sheikh Yassin with studied reluctance. "How do you propose that we entice the *kawaga* spy to visit us? One rarely receives an engraved invitation to wander the alleys of Boulaq." The Sheikh had chosen his words carefully, taunting the hot-head by refusing to address him directly and then baiting him with mockery.

An uncomfortable silence descended on the table. The solution was obvious, but who would risk affronting the Sheikh by suggesting that his granddaughter lure the *kawaga* to their lair? Finally, with great reluctance, a balding middle-aged man suggested with great temerity, "Perhaps your informant could persuade him to visit us."

"Perhaps that is possible," whispered the Sheikh in a voice laden with sadness and dropping all pretenses about the identity of his informant. "But I cannot ask that of her. She has already suffered humiliating gossip, and it is the time for marriage."

"Perhaps in we all testified to her innocence," suggested one on the older members of the council. "Once the crisis has passed, we will honor her as a saint."

"A fallen angel," came the scathing rebuke of the Sheikh. It was a risk, but Sheikh Yassin could not make it easy for them. They would not believe without suffering. Besides, he needed something more than good intentions. All would have to swear to her innocence. The hot-head and younger members of the council had publicly committed themselves. They couldn't retreat. It was on the record. The conservatives had remained silent, showing little emotion other than a guarded nod of the head. That was not adequate. There could be no vacillation in the heat of battle; no denials of culpability or pointing of fingers. It was to be the conservatives, moreover, and particularly the doctor and the elderly sheikh, who would have to certify Zahra's purity.

The group sat cross-legged in stony silence, joints aching and eyes cast to the ground. Minutes passed, each seeming like an hour to Sheikh Yassin. But he remained expressionless, demanding consensus.

Finally, when all seemed lost, the elderly sheikh spoke. "Zahra has been the victim of vicious lies. She is as pure as the day of her birth. May God destroy those who doubt her service to his glory."

"I am the family doctor," intoned the physician. "Her purity is beyond question."

Consensus had been achieved. It was thus recorded.

Chapter 13

Enter Gloria Goldensickle

Feminism and biblical prophesy had become the all consuming passions of Constance Parker. To her they had become one. The ladies of the Bible were as strong as they were devout. They conquered adversity with sacrifice and they conquered the devil with their faith. They slept with their men to rule them. How like them were the pioneer ladies of the American West, their fire still burning in the soul of Constance's mother and her aunts. And now, it burned in her soul as well. Her trip to Cairo had not been in vain. She had not discovered the soul of Egypt. She doubted that Egyptians had souls, but she had discovered the soul of Constance Parker.

She, like the ladies of yore, was not particularly subtle. The name Constance spoke of duty as did the biblical names Esther, Ruth, and Rachel, the names of her mother and her aunts respectively. Her intensity became a source of worry to the preacher whose main source of income was the generosity of the plump executive wives who blended faith with cocktails and docility. Eyebrows were raised, but the preacher could not find a replacement for Constance. He made do by urging her to be more Christian in dealing with the "ladies." He made a few other suggestions as well, but received no encouragement.

Eyebrows were also raised at the school as the more susceptible of Constance's female students assaulted their parents with demands for greater moral responsibility. The director of the school urged her to be more restrained in her club activities and consoled himself with the knowledge that she would soon be gone. He was also a practical man, and found Constance's biblical feminism to be less of a headache than the disciples of Miss Southern Geniality, their ideology engraved on their tight young thighs. The Americans were accustomed to these things, but the Egyptians couldn't handle it.

The difficulty was that Constance Parker felt isolated. Aside from the plump ladies who would attend anything the church offered to ease their boredom, there was little interest in either biblical prophesy or feminism. Few could see the connection between the two. But then, few had grown up on the stark plains of rural Nebraska.

In desperation, she had revived the church's moribund speaker series, regaling meager audiences with an endless series of oppressed Copts and frustrated Egyptian feminists. Both came free, a matter of some importance to a church that had canceled its speakers budget for a lack of funds. Neither satisfied her passions. She tired of Copts whining about their poor treatment and found it difficult to identify with this most ancient of Christian sects that traced its origins to the Patriarch of Alexandria. They were Christians, but not born-again Christians. They also seemed so Egyptian, which of course they were, having predated the Muslims by some 600 years. The Egyptian feminists suffered from the same problem. They were too Egyptian and too concerned with motherhood and their families. She wasn't sure why she didn't like the Egyptians. Perhaps it was because she had been dragged to Cairo against or will, or maybe it was because Cairo was so different from the pastoral sereneness of rural Nebraska. Or maybe, although she refused to admit it, she hated the Egyptians precisely because Parker loved them.

And so it was that Constant Parker had perused the list of guest speakers offered by the Israeli Embassy with more than passing interest. She admired the Israeli intellect and the speakers came free. Parker had dismissed the speakers as a propaganda tool. That, from Constance's perspective, added to their appeal.

The offerings on the Israeli list, however, were disappointing. Some were too intellectual for the plump ladies and others were too Jewish. She had been on the verge of trashing the list when a brief entry at the bottom of the page caught her attention. "Biblical Feminism and World Peace," a discussion by Gloria Goldensickle. The entry appeared to be a late addition to the list and had been scribbled in by hand. In contrast to the other entries, few details were provided other than Gloria's position as a lecturer in psychology at a small Hebrew college. The lack of detail was irrelevant. The very name Gloria Goldensickle had mesmerized her.

"What a marvelous name," she thought to herself, "I can just see her mowing down the terrorists."

* * * *

The Israeli Embassy had been delighted with Constance's request for a speaker, for takers were few. The Cultural Attaché, however, had seemed a bit hesitant about the name suggested. A stooped, balding man with thick glasses and obvious intellect, he felt that a famous professor of religion might be better suited to the intellectual environment of the community church than Gloria Goldensickle.

"Perhaps there could be an inter-faith discussion between Christians, Jews and Muslims," he had suggested to Parker' wife with enthusiasm. "We are all people of the book and greater understanding between the three faiths is essential to world peace." Noting that his burst of enthusiasm was unrequited, he added, "I don't know this speaker personally, but her topic might be somewhat controversial for a first visit."

He had, of course, lied. He knew Gloria Goldensickle well and had shuddered when her name had appeared on the speakers list. But Constance Parker had persisted and, reluctantly, he had agreed. His job was to promote the Israeli cultural presence in Cairo by every means at his disposal. For the moment, that was Parker's wife.

The lecture was reasonably well attended, for the plump ladies had little else to do in the afternoons other than sip cocktails. Many had already sipped, and relished an afternoon of male bashing.

Gloria Goldensickle did not disappoint. Her lecture roamed from feminism to biblical prophesy and from there to the threat that Muslim fundamentalism posed to the existence of Israel. "If Israel disappears," she lamented, "it could well mean the end of Judaism. Only 13 million Jews remain in the world, and Jewish males are assimilating at an alarming rate." She had wanted to say are chasing *shikses* (Christian ladies), but had toned down her rhetoric in deference to her audience.

"Do you know why there are less than 13 million Jews left in the world?" she had challenged her audience. "I will tell you why," she thundered. "Because men are weak. They crave dominance and flee from women who demand a sexual relationship based upon morality and equality. Israeli men are no better than the rest."

"The Bible is not against sex. It is our duty as females to perpetuate the faith. "But," she hissed, "the Bible is against masochism, that disease of the spirit forced upon females by male insecurities. I dare you to search the Internet. There are thousands of web sites that pander to male sadism. If the glorious prophesies of the Bible are to be fulfilled, prophesies shared by Islam and Christianity as well as Judaism, women must assert their equality and force men to follow the word of God. Women of all faiths must unite and confront males with a common commitment to the sexuality of morality and equality. Only in this way will the world realize the prophesies of God."

Lest there be doubt on the matter, Gloria regaled her audience with stories of her own suffering. An irate husband had beaten her mercilessly, knocking her to the floor, and kicking her in the breasts. She had complained to the police, but they had done nothing. One suggested that she try to be a better wife. The rabbi had been no more helpful. Her second husband had destroyed her self-esteem with his constant carping about her weight and by running off with a *shikse*. The word had slipped in, but the damage was slight, for few of the plump ladies had ever heard of the word. Those who had, hardly noticed, for it was at this point that Gloria launched into a description of clitorodectomies so graphic that only a female audience could appreciate it.

"Our women remain strong," she concluded her lecture, "but we must be stronger. If Israel falters, biblical prophesy and its glorious promise for humanity must also falter."

The plump ladies filed out of the assembly hall primed to assault the first male that they encountered. Evening cocktails would never be the same. The Israeli Cultural Attaché wept. The preacher, never a strong man, felt a strange inability to control his bladder.

* * * *

Whatever Gloria's lectures lacked in coherence was more than made up for by a personality that blended zeal, compassion and an undeniable charisma for those who wanted to believe. Part psychologist and part fortune teller, she had become an expert in female insecurities and had written her thesis on male dominance and female masochism in Jewish literature. The departure of her second husband had deprived her of both. She embraced victim hood with the same zeal that she embraced everything else, and had pledged her life to the restoration of sexual sanity in a world of equals. Her courses were immensely popular among female students but were soon dropped by males who, venturing in only to snicker, soon found themselves in danger of psychological castration. The danger was real, for both of Gloria's ex-husbands bore the scars of her of masochism. The exception was a smattering of gays who found her lectures exhilarating and nodded approvingly throughout her sermons.

Parker's wife listened intently to Gloria's lecture, finding sympathy in her suffering and relishing her skillful blending of biblical prophesy and feminism. It was if Gloria were reading her mind, justifying her own sexual desires and rekindling her faith in herself. "Yes," she vowed to herself, "Scott and I will build a relationship based upon sexual morality and equality."

"Her college years had been neither," she admitted to herself, now lost in her own reality, "and that was why their marriage had failed." She couldn't accuse Parker of sadism during the Wisconsin years, but there was no question that his domination of their relationship had been total. She was in love and his dominance hadn't seemed important as long as they were together. Marriage to Parker had become her goal and she had succeeded.

Nor, was he sadistic in the years that had followed. Each had drifted into their own worlds and when the strength of her personality had reasserted itself, he had simply lost interest in her. She had no proof of his infidelities, and he mocked her when she raised the issue. Was humiliation not a form of sadism? Perhaps, but at least he had never beaten her or kicked her in the breasts. She doubted that thought had ever occurred to him. He was not an angry man seething with frustration.

Her resolve lightened her burden, but hope soon faded. Indifference was worse than sadism. Perhaps it was the ultimate form of sadism. Her version of Christian feminism, although yet to be fully articulated, didn't deny Parker his masculinity. Rather, it sought the perfect blend of force and submission expressed in a spiritual framework.

* * * *

They had lunched together after Gloria's lecture, each recognizing in the other a kindred soul. "You seem to know a great deal about Muslims," Gloria had smiled as they ordered a second glass of wine at the outdoor courtyard of the Nile Hilton. "Are you a scholar?"

"Worse," Parker's wife responded, "I am married to one."

"Ah," responded Gloria with interest. "No doubt he teaches at the American University."

"No," responded Parker's wife, "we have friends there, but my husband works for some place called the Institute. He has some big project there, but I don't know much about it."

Over the course of the lunch and the ensuing day Gloria learned a great deal about the Parkers' strange relationship. It was as if she were consoling one of her students. "What a weird attitude Protestants have toward sex," she marveled to herself. "No wonder they are so frustrated. At least Jewish women know what they are here for."

* * * *

"How was your speaker?" Parker asked as they sat gazing across the Nile that warm autumn evening. He didn't really care, but expressed interest in the spirit of their new amity. The tension between them was easing and intimacy had increased apace. They still lived in their own worlds, but without the rancor.

Parker listened with unexpected interest as his wife recounted Gloria's skillful fusion of biblical prophesy, feminism, and sexual license. It was not so much the content of Gloria's lecture that had piqued his interest, although that was clever, but the intensity of his wife's emotions. Her recounting of earlier lectures had been the starting point for their evening discussions and, more often than not, requests for greater information. Parker was the teacher and she a gifted pupil. It had been a coming together, a grand effort to recreate moments long past.

This night was different. His wife was animated and had little interest in debate. Nor was she the clever student initiating sexual play by seeking the wisdom of her tutor. It was as if she had been born again into some strange cult that had seized control of her mind. Parker found this strange, for his wife was confident of her faith, perhaps too confident.

Parker was right. His wife had fallen victim to a sorceress who conquered by preying upon the insecurities and sexual fantasies of the innocent. She eased their self-doubts and encouraged them to sexual excess in the name of feminism. It had been the trick of fortune tellers from time immemorial. It wasn't Gloria's crystal ball that revealed their secrets, but the worry lines on their foreheads and their tortured fingernails. A lucky guess was helpful, but seldom necessary. They came to bear their soul and seek advice. They left as her disciples.

Parker blamed Gloria for his wife's transformation, but that was unfair. Gloria had given the same lecture that she had always given and, aside from their lunch, there had been little time for chit-chat. But, maybe Gloria was to blame. She had been far more animated than usual. This was her first venture before a Christian audience and it would test her belief that the sisters were all the same, that they had the same desires and the same insecurities. The real test would be a Muslim audience, but that would take time and preparation.

Parker's wife had sought her advice, much as her forlorn students sought her advice. The lunch had been a polite pretext, but hardly had they finished their first glass of wine than Parker's wife had begun to confess.

Gloria's exhilaration had been no less than that of Constance Parker. She had expected the litany of psychological abuse, sexual frustration and the yearning for reaffirmation. She was not to be disappointed. Confessions come easy to strangers thrown together for a brief instant by a rare convergence of the planets, individuals from different worlds never to be seen again. What Gloria had not expected was the convergence of their views and their passions. They had reached the same conclusions by their own means. The only difference was that Parker's wife was confused and lacked a plan. A brilliant student, she needed a teacher. Gloria was not confused. She had a plan and she knew how to guide her students.

"What a pity we may never see each other again," said Gloria as their lunch ended. "I've enjoyed our chat so much. It seems that we have so much in common." It was blatant appeal for a second invitation to Egypt and, if all went well, an exchange visit to Israel. What a marvelous treat Parker's wife would be for her students. Where else could they find a living, hands on testament to the convergence of feminism and the Christian concern for the fate of Israel? Perhaps Parker's wife could become a disciple, spreading her philosophy among the plump ladies and even exporting it to the United States. So excited had Gloria become by her own thoughts that she almost missed the words she was longing to hear.

"I wish there were some way to arrange another talk," responded Parker's wife in a rare display of emotion, "but the church has no money for speakers and I'm embarrassed to approach your Embassy again. I know that your country is short of money."

Gloria remained pensive for a moment before responding. "Let me ask," she said. "The Embassy always has money to impress influential Americans. Perhaps your husband qualifies."

*   *   *   *

Gloria had asked, and the Cultural Attaché said he would look into the matter. "First," he cautioned, "we must see how well your lecture was received." His thoughts were focused on damage control, not a second visit. He had heard Gloria's lecture and shuttered at the memory. It had been a declaration of war against Islam and a declaration of war against men. One lecture to the women's club of an American church might go unnoticed, but not a continuing dialogue. A single leak to the press could destroy years of good work. Gloria, moreover, was not merely an academic. She was a woman possessed by demons.

This said, the Cultural Attaché was a conscientious man and, fearing the worst, made polite inquiries about the success of Gloria's lecture. That was his job and he had little choice in the matter. It was with some difficulty, accordingly, that he attempted to come to grips with the rave reviews that Gloria's performance had engendered, not to mention the request for a repeat performance. It just didn't fit. Gloria's lecture may have pleased the women's club, but it sure as hell wasn't going to please their husbands. It was they, in this most imperfect of worlds, who counted. He dispatched the reviews and the request for a repeat visit to Jerusalem, but said nothing of the sense of foreboding that dampened his spirit. His successes in Egypt had been few, and the Foreign Office would be pleased. With luck, the request for a second visit would get lost in the bureaucratic morass like all of his other requests that cost money.

It was not to be. The Foreign Office had agreed with remarkable speed and even suggested a possible exchange program. As always, their logic remained opaque and they hadn't bothered to explain. Obviously, they hadn't heard Gloria speech. Like all men of conscience, he was filled with remorse. He could have killed the matter, but didn't. He had put his career before his country. To ease his conscience, he invited the Mosad agent to coffee and explained his concerns about Gloria.

"It is worth the risk," the agent had consoled him. "Her husband's position at the Institute was all the justification that the Foreign Office needed to open their wallet. He is an important scholar and is known to have friends among the Palestinians. That, of itself, requires watching. More importantly," the Mosad agent continued, "was the change in patterns. Why was an American scholar with obvious ties to the Embassy suddenly allowed entry to the heart of Egypt's liberal establishment? Perhaps the Americans are planning something that we don't know about?"

"A liberal coup would be to our benefit," offered the Cultural Attaché. "Anything that stuffed the Islamists would be to our advantage."

"Beyond doubt," mused the Mosad agent, concerned that the Americans had not informed him of their plans. "We could help pave the way. I have checked with my usually reliable sources, but they know nothing of the matter. It's all very strange. Perhaps your friend Gloria can find out something"

The Cultural Attaché doubted it, but nodded in agreement. The survival of Israel required vigilance. It also required the unbridled support of the United States. While the rest of the world clamored to throw the Jewish state to the wolves, the United States held firm. But for how long? Perhaps the Americans were tiring of their petulant offspring. Thus it was that the Israeli Foreign Office watched the comings and goings of Americans in Cairo with great care. There was no choice in the matter.

Chapter 14

Laments

The deepening friendship between Smith and Parker was not difficult to understand. Smith was intrigued by Parker's tales of the Institute and Parker relished Smith's candid discussion of Embassy intrigues. It wasn't what they taught you in Political Science 101. In reality, each longed to be the other. Smith, a scholar at heart, closed his eyes and visualized himself lecturing to bright young minds, his hand gripping a best seller that dared to tell the truth unrestrained by diplomatic niceties or the fear that the Israelis would place him on the black list of American diplomats deemed pro-Arab. Arabists, the Israeli's called them, as if it were somehow a crime for American diplomats to be versed in culture of the people they were struggling to rule. The list was powerful, its members quietly being retired from the Corps.

Smith loved the glamour of the diplomatic world in which nothing was what it seemed, but suddenly realized that he had become its captive. There was no exit. When Parker had lamented the scholar's lack of relevance, Smith cringed. What was his relevance? Israeli pilots challenged their government by refusing to bomb Palestinian civilians, and Israeli reservists refused to serve in the Occupied Territories. That was courage. But he lacked that courage. Israel had learned to tolerate dissent. Not so with the U.S. Department of State.

Smith's confessions had cheered Parker for the moment. It was nice that people in high places found scholars to be relevant, but he knew better. He closed his eyes and visualized the rows of bright young minds sitting before him. He saw beautiful girls who never age, each embarking upon a new college adventure, most yawning from the strain. Inquisitive young men slumbered in their chairs, baseball caps shading their eyes from the glare of the fluorescent lighting. Two jocks were snapping the bra strap of the girl sitting between them.

A few students were intellectually curious, but there weren't many. By and large, the university had become an extension of high school. It was just another hurdle to be crossed before taking a job at Wal-Mart or McDonalds. The important thing was a decent grade. Professors who gave hard tests were trashed on student evaluation forms. Parker's books were praised but, as far as he could tell, had little discernable influence on anything. It was as if the world consisted of two groups of people: those who thought and those who acted. As for daring to tell the truth, what difference did it make when no one was listening?

Even the right to be irrelevant was under attack. Right wing fanatics were making large grants to universities on the condition that they hire professors who parroted their philosophy. Zionist groups encouraged students to monitor affronts to Israel in their courses. A book had even been written on Arabists in the ivory tower. To the author's surprise, he had found most of the Arabists whom he interviewed to be reasonable people. Few were antagonistic to Israel. They merely felt that a balanced approach to the Arab-Israeli conflict would be good for the world at large, Israel included.

Smith and Parker hadn't intended their discussion to take the track that it had, but both were angry. Smith was fuming because Jake had called him a jackass and suggested that he take lessons in diplomacy from Mandy. He could almost see Jake's hand going up her skirt, although he knew better.

Parker, for his part, had just learned of his wife's impending trip to Israel as the guest of the Israeli government. His colleagues at the Institute were paranoid enough without the Israelis entering the picture. She hadn't consulted him in advance, and to make matters worse, Gloria Goldensickle was to be her hostess and guide. So the scotch at Smith's villa had flowed and with it their frustrations.

Neither really wanted to change careers. Each simply wanted to fulfill his dream of making the world a better place. Both had the knowledge and experience to help things along, but to what end? Academics had little influence on policy, and Smith was stymied by diplomatic correctness. His job was to gather information and carry out the Secretary of State's orders, nothing more.

Thus, they formed a pact. When Smith retired some fifteen years down the road, they would write a book on the Middle East that combined the diplomatic and academic perspectives. It may even be two books, and if they disagreed, so much the better. A national debate would erupt and people would become concerned. What a glorious dream.

But even dreams have their uses. Their dream was a bond, a curious fiction that allowed each of them to enter the world of the other. Smith became the dispassionate academic and Parker the hands on problem solver.

"So, my co-author," asked Smith with the resoluteness of one flirting with intoxication, "how do we solve the Egyptian conundrum? The government is spinning out of control and pushing people into the hands of the jihadists. If things don't change in short order, we'll lose Egypt just as we lost Iran and Iraq. If Egypt goes, the Saudi monarchy won't be far behind. Far worse, the war on terror is a stalemate or worse. We can't even get the Egyptian government to break its truce with the jihadists. Whose side are they on? Jake wants a coup, but Washington is afraid to rock the boat. Anyway, the army already runs things and a coup wouldn't change anything. We would just be dealing with different thieves. The longer we dally, the worse things get."

"It seems, my co-author," smiled Parker, also reveling in that brief period of lucidity that precedes intoxication, "that you have eliminated all of the options but democracy. Give democracy a chance and let the Muslim Brotherhood take over. You know that you can't stop them, so why not be on the winning side? That way you will be in a position to encourage their moderation.

"You're being an idealist," chided Smith. "You know damn well that democracy can't work in the Islamic world."

"Don't think of democracy as an ideal," responded Parker, "Think of it as a Machiavellian ploy. The Brotherhood will take over and the jihadists won't have a leg to stand on because Egypt will have an Islamic government. Better yet, the Brotherhood hates the jihadists and knows how to take care of them. Don't forget, they come from the same swamp. The liberals will bellyache, but it serves them right for deserting us. The best part is that the Brotherhood will screw things up just like the mullahs did in Iran. Nothing can stop the wave of Islamic fanaticism as fast as an Islamic government."

"You're drunk," slurred Smith. "We can't put an Islamic government in office. What in the hell do you think we have been fighting against for the last 30 years."

"And with great success, I might say," chided Parker with unaccustomed brutality. "All you have done so far is to piss off a billion and half Muslims by convincing them that the US had launched a crusade against Islam. No wonder the jihadists are so hard to track down. You are creating terrorists faster than you can kill them. Even the liberals, our natural allies, call us fascists. You can't swim against the Islamic tide forever. Give them democracy and let them have at it. Anyway, what choice do you have? Even if Jake gets his coup, it will only keep the lid on for a year or two. When the explosion comes, it will reach all the way to your cabin in Vermont. Remember, the greater the pressure in the boiler, the greater the carnage when it blows. You're sitting on a volcano. Have a fair election and ease some of the pressure."

"You're preaching to the choir," responded Smith with bitterness. "I know what we've done. The choices aren't easy. I floated the idea of working with the Brotherhood but it didn't find any takers. There is no guarantee that the Brotherhood wants to play. They may even be in cahoots with the jihadists. One beguiles the masses with slogans of moderation while the other spews violence. The end result is the same: an Islamic government. As you said yourself, they come from the same swamp."

"I don't think so," responded Parker, attempting not to slur his words. "The jihadists know that they can never achieve their warped dream of a jihadist theocracy as long as the Brotherhood offers the masses a peaceful road to an Islamic government. It is Islam without pain, so to speak. The jihadists need the government's oppression to restore their popularity and they need the government to destroy the Brotherhood. They bide their time, but not without rearming."

"Don't be so damn holy," snarled Smith, more accustomed to alcoholic debates than Parker. "I told you that the idea had been floated. It is just too risky. If it didn't work, we'd have a real mess on our hands."

"Not a bigger mess than you have now," countered Parker. "Play hard ball and open negotiations with the Brotherhood. That will scare the hell out of the government and they will back down from their truce in big hurry."

"We can't be seen negotiating with the Muslim Brotherhood," replied Smith, allowing himself a hint on condescension. "That would be a sign of weakness. The Muslim world already thinks that we are on the run. Besides, we can't negotiate with the Brotherhood without the agreement of Jake, not to mention Washington."

"It seems," concluded Parker with resignation, "that you people always have an excuse for doing nothing until the world falls apart and then you send in the bombers. And after that, what? You've tried occupation and we all know how well that works."

It wasn't Parker's logic that troubled Smith, but the fact that it paralleled his own. One more time the US was going to go down the tubes because the Jakes of the world had no idea of what they were doing. Once again the US was propping up corrupt and incompetent dictators against the will of their people. When things got out of hand, the US would stage a coup. But to what avail? American support among moderate Muslims would evaporate and the jihadists would reap the harvest. Sooner or later all hell would break loose and the United States would have another Islamic republic on its hands. How many times had he pursued the same logic with his colleagues in the Embassy only to have it shot down as impractical and unworkable? "Get real," they scoffed, "and stop dreaming. Jake is on your case as it is. Don't make things worse."

Looking at Parker he made a suggestion that he would not have made if he were sober. "Perhaps you could help us with this, Scott. You could be a silent intermediary between us and the Brotherhood. No one would suspect it because you are at the Institute, and they hate the Brotherhood. Besides, you are on the inside and have no real ties with the Embassy."

"Precisely," responded Parker. "How convenient when they fish my body from the Nile." Parker was drunk, but not that drunk.

* * * *

Curiously, Parker had much the same conversation with Mandy a few nights later. They didn't need alcohol to ease their inhibitions, for when she was in his arms, there were no inhibitions. She was in love with Parker and she was in love with her job. Eventually she would have to choose between them, but for the moment, they were one in the same. He was her window on an Egypt that she, as a diplomat, could never know. He was the insider, she the outsider. She had attempted to penetrate the soul of Egypt with Egyptian men, but their focus was to narrow: sex and exploitation, but nothing else. It was also dangerous, and called into question her capacity for independent judgment.

With Parker it was different. She reveled in the power of Parker's body and his quiet self-confidence. He dominated without being demeaning, and when they discussed Egyptian politics it was as a team, each bringing their special knowledge to the table. She knew of Smith's friendship with Parker, and she delighted in upstaging her senior by alluding to "private" information that exceeded the bounds of male bonding. She wanted their affair to be secret, but not too secret.

Marriage, of course, was never mentioned. He was already married and she wasn't sure that she wanted to be married. There was still time to think about it, but not too much time. Once scoffing at make-up, it had recently become her friend. She was a classy thirty with her petit frame, blond hair and perfect skin, but what would forty look like, especially with the grind of the Foreign Service?

Perhaps it was this thought that hovered in the back of her mind as they sat on her balcony overlooking the grand sweep of the Nile and discussed the Brotherhood option. "Will you take care of me when they throw me out of the Foreign Service for not following the chain of command?" she asked scarcely aware that the words had escaped her mouth. Parker kissed her gently and whispered, "Follow the chain of command."

* * * *

Male bonding can't compare to the strength of a relationship between a man and a woman, but it does have its advantages. Parker found it easy to build Zahra into his stories of the Institute that Smith found so intriguing. The Arabian Nights, he called them. Not so with Mandy. Zahra's name was mentioned in passing, a minor figure in a panoply of bizarre characters. Honesty required no less. Always the good storyteller, he studied his audience with care and found Mandy to be fascinated by the grand Nubian with his bald head, huge belly, and Swedish wife. He even mentioned the Nubian's torment of Zahra with his guttural impersonations of ecstasy. This, of course, was a mistake.

"Perhaps you would like me to moo like a cow, too," she snapped in wounded sarcasm, revealing emotions she would have preferred to have left unexpressed. She knew Egyptian women were attractive with their huge brown eyes and opulent breasts. Parker had dropped the subject.

Smith, smarting from Mandy's allusions to "private information," took his revenge by dropping hints casual hints about Parker's special informant at the Institute. Nothing direct, of course, for that would be a breach of confidence. When Mandy finally put two and two together, she was livid. Smith had scooped her and Parker had deceived her.

She had erupted in tears, which angered her, and then berated Parker for his duplicity, which angered her more. It showed just how much she cared. "Control your emotions, her father had warned he as he groomed her for the Diplomatic Corps. Use them as a weapon, but don't let them betray you. Success in the Corps demands it. Now, when it mattered most, she had failed. Stripped of her defenses, she had spewed emotion from every portal: anger, jealousy, pain, despair. "The down sides of love," her mother had called them, suggesting that her father was more human than her daughter was willing to believe.

Chapter 15

Schemes and Plans

It would be unfair to say that Smith and Mandy were adversaries. That was not the case. Their first year together had been one of harmony and mutual respect. He was the golden boy on the fast track to success and she was an admiring junior. They agreed on most issues and, more often than not, she was his ally on internal debates. Perhaps there were hints of a flirtation, but nothing serious. Scandals were verboten. The former Ambassador had little use for women in the Diplomatic Corps and had largely ignored her.

It was Jake's arrival that had created the tension between them. Smith was everything that Jake wasn't: suave, erudite, subtle and adroit at working within the system. He was an organization man par-excellence to be relied on for his tact and discretion. In Jake's eyes he was an effeminate shit, a pisant bureaucrat using a million rules and regulations to keep Jake from lashing out at the enemies of the United States. Somehow he figured that the Foreign Service would be different, but one look at Smith and the DCM told him that it wasn't. If Jake were to kick ass in the Middle East, he knew right where to begin.

They had recognized each other immediately: the gun slinger versus the faceless bureaucrat. Jake had fired first. "Glad to meet you son. Do what I say and we'll get along just fine." Actually, Jake hadn't meant it to be an insult. That was how he treated all of his employees. Smith bristled, but kept his composure.

"Thank you, Mr. Ambassador. I look forward to working with you." An innocuous bit of bureaucratic drivel, or at least it would have been if Smith had not stressed the word "with." It was a challenge and Jake recognized it as such. He welcomed it. He would crush Smith just as he had crushed better men. That's why he was rich and the friend of the President.

One look at Mandy, by contrast, had melted Jake's heart. She was the daughter that he had always longed for. She had feigned a professional handshake, and then threw her arms around him in a daughterly embrace. Catching herself, her face flushed with embarrassment, she had stammered, "I'm so sorry. That wasn't very professional of me." The battle was over before it had begun. This said she retained a sincere respect for Jake. He was rich, intelligent, a friend of the President and a fount of raw energy; a mover and shaker in a world that needed to be shaken.

She had attempted to put in a good word for Smith, but one look at the anger mounting in Jake's eyes dissuaded her. "If you want to succeed," he had said with the firmness of a stern father, "you must put aside your emotions." She hadn't made the same mistake twice. She respected Smith, but saw little need to sink with his ship.

The meetings in the Embassy were all the same. Jake hammered on the growing threat of the jihadist and stressed the need for a military coup. The DCM urged patience and Smith argued that another military coup would simply unleash a rush of support for the jihadists and discredit the US in the region. "And that," he would taunt Jake, "was not what the Secretary of State wanted. Anti-Americanism was already at fever pitch, and the Secretary was doing his best to calm things down." Smith wasn't bold by nature, but his only hope for the future was to distance himself from Jake's policies.

It was at this meeting. Jake had dismissed Smith and the DCM with a wave of the hand, and asked Mandy to stay behind. He trusted her and her views made sense. Smith and the DCM were out of the loop. She agreed with Smith, but didn't attack Jake's plan directly. Rather, she warned him that the Secretary of State wouldn't buy in until he had his ducks in a row. Everything had to be in place and nailed down."

Jake, an avid hunter, was impressed. "Right on," he said thoughtfully, "we've got to get our ducks in a row. Work on it, and come back with a plan."

Mandy did have a plan. It was her plan, but it was also Smith's plan and Parker's plan. Elections would be held, but they would be held in a controlled environment that would lead to a partial victory by the Muslim Brotherhood. The Brotherhood would participate in governing Egypt, but the military, much as in Turkey, would keep the Islamists from going to extremes. Both, whatever their mutual hostility, would have a stake in preserving the system. The corrupt despots would be gone and Egypt would have a more Islamic government. The jihadists, having been outflanked by the peaceful approach to an Islamic state, would lose the sympathy of the masses. They would also suffer the vengeance of the Brotherhood and the generals. The United States, for its part, could take credit for being a friend of Islam. It wasn't perfect, but it seemed to work in Turkey. If the Brotherhood screwed things up, so much the better. They would be discredited and liberal democracy might have a chance.

They had their plan, but that was the easy part. The problem was how to implement it. Jake had to be convinced, a Herculean task in itself. There was also the problem of the Brotherhood. The Brotherhood had been burned by their last foray into cooperation with the Embassy and seemed content to watch the US stew in its own juices. The Embassy was also prohibited from initiating contacts with the Brotherhood without clearance from Washington. Incidental conversations were ok, but nothing that would jeopardize Washington's delicate relationship with the Egyptian government, not to mention the Israelis. The Embassy's orders were to keep the lid on, not blow it to kingdom come.

"You know this is crazy," said Mandy as she and Smith had a hurried conversation in the courtyard of the Embassy. He was on his way to a reception, and she on her way to meet Parker for a drink. "Our job is to do what we are told, not to make policy. Hell, even Jake can't do that and he is a friend of the President."

"Don't think of this as making policy," replied Smith. "We are simply giving Washington another option. Besides, Washington is screaming about the need for democracy. All we are doing is paving the way."

"You know damn well that they don't mean it," snapped Mandy. "It could be the end of our careers if things go wrong."

"If could be the end of our careers if we do nothing," responded Smith. "The CIA is ranting and raving about the jihadists and we will look like complete fools if we keep saying that things are fine and dandy. Don't forget Iran and Iraq. We also have to distance ourselves from Jake's fixation with a coup. He keeps haranguing the Secretary of State with the topic and spends all of his time at the receptions talking to Egyptian generals. They don't know any better and think he is speaking for the President. He's even invited some of his favorite generals for a special session on regional planning. He is a man in a hurry and only has a year left. He will throw all of his chips in the pot and go out with a bang. If he wins, he will be Secretary of State. If he loses, he goes back to counting his millions and we'll be left holding the bag."

Mandy remained silent. Smith had been unable to disguise his resentment of her influence with Jake, but that didn't alter the fact that he was right. More than one friend in the State Department had told her to cool Jake down. "Easy tiger," one had cooed. "People are beginning to think that you are giving him more than advice."

Smith was also right about the generals. Jake entertained them all. He would know when he had the right man. For the moment, an ex-general named Ali al-Nimr was the top of his list. He was tough, rich, and maintained strong support in the military despite his pious calls for greater democracy. He was also one of the few people in Egypt who was not afraid to stand up to the Minister of Interior. Jake knew by Ali's very demeanor that he was a good man. He could tell by looking in his eyes. He wasn't worried about Ali's liberal facade. On more than one occasion, Ali had cautioned him that democracy and human rights would take time to mature in a country like Egypt. Jake had conveyed his message to Washington.

* * * *

"What we need," Mandy spoke softly to Smith, "is someone outside of the Embassy to serve as an intermediary between us and the Brotherhood. That way we can take the credit if things work out and feign ignorance if they don't. It also has to be someone that the Brotherhood trusts or at least will feel comfortable talking to, preferably someone they can talk to indirectly without committing themselves. It might also be helpful if that somebody were able to convince the liberals that they would be able to play if they went along." She didn't mention Parker by name. There was no need to.

"He laughed in my face when I suggested it," said Smith, "unless you have some special means of persuasion."

"No," said Mandy ignoring the jibe, "we had a fight over his girl friend and don't discuss the issue. You're his buddy. It's up to you."

"Can you handle Jake?" asked Smith.

"I think so," responded Mandy. "I will help him put his ducks in a row."

Smith looked puzzled, but didn't ask for a clarification. It was obviously a private matter.

* * * *

Smith and Parker had talked a few days later following a reception at Smith's villa. Each had sunken into one of the soft leather chairs surrounding the fireplace in Smith's study and waited for the other to speak. The fire wasn't needed, but there was a slight chill in the air and it contributed to the ambiance of the fine cognac and Cuban cigars.

The time for dancing was over. Smith inhaled a glorious plume of rich smoke scented with the bouquet of cognac and came to the point. "All of our information indicates that the Brotherhood won't play. Why should they? The way things are going now, they can just sit back and pick up the pieces. They know that sooner or later the Americans will force the government to turn on the jihadists. The Brothers bide their time while we do the dirty work and then come in as the good guys. The US would have to embrace them. We would have no other choice."

"Maybe not," replied Parker, attempting to show enough cooperation to keep Smith on board without committing himself to serving as an intermediary with the Brotherhood. "Nothing tangible," he rationed his words, "but the Brotherhood is nervous. The truce between the government and the jihadists is taking its toll. Both, moreover, are preparing for the final battle with the Brotherhood: the Minister of Interior by demanding more American weapons and the jihadists by strengthening their ties with the global jihadist networks. My informant has openly raised the question of the Embassy's logic in allowing the Minister of Interior to honor his truce with the groups responsible for 9/11. That, of itself, is a sign that the Sheikh is worried."

"What did you say?" questioned Smith, alarmed that the Brotherhood had reached the same conclusion as the CIA and more envious than ever of Parker's position at the Institute.

"That the US hadn't agreed to the truce and was hostile to it."

As he spoke, his mind reverted to his conversation with Zahra. He had seen his words recorded in the depths of her eyes. "I don't believe you," she had responded quietly. "The United States controls the government. There could have been no truce without a nod from the Embassy."

Reading the sadness in Zahra's eyes, he realized that the important thing was what the Arabs believed, not its accuracy. They were not responding to the world as the United States saw it, but to the world as they saw it. In reality, both images were flawed. Both were vague approximations of reality, dream worlds in which each saw what they wanted to see. "As you like," he had replied gently, knowing that his comments would find their way to Sheikh Yassin.

"You were saying," coughed Smith shaking him from his reverie.

"Sorry," responded Parker. "It's just that I have this gut feeling that the Brotherhood would be willing to discuss the issue if it could be done in a discrete manner. The government is closing in on them from one side and the jihadists from the other. Even worse, the jihadists are regaining their popularity. They may have declared a truce locally, but they are sticking it to the US globally. The people love it. The 'kill American' strategy, they call it. Curious, isn't it? The Embassy and the Brotherhood are in the same boat. To succeed, you both have to break the government's truce with the jihadists and get rid of the Minister of Interior. The longer the Minister of Interior stays in power, the stronger the jihadists become. They've learned the lessons of the past and have become a much smoother operation."

* * * *

"How does he know?" asked Mandy, her voice taught with the pain that she knew was coming.

"He didn't say," responded Smith dryly, "and I didn't ask."

"Don't lie," hissed Mandy. "You know damn well that his girlfriend told him."

"I'm not sure," cautioned Smith in a calming voice. Mandy had long ago given up pretenses when it came to Parker, and little was to be gained by inflaming her jealousy. A few weeks earlier it would have offered an opportunity for sweet revenge, but things had changed. For the moment, they were on the same side and he needed her to handle Jake. "She is obviously part of the equation, but I think Parker is doing a lot of reading between the lines. He said as much himself. Besides, she's secular. The only connection is an occasional family get together. I've had it checked out. Let's see how things develop."

"And if they do develop?" asked Mandy pointedly. "Then what?"

"Then," said Smith solemnly, "you handle Jake and I'll persuade Parker to serve as our intermediary."

"I don't think he will do it," replied Mandy skeptically. "Trust and honesty with the Arabs are big with him."

"We all have our faults," smiled Smith enigmatically, "but we're not asking him to spy. We merely need him to serve as a messenger between two interested parties, if such they are. Besides, we are co-authors."

The reference to he and Parker as co-authors caught her off guard. Her eyes flashed with irritation. "Each of us," the faint smile on his face seemed to say "controls a different end of our mutual friend." But his thoughts went unspoken. There was work to do.

CHAPTER 16

A Pregnant Spy Won't Fly

Having decided on a course of action, Sheikh Yassin surveyed the terrain with the practiced eye of a field general. This, of course, was exactly what he was: a field general in the army of God. "Patience," he cautioned his council. "Patience. Let the situation evolve. Wait for the enemy to expose his flank and then pounce." But the hot-heads would have none of it. He had promised action and they demanded action.

The hot-heads didn't understand how many enemies the Brotherhood had or just how dicey the situation had become. There were so many enemies: the Minister of Interior, the jihadists, the Embassy, and Mizjaji's thugs. Each had a plan. The Minister of Interior would turn the elections into a farce and use his fraudulent victory to step up his attacks of the Brotherhood. Sheikh Hassan and other jihadists would provide the Minister of Interior with information on the Brotherhood's secret arms caches. The Embassy would see the elections results as a sign that the government was firmly in control and back away from a possible agreement with the Brotherhood, if such there were to be. Zahra's informant, he couldn't bring himself to use the word lover, had intimated that such an agreement was a possibility. He had his doubts. As always, the Americans would cling to their corrupt puppet government and plead with the Minister of Interior to attack jihadists. No wonder they were losing the Middle East. "Live in hope and die in despair," his acerbic mother would have said, may God bless her soul.

Then, there were the rumors swirling around Zahra. Rumors were the oxygen that Egyptians breathed. They were also dangerous, for they were believed by all, even those who should know better. Indeed, those who should know better were the source of most rumors, but none more so than the Minister of Interior. He slandered when he could not kill, but he was not alone. Rumors were the first line of battle, turning neighbors against neighbors, faith against faith, and nation against nation. Were they not also the stuff of the Embassy receptions and the CIA reports?

Sheikh Yassin listened carefully to the rumors that swirled through the alleys of Boulaq. They were his warning signals. The rumors surrounding Zahra had become increasingly vicious. Some attributed her prudent dress to an unexpected pregnancy. Even her friends, it was said, were alarmed by the swelling of her girth, and they should know, for they tracked it on a daily basis. "Dangerous," the Sheikh murmured to himself "Very dangerous. A pregnant spy?" He could wait no longer. Parker's visit would be the call to arms.

✳ ✳ ✳ ✳

"I think, my princess," said Sheikh Yassin, as they sat in the alcove of her father's house, "that it is time to invite your American friend to visit the mosque. The rumors and gossip have gone far enough. We need to keep people guessing before they get bored and take matters into their own hands. You know how emotional our people are. The slightest incident erupts into violence. Their lives are so dismal that they cannot survive without the fantasy of their soap operas. Some get so frantic that they even attack the actors. Our little soap-opera is so much more enticing. It is real. Even the Minister of Interior is interested. Just think of the stir that a visit to the mosque will create in their fevered minds!" The Sheikh's voice was animated and to Zahra it seemed almost euphoric. "You must understand that your little adventure," the Sheikh continued, "has become the talk of Boulaq and beyond. Let people see that the grand romance of their fancy was God's will."

If the Sheikh had been animated, Zahra was not. She sat stunned, her mind refusing to acknowledge the Sheikh's words. Her rebellion had been demeaned as a little adventure. Her grand romance scorned as a petty soap opera. Veiled threats of people taking things into their own hands filled her with terror, but none more so than Mizjaji's rumor that the angel of death was about to strike. "If

Sheikh Yassin is too soft to kill the whore," so the rumor went, "it is the angel's responsibility to do so."

But even that rumor, as ghastly as it was, proved too simple for the good folk of Boulaq. Rumors begot rumors and it was soon predicted that she would not die sound. The mid-wife would assure that there would be no orgasms in hell, but not before the angel of death had received his due. It would be her last glorious memory as the devil took her for his own, for was she not the Goddess of the Nile?

Zahra's fear of death paled in comparison with the depth of her shame. She had brought disgrace on her family and jeopardized the life's work of her grandfather. Had he not referred to "our" soap opera? More than ever, their fate was inextricably linked. He was the puppet master and she was the puppet. She had not played by the rules and now her folly had triggered a chain of events over which she had no control. Had she placed Parker at risk as well? She dared not answer. Her mind became clouded and she closed her eyes. The angel of death was calling her. Not Mizjaji, but the true angel of death.

Sheikh Yassin read her thoughts and placed his hand on her shoulder. "Not yet my beautiful child," he whispered. "Everything is the will of God. You must follow your heart. It is ordained."

Brushing away her tears, Zahra looked at the Sheikh with the eyes of one who had received a stay of execution. "Yes, my grandfather," she wept, "I will follow my heart."

She dared not ask the question that now tormented her mind, "What does my heart want?" Rather than easing her mind, the Sheikh's command had thrown it into turmoil. She had been a rebel, rejecting the East by enveloping herself in a veneer of westernization. She had enjoyed being the center of attention, saying what her friends were afraid to say and doing what others longed to do. She could do it because her father was rich and powerful. It was all so easy.

It was also an illusion. She was not Western. Her life had been shaped by her farther and grandfather. It was they who had inspired her to press the limits. It was also they who had dictated every key decision in her life. They had chosen her schools and selected her major in college. Now, faced with decisions, she realized that she had always been an actress, reading scripts prepared by others. When she had strayed from her lines, or pushed them too far, its was her family who had come to the rescue. Western girls were raised on romance and independence. They could cut the cord with their family and branch out on their own. In the East it was different. Marriage was a family affair. Romance was the enemy of logic. She knew that she would marry well and vacillated between dreams of a hansom tyrant who would beat her and a weakling whom she could dominate.

But that was in the past. She had strayed from her script and become a pawn in a vortex of intrigue. What did her heart want? It wanted her family, it wanted Parker, and it wanted to run. But to where? Women couldn't leave Egypt without the permission of their father or husband.

The sheikh looked at his granddaughter with quiet concern. He had no idea of what went through the mind of a young girl. He thought he did, but now he was not sure. As she rose to leave, his eyes strayed to her waist. Perhaps it was that time of the month. "God, my princess, created beauty," he said as if to make her smile. "Prudence should not hide your beauty." Dare he say more? He had to know.

There was no need to say more. Zahra had heard the rumors and seen the tell-tale glances of her friends, if such they were. They had lived in the shadow of her glory, thrilled by her friendship and encouraging her to new heights. They were not close friends, for it was dangerous to be too close to her. Parents and potential suitors disapproved. Now, in her moment of need, they shunned her, praying that past friendships had not been an act of folly. Eyes avoided her when she entered the room, all except the eyes of the Nubian and the Wisp.

*   *   *   *

"Why is it," Parker wondered to himself as he held Zahra's trembling body in his arms, "that love affairs that begin as soaring adventures soon degenerate into maudlin soap operas?" He doubted that their affair would soar forever, but prayed for it to have a soft landing. His marriage was a tragedy and his affair with Mandy was heading in the same direction. Mandy demanded to receive news of the Institute before Smith, yet the very mention of Zahra's name chilled their conversation. Where else did she think he got his information? If he didn't mention Zahra, she did. Cooperation between Mandy and Smith had ground to a halt and with it their plans for aborting Jake's coup. Now, his relations with the Embassy souring, he stood there comforting an Egyptian girl whose only sin had been a dalliance so trifling that it would evoke pity in rural Nebraska.

Parker listened intently as Zahra poured out her heart. He was the only one that she could turn to. She described the ring of fear that had enveloped her: the rumors, the desertion of her friends, the eyes that measured her waist, the growing boldness of the Nubian and the Wisp, and the concerns of the Sheikh. Parker listened, and as he listened, he counted the seconds before the click of the secretary's heels would send them scurrying or the Wisp's knife, propelled by soles of gum rubber, sank between his shoulder blades. Or, would it sink between her marvelous breasts, and they were marvelous. Zahra seemed unmindful of the threat. It was as if she didn't care.

"What did your grandfather say?" asked Parker with a gentleness that disguised his growing unease. He felt the circle of fear that was tightening around her more intensely than she could ever guess. It was tightening around him as well. Everyone pretended that things were the same: the Boss, the Nubian, the Wisp, the general's wife, and the secretary. But they weren't. Everything had changed.

"He suggested that I wear clothes that are modest but chic," she replied with embarrassment.

"Your grandfather is a wise man," approved Parker. "Perhaps you should dress like a nun one day and display your navel the next."

Parker listened to his own words with disbelief. What had motivated his insensitivity? A Freudian slip? He was emotional to be sure, for he could not deny his affection for Zahra. Or was it his own fear? He often joked to build his courage. No matter, he chastised himself for having missed all of the clues to what was happening around him. Was he doomed to be an outsider much as all who had preceded him, describing but not understanding?

She choked back the tears triggered by his coarseness, and whispered, "My grandfather thinks that the best way to put an end to the rumors is for you to visit his Mosque. You are my only friend, Scott. I have no one else to turn to. Please do not desert me. I love you, Scott."

"No," he whispered softly as the click of the secretary's heels sounded her approach, "I will not desert you." They had been spared again, but for how long? Perhaps he was becoming a fatalist. What will be will be.

* * * *

"How clever you are, my angel," Sheikh Yassin beamed as Zahra recounted the scene.

"No, Grandfather," she responded, finding little cheer in praise that implied that she had deceived her lover, "I followed my heart as you instructed. I no longer have the capacity for thought."

The Sheikh remained in the alcove for a few minutes after Zahra's departure. More than ever he saw the hand of God guiding the course of events. He even marveled at Parker's suggestion of a naked belly button. There could be no naked belly button, but he had a friend among the Islamic tailors who could work wonders. Hints of translucent gauze would be far more convincing than a naked belly button.

Chapter 17

Ducks in a Row

"Up for a drink after the dance?" Smith asked. "I'd like to continue our conversation about the Brotherhood."

Smith's reference to the dull Embassy receptions as a dance never failed to bring a smile to Parker's face. It had become a standing joke between them. "Sure," he replied in kind. "Always glad to serve my county." Each returned to their rounds, changing partners at five minute intervals. Interest in Parker had increased with time, and he enjoyed his new found importance.

His humor faded when an Egyptian diplomat of long acquaintance made an oblique reference to his relationship with Zahra. He knew that it was a warning, but he was tired of being the lead actor in a second rate soap opera. His humor disappeared all together as he anticipated another row with his wife. She would be furious that he was spending the night away from home, but so be it. He needed some comfort after the session with Zahra, and his wife's announcement of her trip to Israel had sent their relationship into a tale spin. It was not that he minded her absence. She could have gone to the moon for all he cared, but the trip to Israel was sensitive and she should have discussed it with him before accepting Gloria's invitation. He didn't like being confronted with fait accomplis, and especially a fait accompli that bore the stamp of Gloria Goldensickle. Just how comforting Mandy would be remained an open question.

* * * *

"What's new in Egypt, my co-author?" queried Smith as they sank into the padded leather chairs of his study, drinks in hand. Mandy, sitting are the arm of Parker's chair, glowered at the Smith's reference to Parker as his co-author and moved to a hard back chair next to the fireplace. They would spend the evening together, but his hopes for comfort had begun to fade.

"I've been invited to visit Sheikh Yassin," responded Parker with nonchalance. He had started to say summoned, but thought better of it. It was a godsend that he was able to break the news to them simultaneously.

Parker didn't mention the rumors of Zahra's pregnancy. His relationship with Mandy would have dissolved in a pool of emotion and Smith, sensing danger, would have severed their ties. He also saw little reason to mention his wife's invitation to visit Israel. It was still theoretical and he would deal with it when the time came.

Smith and Mandy exchanged a quick glance. The time for decision had come. They had their intermediary, the perfect intermediary. He had declined to play, but Sheikh Yassin had taken care of that. He was playing whether he liked it of not. Why else would Sheikh Yassin have invited him to the mosque? The Sheikh had tipped his hand, and now they had to respond. It was now or never. But, was Parker really the perfect intermediary? Could he be trusted to follow their orders to the letter, saying what he was told to say and nothing more? He was on the outside and didn't understand the intricacies of the Embassy. Far worse, he was a free spirit. Could they turn him off if things started to go sour? What was the escape route? There had to be an escape route.

These were professional questions, instantaneous and simultaneous. They were questions pre-programmed by their training, by the culture of the Foreign Service, and by their sharply honed instincts for survival. They were also questions that had to be answered. That was the hard part. Smith and Mandy were locked in a mutual pact to serve their country and save their careers, but they didn't trust each other. Talk had proven difficult. Each feared a double-cross and each feared that the other was using a special relationship with Parker to extract privy information unknown the other. Rather than working together to manage Parker, it was Parker who was managing them. Not intentionally, of course, but he had become the intermediary between them just as he had become the intermediary between the Embassy and the Brotherhood.

Parker had expected a surprised reaction to his announcement, but not the stunned silence that had ensued. He tried to read their emotions but failed. They had been steeled to keep their emotions to themselves. "We'll see how steely she is in bed," Parker consoled himself, hurt by the sudden reminder that he was an outsider. Their worlds had come together, but only for a moment.

"Are you going?" asked Smith, repeating Mandy's question with a tinge of concern and envy.

"I haven't decided," taunted Parker, unwilling to give information for free but glad they knew where to look for his body.

Mandy smiled warmly, the chill of their earlier tensions having been banished by the news of the Sheikh's invitation. It would be a comforting evening after all.

*　　*　　*　　*

"Anything new?" asked Smith plopping down on the corner of Mandy's desk.

"Not really," she smiled with studied ambiguity. His inference that she had used their lovemaking to pump Parker for information rankled, and she resented it. That wasn't the case. The invitation to the mosque had simply provided a professional and much needed excuse for her to banish the jealousies that threatened to destroy their relationship. He had sketched the tenuousness of his relationship with Zahra and the fears that engulfed her. He didn't deny that he loved her, but neither had he said that he did. Even if he did love Zahra, Mandy no longer feared her as a rival. It wasn't anything that Parker had said, but the strength of his body as he possessed her.

Then relenting, she added, "He thinks that we are hiding something from him. He didn't say anything specific. Just women's intuition. I don't know if he will go or not. I almost hope that he doesn't."

"He'll go," laughed Smith. "He's a romantic searching for the soul of Egypt. It's a chance of a lifetime. I'd go in a shot, come what may. The question is will he play the role that we want him to play?"

"Not if he's suspicious," warned Mandy, closing her eyes and reliving the night without sleep. He was never the same. Sometimes he was gentle and playful, others intense and assertive. Last night he was cruel, punishing her for her duplicity. Which would he be after their marriage?

"What should we do?" asked Smith, forcing her back to reality.

"Be up front," responded Mandy. "Tell him our plans and his role in them."

"What plans?" frown Smith. "All we have done is to agree that it would be in the best interest of the United States to open lines of communication with the

Brotherhood in a way that doesn't embarrass either party. Parker supports the idea and now finds himself in a position to serve as the perfect intermediary. We can't ask him to play that role officially because that would be a staggering breach of our authority. If the Sheikh makes overtures, we can take note of that information and recommend action by Jake and Washington. If they go along, we will pursue the matter and be in the driver's seat. If they don't, we will have staked out a position independent from Jake and can say 'told you so' when the government goes down the tubes and the Brotherhood seizes power."

"Which option do you prefer?" asked Mandy making no effort to hide her repugnance.

"As a romantic," responded Smith ignoring her attempt at self-righteousness, "I would prefer to be in the driver's seat. The next stop could be an ambassadorship. As a good bureaucrat," he continued, "I incline toward the latter. A step up the ladder with no risk. How about you?"

"It's too bad that you can't have it both ways," chided Mandy, ignoring his question. "If things work out, you take the glory. If they don't, Parker is left holding the bag."

"Not at all," responded Smith. "If things work out Parker will be a big time consultant. Don't forget, the Brotherhood trusts him, not us. He'll be the world's leading expert on the topic and write his own ticket. If things don't work out, he gets on an airplane, richer for the experience. Which," he added with a touch of malice, "is what he is going to do anyway in a few weeks, or is it months?"

He had expected Mandy to wince with pain, but she hadn't. To the contrary, a faint smile played across her lips. "If Scott were a global consultant who could write his own ticket," her mind raced, "there would be no conflict in our careers." Whatever hesitancy she had about their plan now vanished.

"That's a funny way to treat a co-author," responded Mandy, returning his jibe and more anxious than ever to square herself with Parker. "You know damn well that you want him to do more than make a courtesy call on the Sheikh. That's merely the opening salvo. It will take more than an American scholar having tea with a Muslim cleric to convince Washington that they should flirt with the Brotherhood."

"What do you suggest?" replied Smith, restraining his irritation. He needed her support and that was fragile at best. She was going to survive whatever happened, and her interest in adventuring probably had more to do with Parker than logic.

"Make him a full partner," she responded quietly. "Tell him what you want him to do and admit that you can't support him if things go wrong. I'm sure that he's already figured that out, but it would be nice to hear it from you. Also tell him the risk of having Jake involved. God knows what that man is going to do if we don't get him on board. He could blow the whole operation and the Brotherhood would blame Parker."

"You are leading with your heart," mocked Smith with exasperation. "We're not asking the man to be a spy, merely to serve as a go-between for two sides that may want to talk."

"Yes we are," she hissed. "Not a day goes by that one of us doesn't pump him for information. What do we give him in return? Nothing! He has had it with our duplicity. Believe me, I took the brunt of his anger."

Smith paused, knowing that he had been bested. "When do you want to play true confessions?"

"This weekend. I will host a cocktail party for a few friends, Jake included. We can talk afterwards."

"Should I give Parker a ride home?" ventured Smith in a final effort at parity.

"In the morning," she smiled. "You can sleep on the couch."

* * * *

Mandy was at her charming best at her cocktail party, and that was charming indeed. She introduced Parker to Jake as a distinguished professor and a leading specialist on Middle Eastern affairs. Sensing Jake's distaste, she leaned forward revealing as much cleavage as she could muster and whispered for all to hear, "He's our man at the Institute and America's leading expert on the Muslim Brotherhood."

Jake, always fond of spies, shook Parker's hand enthusiastically, relieved that Parker hadn't tried to hug him. "So, professor," he said with a meaningful wink, "how far can you trust those people?"

Smith held his breath, hoping that Mandy would jump to the rescue if Parker got too academic of worse, too liberal. They had already agreed that he would stay in the background. A kind word from Smith would be the kiss of death and Jake would smell a plant.

Smith had worried in vain. Parker had heard so many Jake stories that he knew his prey well. "You can't," he responded without hesitation. "It is all a poker game. They are being squeezed by the Minister of Interior on one side and the jihadist on the other. For the moment, they have the most chips, but it's touch and go. A good draw by the jihadists could put them out of the game."

A warm glow came over Jake with the mention of his favorite game. "Who wins if they're out?" he asked with the intensity of kibitzer placing side bets.

"The jihadists," responded Parker with conviction.

"What makes you so sure?" countered Jake.

"The government's easy money," responded Parker almost automatically.

"And if the Brotherhood takes the pot?" asked Jake.

"They stay in the game and the jihadists go home."

"And the Minister of Interior?

"He's dead meat."

"What are the odds in favor of a military coup," asked Jake working the conversation around to his favorite topic.

"I'm not sure," replied Parker after careful consideration and making every effort to avoid sounding like Smith. "Looks good on the board, but nothing in the hold. The right general could keep the lid on for a year or two, but even that's iffy. The Army has been infiltrated by both the jihadists and the Brotherhood, and key officers in both are shifting arms to their militias, especially the jihadists. The generals all kiss ass, but even the Minister of Interior doesn't know who is who. It's a crap shoot."

Jake said nothing, but gave a brief nod of understanding. Jake didn't like crap shoots. He wanted the odds stacked in his favor, and that didn't include the risk of placing a jihadist sympathizer in office. He left the reception a few moments later, but was not smiling. He had even lost interest in Mandy's cleavage, such as it was. The thought of US weapons being filtered to the jihadist militias had shaken him as had his growing concern for the reliability of the generals who attended his private sessions. Ali al-Nimr still stood tall in Jake's mind. He was the only one that talked straight. As for the rest, he would have to watch them more closely. In the meantime he would deal with the Minister of Interior. "He's played me for a fool for the last time," Jake vowed to himself. "Time to make that sumbitch sweat."

Smith and Mandy weren't sure that they had followed the conversation, but it was clear that Jake had.

* * * *

Smith didn't spend the night on the couch, but with the sense of intimacy that comes with too much booze, he laid his cards on the table. Mandy, draped on the arm of Parker's chair, monitored the conversation, daring Smith to hedge his bets.

Smith had played it straight. "You want to put your ideas into action, and now is your chance. There may be risks, but I don't think so. Mandy is less sure. If things do go sour, you are on your own. We'll do our best to help you from behind the scenes, but there are no guarantees."

Parker was mollified by Smith's show of honesty, but that did little to calm the turmoil in his stomach. "It seems that I am already serving as go-between," he responded, "but I'm not sure that's what the Sheikh wants to talk about." Parker didn't elaborate. Neither did he say that he was going to the mosque.

"Will you be gentle with me tonight," whispered Mandy as they entered the bedroom?"

"Aren't I always gentle with you," laughed Parker, kissing her on the forehead.

*　　*　　*　　*

"What do you know about this Parker?" Jake asked Smith during an incidental meeting.

"He's a friend of Mandy's," Smith replied with studied distaste. "She can give you the details."

"I'm glad that someone around here is on the ball," growled Jake, "It'll look good on her record."

Chapter 18

A Flaming Reception

Parker made his way to the Institute along Galal Street much as he had every other day, his stoic attempts to navigate the sidewalk soon giving way to the gutter. He felt Egyptian, and accepted the swirling dust and insane traffic with a serene sense of fatalism. What will be will be. Lost in thought, he collided with a street vendor plodding in the opposite direction. He turned to apologize only to see a motor bike careening toward him out of control. The vendor had saved his life, or was it fate?

"You should use the sidewalk, my friend," scolded Ahmed the bootblack as Parker stopped for his ritual shoeshine. "It is much safer." Then, adding a final snap of his rag to the glistening shoes, he looked up at Parker with a curious mixture of awe and curiosity and said, "Permit me, oh *kawaga*, to introduce you to my friend Salim. He will guide you to his piety, the great Sheikh."

Parker was a big man, but his guide was bigger. He was huge, towering over Parker and dwarfing him with his bulk, bigger even than the Nubian. Parker's first instinct was to size him up in case worse came to worst and he was forced to play James Bond. It was folly, of course, for Parker was not James Bond. He was a lover and a poet, but not a gladiator. He had fought when forced, giving as well as he took, but that was of little solace. Getting battered had always seemed like a dumb thing to do and Parker had concentrated on words.

The deeper they penetrated the gloom and filth of Boulaq, the greater Parker's sense of foreboding became and the more he steeled himself to the inevitable.

"What a fool I've been," he worried. "The invitation was a trap to lure me into depths of Boulaq from whence there is no return. I will never see Sheikh Yassin and Ahmed will say that he shined my shoes and watched me disappear into the Institute."

Parker studied the movements of the giant with the instincts of a trapped beast. He would have to strike with lightening force, but where? Where else? He would poke the giant in the eye and knee him in the balls. Parker also considered a karate chop to the neck but soon abandoned it. He had never studied karate. It also occurred to him that the only view that he had of the giant was his massive back side. There were no eyes to gouge and no balls to knee. "What if he is eunuch?" flashed a warning from his addled brain. "There will be no balls at all."

The giant lumbered forward, clearing a path through the rabble scurrying to get a glimpse of Parker. He showed neither weakness nor any particular interest in the *kawaga* struggling to keep pace. Parker stumbled, but the giant's hand righted him before he touched the ground. Parker's fear eased, but he remained alert. Push him and run like hell. That was all he could do. But run to where? He was lost. Never mind, he would cross that bridge when he came to it.

When the giant did whirl around, it was with such deftness that Parker had not seen the blow. Pinned by the bulk of the giant, his face ground into the putrid mud of a narrow ally, he looked up to see a wave of flame sear the adjoining wall and, most likely, the back of the giant.

Sorry, *ya kawaga*, muttered the giant in obvious pain as he dislodged himself from the mud and pulled Parker to his feet. Parker stared in disbelief as he watched as a gang of youth wielding flaming *butagaz* (propane) canisters scorch all before them as they disappeared around a corner. Two bodies lay in the mud, but the giant ignored them, and led Parker into the courtyard of the mosque complex. The giant was not a guide, but one of Sheikh Yassin's body guards.

"Thugs," mumbled the giant as he delivered Parker to the Sheikh who had emerged to greet him. The Sheikh gave a command and what appeared to be a medic appeared from an adjacent building and led the giant away, the molten flesh of his back now visible."

"I am very sorry," apologized Sheikh Yassin with the concern of a covetous father fearing the loss of a prospective son-in-law. "I will have the doctor examine you."

"I'm fine," responded Parker, still wiping the putrid mud from his face, but visibly relieved that he had been neither seared by the flames nor ground to a pulp by the weight of the giant. "It's nothing but a few scratches." Then, with heart felt sincerity he added. "Please give my deepest appreciation to the giant. I pray that his wounds are not too severe."

"His recovery will take some days," responded the Sheikh, "but our clinic is well staffed. Our doctors charge the rich outrageous fees, but buy their entrance into heaven by administering to the poor a few hours each week. They live well and God is served." Then, assuring himself that Parker had suffered little more than a few scratches, said with the dispassion of a general reviewing a favorable casualty report, "It was a revenge killing. The people of this quarter are still very tribal. You were not the target. The police should handle these things, but they fear to penetrate the alleys of Boulaq."

The unpleasantness of the butagaz attack out of the way, the conversation became a study in circumlocution. They discussed everything and nothing. The Sheikh, gracious to a fault, prayed that Parker's family was well and that they found their experience in Egypt to be a pleasant one. Parker, adopting a strategy of sincerity and honesty, responded that he had always been enamored of Egypt and hoped to return often.

"I pray that your wife also finds it charming, too," teased the Sheikh.

"Perhaps less so," responded Parker, confirming what the Sheikh already knew.

The existence of a wife noted, they moved on to the Institute as a second cup of tea was served. The third cup, if tradition held, would signal the end of the interview. "My good friend, the Boss, is most pleased with the project," continued the Sheikh with gentle flattery. "He will be saddened when you soon leave for the States."

"The Boss is an old friend," responded Parker. "It is he and interviewers who have made the project work. I merely offer technical advice."

"But you are too modest," chided the Sheikh. "It must be your mid-Western background. I studied at the Iowa State University, you know. What a wonderful place it was. Everyone was so polite and so welcoming. I studied economics. My son was born there. That makes him an American citizen, I believe."

There was a pause as the Sheikh became lost in memories of Ames in his youth. His point had been made. He knew that Parker would be leaving in a few weeks, perhaps two months, and he was in touch with the Boss despite their philosophical differences. Whether they were friends or not remained an open question. More importantly, he had indicated a quiet affection for the United States, a sentiment seldom found in the rhetoric of the Brotherhood. Was this merely the politeness of a very polite individual or an invitation to dance?

The conversation then drifted to religion, and the Sheikh noted that he had participated in a seminar on interfaith understanding and found it exhilarating. "The three faiths are so similar," he lamented. "What a pity that we are in conflict. We worship the same God and honor the same prophets. Abraham and Moses are sacred to us and the Koran even has a separate chapter devoted to the Virgin Mary. We don't believe that Christ is the son of God, but he is clearly a major prophet and his virgin birth is beyond doubt."

"The important thing, professor, is that we all agreed that the salvation of the world required more religion in government. Catholic, Protestant, Jew, and Muslim. We were all in agreement. The decline in religious morality is a threat to world civilization. Surely you must believe that, professor. You attend church on a regular basis and your wife is very active in interfaith programs. Isn't that so?"

Another point scored. Parker had attended church from time to time, primarily to keep tabs on his wife's Israeli connection and find out more about Gloria Goldensickle. Nothing in Parker's life had gone unnoticed by the Sheikh.

Polite to a fault, the Sheikh spared Parker the need for a response. Jumping to his feet, he peered at the open wound on Parker's wrist and begged forgiveness for his insensitivity. "Forgive me, professor, I hadn't noticed your wound before. God knows what filth is in it. Come quickly to the clinic. The third cup of tea sat empty on the table. Zahra, the main topic of discussion, had not been mentioned by name, only the unfortunate tribal customs of blood feuds and honor killings.

"You must come again," said the Sheikh, shaking his hand in a warm farewell, "I have enjoyed our conversation."

The return trip to Galal Street was uneventful. Eyes peered, but eyes always peered in Egypt. Parker searched for the scars of the butagaz attack, but failed to find them. Boulaq was a collage of scars, each indistinguishable from the others.

* * * *

A chill breeze swept the Nile as Parker crossed the bridge to Zamalek, descended the winding stairs leading to corniche, and selected a table graced by the afternoon sun. The casino was empty, yet the waiter seemed to resent the interruption. When he finally arrived, Parker ordered a pot of tea. He needed time to sort things out before he met with Smith and Mandy that evening.

Parker's exhilaration at being relevant had faded with the stench of burning flesh that choked his nostrils as his face lie buried in the sewage of Boulaq. Sheikh Yassin had dismissed the attack as an unfortunate incident, but nothing of importance. Parker had his doubts. He had not wanted to become the intermediary between the Embassy and Sheikh Yassin, but his affair with Zahra had left him no choice in the matter. When the Sheikh commanded, one obeyed.

Curiously, he thought, no mention had been made of the Embassy. Or was it curious? Mention of the Embassy would have been a premature show of interest and that was against the Arab way of bargaining. Nothing could be what it seemed. His role as an emissary of the Embassy had been assumed. Zahra was the excuse. That is not to say that she wasn't on Sheikh Yassin's mind. She had to be.

Sheikh Yassin had more than lived up to his billing. Although not easily awed, Parker admitted to having been moved by this biblical like figure of imposing size, long white beard, and piercing brown eyes that bristled with intelligence and passion. His voice had matched, exuding compassion while threatening damnation.

Yet, for all of his experience and sagacity, the Sheikh had assumed that Parker's role at the Embassy was greater than it was. He had also mistaken Parker's periodic attendance at church as a sign of religiosity. Parker's actions had been observed but his motivations misunderstood. Sheikh Yassin had studied in America, but he didn't understand Americans.

The message was not lost on Parker. Perhaps he, too, was deluding himself by believing that he understood a culture so different from his own. Perhaps the Brotherhood's disavowal of terror was a charade; a temporary stratagem that masked a more sinister intent. Was he seeing what he wanted to see and interpreting events to fit his own naive theories? Such issues mattered little in academic debates, but he was no longer engaged is sterile debate. What he told Smith and Mandy would unleash a chain of events beyond his control. He thought he knew what the outcome would be, but there were no guarantees. Anything could screw things up. Everything could screw things up.

But what to tell Smith and Mandy? How to convey the essence of the interview without inserting his own prejudices? Why not just give them a blow by blow description of what had happened and let them draw their own conclusions? That, after all, was his role. But that, too, was flawed. Even if Smith and Mandy could appreciate the subtlety of Arab negotiations, Jake could not. He would need something stronger before he placed his bets. Parker made his decision.

*   *   *   *

Mandy and Smith listened in fascinated horror to the Parker's recounting of the butagaz attack. "Were it not for the giant," he grimaced, recalling the terror of the moment, "I might be dead." Then, turning pointedly to Smith, he added, "So much for your theory that there was little danger in being the messenger. You know damn well that everyone kills the messenger. He's the only one that they can get their hands on."

"Sorry, old friend," said Smith with a weak smile. "But as you said, it wasn't the Sheikh who caused you grief."

"The Sheikh lives in Boulaq," replied Parker, "and Boulaq is dangerous."

"Granted," said Smith, running short on patience. "What happened in the interview?"

"The Sheikh had many kind words about his college days in the US," replied Parker, "and he spoke eloquently about his desire for greater inter-faith dialogue. He saved his wrath for the jihadists and the Minister of Interior and indicated a desire for second meeting."

"What did he say about us?" interjected Mandy.

"Nothing," replied Parker. "He mentioned neither the American government nor the Embassy. That, in itself, was remarkable given the hatred of the US in the region."

"My God, man," snapped Smith, "We can't go to Jake with a lot of mush. Does Sheikh Yassin want to play or not?"

"Are you asking for my impression or for a statement in blood?"

"You know damn well there are no statements in blood in our world," replied Smith making little effort to hide his irritation. "It's go or no go. If you say go, we go to Jake. You and Mandy will have to sell him."

"It's a go," said Parker quietly but without hesitation. He had recounted the interview faithfully and when he was forced to give his impression, he did so. Honesty was served.

Mandy, with a woman's intuition had wanted to ask about Zahra, but didn't. How could the Sheikh say nothing about the relationship between Parker and his granddaughter? Was Parker hiding something from them?

Chapter 19

Chain Reaction

Parker's visit the mosque of Sheikh Yassin was the talk of Boulaq. It was also the talk of the Ministry of Interior. "The interview was staged," glowered the Minister of Interior to his adjutant. The *kawaga* is too close to the Embassy for it to have been a social visit." Then with a snicker triggered by visions of Mandy, he leered with a touch of envy, "Very close, indeed."

"Quite," responded the adjutant, in an affected English accent. "Almost as close as he is to the granddaughter of Sheikh Yassin. But why would the Sheikh invite the lover of his granddaughter to his mosque?

"I'm not sure," responded the Minister of Interior pensively. "It wasn't to eliminate him, for it was the Sheikh's bodyguard who saved the spy's life. To announce a wedding? Impossible," the Minister of Interior answered his own question with a cynical sneer. "Muslim virgins can't marry infidels. Get me the Wisp."

✶   ✶   ✶   ✶

Parker's zeal for relevance would have all but disappeared if he had been party to the exchange between the Minister and his adjutant, but he wasn't. Nor had he been party to the even more interesting tête-à-tête between Mandy and Jake.

"Your friend Parker is a most interesting person," smiled Jake. "I like the way he thinks." It was an enigmatic smile, less fatherly than usual.

"He's a little too Machiavellian for my tastes," responded Mandy, knowing that her words were music to Jake's ears. If Jake had a hero other than John Wayne, it would be Machiavelli. She had steeled herself to the task of selling Jake on their plan, but found his smile unnerving. Perhaps she had shown too much cleavage at her reception.

"You are sure that he is on our side," asked Jake, his eyes playing on her breasts.

"A hundred percent," replied Mandy crisply, aware that Jake was attempting to unnerve her with his sexual innuendos. He was testing her, hoping to shatter her facade of loyalty and force her to admit that she was a mouth piece for Parker and Smith. She sensed his game, but had little experience with the Jakes of the world. They played by different rules than diplomats, and she found his stare menacing. What would he demand as the ultimate test of her loyalty?

"But he's an academic," Jake pursued his prey, his eyes moving to her thighs. "They live in a dream world." How many of Jake's victims at the poker table had withered under his stare? He knew that he could break her, but did he want to break her? He might need Parker down the road, as an ace in the hold, so to speak. He had to win. He couldn't screw her, but he could force her to betray her lover.

"He's better than most," replied Mandy, her mind searching for an out. She felt her nipples harden against her will. Nothing sexual. It always happened when she found herself under stress.

"Meaning?" asked Jake, noting the growing prominence of her nipples.

"He's solid," Mandy replied, maintaining her facade of perkiness, "but he's a chess player, always thinking two or three moves ahead. He doesn't understand that a couple of months are a long time for us. Things come up and we do what we have to do. Sometimes there are mistakes and we pick up the pieces later." Parker's stock had declined, or had it? Jake played poker, but he also played chess. He understood the need to think two or three moves ahead of the Minister of Interior.

"At least your friend Parker understands that things can't go on the way they are," nodded Jake, turning the tables on Mandy and giving Parker the benefit of the doubt. That, too, was one of his tricks. Torture his victims and then switch positions with lightning speed and force them to make a hurried recovery. Checking an urge for profanity, for he didn't swear in front of ladies, he asked, "What do you think of his talk about working out a deal with the Muslim Brotherhood? Smith is always harping on the topic and your friend thinks it might work in the short run. At the very least he thinks that it will keep us in the game.

Myself, I don't trust any Muslim and I am not too sure about the Jews. Christ is the only way to go, but at least the Jews worship the same God."

"So do Muslims," responded Mandy, desperately attempting save her pride while finding a middle ground between Jake and Parker. "All three faiths worship the same God, but I share your concern. Things can't keep on going the way they are now. The jihadists are just biding their time while they wait for the right moment to strike. The military can't be trusted, but we've got to do something before there is disaster and our President takes another hit."

"That's what your friend said in so many words," replied Jake, cringing at the thought of a wounded President. If the President were defeated, there would be no hope of his becoming Secretary of State. "He said it will keep us in the game long enough to get a new deal, but made no promises beyond that. It's pretty clear though, that he's soft on Muslims. Otherwise he wouldn't be sucking up to them. God knows I don't trust those people. I tell you, Mandy, a coup is the only way to go. The military has got their head on straight. They'll get those suckers. And now, my pretty," his eyes demanded as they played on her protruding nipples, "Make your choice. Are you going to side with me on a coup, or are you going to sink with your lover and that ass Smith?"

"Perhaps we could kill two birds with one stone," whispered Mandy, reading Jake's mind. "Use the Brotherhood to scuttle the Minister of Interior, and then use Washington's fears of the Brotherhood to scare the Secretary of State into a coup." Had she betrayed her lover, or merely done what she had to do to get Jake to buy into their plan?

"Damn, you'll make a good ambassador," beamed Jake with admiration. "But it will be tricky. Can't hurt the President and can't let the Secretary of State know what's going on. He'd queer the whole thing. Maybe your friend Parker is the key. How long is here for?"

"Six weeks, maybe two months," responded Mandy, stoically repressing the surge of anxiety triggered by the thought of Parker's departure. "After that it is touch and go."

"Do you think he'll play along?" asked Jake, his voice that of a commander talking to his adjutant.

"Hard to say," responded Mandy, on the verge of mental exhaustion. Even her nipples had become exhausted. "You know these academics."

"You said he was solid," scolded Jake now intolerant of facts that might derail the one strategy that served all his goals. When Jake made a decision he didn't look back. Vacillation was suicidal. Place your bets and hold tight.

"He is solid," reaffirmed Mandy, "but he's got to do it his own way. I can guide him, but these things take time and …" She stopped in mid-sentence as if embarrassed.

"How much money does he want?" asked Jake with sympathy, now confident that she was on his side and relieved that he didn't have to embarrass himself in bed. Nor was he offended by the suggestion of money. He liked to buy people, and he was on the verge of buying a spy and his girlfriend.

"It's not money per se," continued Mandy with embarrassment. "His grant will run out in June and he would like to stay longer. That will take some of the pressure off of us, too. We won't have to worry that he will jump ship at a critical time."

"You won't mind if he sticks around a few more months, will you?" Jake's question was not intended to be cruel, merely to force acknowledgment that a favor had been granted.

"No," she smiled, much as she had smiled when her father had seen through one of her little schemes.

"Fill out the papers," said Jake in a tone that indicated that there was no further need for discussion. "I'll take it from special funds." He didn't ask the amount. In fact, he wasn't sure what spies sold for these days.

Both were delighted by the turn of events. Jake had his plan and Mandy had kept Parker for a few more months. It was not long, but the inevitable had been delayed until things could be sorted out. Love or an ambassadorship? If things went wrong, Jake would take the blame and Parker would be history. If things went right, she could have it all, Parker and an ambassadorship.

* * * *

The Wisp trembled as he wound his way through the dusty corridors that led to the massive office of the Minister of Interior. *Dingy alleys leading to a hidden palace from which few return* was how a long departed poet had described the infamous journey. The Wisp trembled despite the fact that he had been right. Parker's visit to the mosque proved that he was right. Sheikh Yassin's granddaughter was the Muslim Brotherhood's contact with the Embassy. He deserved praise, but being right in Egypt has its dangers. Being right means that you possessed secret information. More information, perhaps, than you had revealed. Only a fool would reveal all of his information before receiving his reward. The Wisp also knew that the Minister of Interior would demand new information, information that he did not have. He would have to invent some. The Wisp also worried that the Minister would want more information about his sources. One does not acquire secret information without being close to the enemy, perhaps too close.

"Why wasn't I warned of the visit?" glowered the Minister of Interior by way of greeting. "I had expected better of you."

"Everyone was surprised by the visit, Your Excellency." stammered the Wisp. "Even his granddaughter didn't know when it would happen."

"True," pounced the Minister of Interior, a sadistic smile playing across his lips, "but she knew that it would happen. You said so yourself. That would have been useful information, don't you agree? We could have been on the alert. How did you know that Zahra knew that there would be a meeting? Did she tell you that when you were intimate with her? You were intimate with her, weren't you?"

Content that he had reduced the Wisp to rubble, the Minister moved in for the kill, his sneer deepening. "Perhaps this pretty woman has played you for a fool. It is known that you love her and that she takes delight in humiliating you. It seems that you are deceiving me to protect a whore. You agree that she is a whore, don't you?"

The Wisp, unable to speak, nodded his head in the affirmative.

"You seem to know a great deal about some things and very little about others," menaced the Minister of Interior. "I don't want any more surprises."

The Wisp staggered through the labyrinth of corridors, swearing revenge on all who had turned his life into a tortured hell. But most of all he swore revenge on Zahra and Parker. He swore revenge on Zahra for making him an object of scorn and he swore revenge on Parker for seducing the woman he loved. His knew of but one solution for both. But first, it was imperative he get the fellowship to the States. Parker, it seemed, was more influential than he had realized.

* * * *

Sheikh Hassan, too, had also been perplexed by Parker's visit to the Mosque. Hassan recognized the ploy for what it was, an attempt to shatter the fragile truce between the jihadists and the Minister of Interior. It couldn't be otherwise, for Yassin could have disposed of Parker well before matters got out of hand. But he hadn't. Instead he had contrived the affair with Zahra to create a circus while he negotiated with the Americans. Hassan didn't like Yassin, but he respected his cunning. "Yes," he nodded to himself giving Yassin his due, "the fake assassination attempt was an act of genius." The Minister of Interior will breathe fire. Our agreement was that there would be no attacks on Americans until he gave the word. Now the Americans will be all over him and we will be blamed. Yassin can take credit for preventing a disaster while making sure that the international press was well informed. He could read the headlines before they appeared. "American official in Egypt escapes assassination attempt by jihadist group. Egyptian government feigns ignorance."

* * * *

Mizjaji's mood was no better. He had hoped to use Zahra's affair with Parker to force Sheikh Yassin to murder his granddaughter, something that Mizjaji knew that he would not do. His honor destroyed, Sheikh Yassin would retire to his son's house and he, Mizjaji, would rule Boulaq and the territories that lie beyond. Sheikh Hassan and the other freed prison sheikhs would say little, for they were playing a waiting game. With a little luck, it would be he and not Sheikh Hassan who emerged as the leader of the jihadists in Egypt.

Sheikh Yassin had outflanked him. Word of the assassination attempt had spread like wildfire and Sheikh Yassin's agents had fanned the flames by spreading rumors that Zahra had duped the *kawaga* into revealing vital secrets about US plans to take over Egypt. The CIA was behind the assassination attempt, so the rumors went, but the grand Sheikh had outsmarted them. Henceforth, the Brotherhood would place a special guard on Parker to assure that their prize stooge remained unharmed. No one asked how the CIA got Parker into Boulaq in the first place. These *kawaga* are very clever people and one can only guess at their means.

Mizjaji's first thought was to put an end to Sheikh Yassin's charade by assassinating Parker, but he soon thought better of the idea. Sheikh Yassin's men would be watching him. It was too dangerous. There had also been the visit from Sheikh Hassan's man warning against an attack on Parker. The prison sheikhs still needed their truce. "Besides," Mizjaji smiled to himself, "let the big boys slug it out. I'll be here to pick up the pieces."

* * * *

Parker stood on his balcony peering into the evening haze settling on Boulaq, the rapturous chorus of evening prayers echoing across the Nile. The gentle beauty created by the subtle merging of a thousand minarets never failed to move him. He knew their gentleness was a mirage, each individual mosque assaulting believers from loudspeakers so amplified that the word of God gave way to electronic squeals. It was better in earlier times when the world was less complex and the prayer leader lured the faithful to the mosque with the beauty of his voice and poetry of the Koran. He felt isolated and vulnerable, knowing that his visit to the mosque of Sheikh Yassin had produced a similar cascade of echoes, each urging insane people to prepare for battle.

Chapter 20

The Shrine of Gloria Goldensickle

His relations with Mandy and Smith more or less in order, Parker turned his attention to his wife's worrisome trip to Israel. He hadn't opposed the trip directly. It was pointless to do so. Given the contorted state of their affairs, his opposition would have invited her defiance. Seeking a middle ground, Parker had suggested that she postpone her trip until their departure from Egypt. That way, he promised, they could go together and would have time to give some thought to their future, a matter of utmost concern to his wife.

When this bribe failed, he had relied on the tried and true, withdrawing his attention from her and losing interest in religion. Her hopes of a new beginning in rural Nebraska would fade and she would relent. She always had. Life would not be pleasant, but then it seldom was.

The trip to Israel, however, was different. It was a pilgrimage to the holiest shrines of Christianity. It was also a pilgrimage to the shrine of Gloria Goldensickle. It was the latter that had overcome his wife's fear of the unknown and bolstered her confidence. It was not for herself that she was going, Constance had convinced herself, but to save their marriage. Her hopes for the future had soared during the period of sexual reunification that had followed Gloria's first visit, but soon faded as she found his sexual demands to be excessive.

Talk of the trip had not helped, and more than once he had called from Maadi, saying that he had been detained at Smith's and would spend the night in their guest room. This wasn't a breach of his honesty policy, merely an act of kindness. She accepted it as such. The truth, if it were the truth, would force a scene if not a divorce. Now, more than ever, she needed Gloria's guidance. She had to be reassured that sexual submission would lead to salvation. She was a literal person, and the parallel between sexual submission and religious submission didn't occur to her. Perhaps there wasn't one.

The trip, itself, was a blur of sights and sounds that assaulted her senses with such intensity that they merged into one. Israel, aside from Jerusalem, had not impressed her. It was too small and too crowded. There were too many soldiers and too many fearful people. Parker's addiction to the news hadn't help. She knew of every terrorist attack and of every Israeli reprisal, each slaughtering more innocents than the other in an unrelenting pageant of carnage. But Jerusalem! Jerusalem dazzled with the beauty of the ages. Christians, Jews, Muslims and pagans had all claimed it as their own. The pagan gods of antiquity were no more unless one worshiped the god Mammon, but each of the three faiths continued to stake their claim to this most holy of cities. Once again, God had placed it under the guardianship of the Israelis, but for how long?

The shrine of Gloria Goldensickle was less elegant than she had imagined. In reality, it was little more than small desk crowded into a closet sized office. Two consulting chairs competed for space and an overflowing bookcase, and they with stacks of books littering the floor. "Offices and apartments are small in Israel," Gloria had lamented. "There isn't much space and land is very expensive." But, in Gloria's presence, the closet became a palace. Parker's wife willed it to be a palace because she needed a palace to convince her that Gloria spoke from on high.

Parker's wife sat in a chair next to Gloria's desk that had hosted a hundred lost soles before her. Pouring out her heart, she begged for guidance. Gloria, guided by the ghosts of the hundred lost souls, listened attentively and plotted her strategy. Extreme measures were required if this most fragile of marriages were to be salvaged. Gloria, moreover, was intent on salvaging this most fragile of marriages. Her responsibilities as a psychoanalyst and priestess demanded no less. More importantly, Parker's wife was part of her plan. It was vital that she remain in Cairo.

Ironically, it was Parker's wife who had inadvertently planted the seeds of the plan in Gloria's mind. It was she who had mentioned vague plans for a feminist demonstration in Cairo and it was she who had described the plight of the Egyptian feminists who spoke at her seminars. It was as Gloria dozed on the long return bus ride to Israel that her plan had taken shape. Israeli feminists would join the Egyptian feminists in their protest. Strong contacts between the two movements would be forged and together they would work for peace and justice in the region.

Gloria had made earlier attempts to establish ties with the Egyptian feminists, but had met with little success. Egypt's feminists, like most Egyptians, had accepted peace with Israel as a necessary evil. Too many wars had been lost and too many people had suffered. There was peace between the two countries, but it was a cold peace. Israel's quest for love and acceptance was unrequited. "Victory and oppression do not bring love," Gloria lamented. "How many mothers on both sides had wept for their dead sons? The females of the two countries had to unite to bring an end to this male madness. There was no other hope. A dream? Perhaps, but the Middle East needed dreams."

It was the pain of Gloria's earlier failures that had made Parker's wife so vital to her plan. Constance Parker's contacts with the Egyptian feminists would allow her to track the plans of the feminist march. The church would also serve as an ideal liaison between the Israeli and Egyptian feminists. The plump ladies would provide wonderful cover. Perhaps they would even trade their tea and cocktails for the chaos of Cairo's streets, but that was doubtful. The Israeli delegation would not come as feminists, but as part of an inter-faith meeting between Muslims, Christians and Jews. The Minister of Interior monitored Israeli contacts with Egyptian protest groups, but he would be able to do little. Peace among the faiths ranked high on the American agenda.

All of this, of course, required that Parker's wife embrace the plan. It also required that she remain in Cairo. Both were iffy. Indeed, it was only as Gloria listened to the rambling confession of Constance Parker that she realized just how iffy her participation had become. This most lonely and guilt ridden of ladies had all but accepted defeat. More and more she spoke of a return to rural Nebraska. It was there, in the bosom of her family, that she would find love, hope and forgiveness. She would teach missionary studies in her uncle's college and throw herself into church work. Her love for Parker was deep, but it was not without limits. Those limits had now been tested. Perhaps she would marry again, but that was not important. She had already made inquiries at the airlines. Her husband, she confessed, would not oppose her departure. That message had become clear as she plotted her trip to Israel. She had come to Gloria's shrine to save her marriage, but even that was a matter of doubt. Perhaps she had come to ask Gloria's permission to leave her husband and devote her life to Christian feminism.

As Parker's wife confessed, Gloria psychoanalyzed. Constance Parker's commitment to feminism and to Christianity was unshakable. Both were the product of the frontier spirit that surged in her veins. It was that ethic that made her a feminist by nature rather than by choice. The same ethic was the bedrock of her faith. Unfortunately, from Gloria's perspective, neither faith nor feminism required Constance Parker to reside in Cairo or Israel. She hated the former and, by all appearances, didn't care much for the latter. The problem was rural Nebraska. It was too ideal, too pure and too tempting.

This realization was inescapable. The more Parker's wife confessed, the less she spoke of her husband and the more she drifted into descriptions of fertile plains, inner peace and a childhood surrounded by love, faith and security. It was to rural Nebraska that she now longed to return. There, in the bosom of her family, she would overcome the failure of her marriage and serve God by inflicting guilt on untold generations of Sunday school students. With God's will, she would marry a sturdy corn husker and together they would sew the plains. Children would follow. The mistakes of youth would be forgiven.

"Was there really a place of such peace and serenity?" Gloria wondered, tears welling in her eyes. She, too, wanted to flee from a life littered with broken marriages, macho warriors, and terror. But to where? She was a *sabra*, a name that natural born Israelis wore with pride. Unlike American Israelis, she didn't have dual citizenship, flitting between the two Jewish havens, their dedication doubted by both. Alas, there was no place for Gloria to run. Her only option was to rededicate herself to the task of bringing peace to Israel through feminism. Fighting violence with violence hadn't worked. Israel had been transformed into an armed camp surrounded by a towering fence. Its grip over the Occupied Territories was crumbling. Violence for what? Only person to person understanding with the Arabs could secure a lasting peace.

Parker's wife interpreted Gloria's tears as compassion and, head bowed, begged for advice. It was a sincere request, for she was a sincere person. But even sincere people can be self-serving. Gloria was to provide the benediction for her departure. The guilt of not standing by her man would be banished. Gloria would tell her that she was a good soldier who had done her best against insurmountable odds. Gloria would tell her that it was time to leave.

As Gloria listened to the confession of Constance Parker, her strategy became clear. "Yes, my lovely," Gloria mused to herself, "I will bless your departure and wash away your sins. But first you must atone for your sins by remaining in Cairo until after the feminist march." It would be guilt that kept Parker's wife in Cairo.

The difficulty, Gloria lamented, was that Parker's wife didn't have enough guilt. All in all, it was mostly self-pity. She had sinned, at least in Christian terms, but far less than the rest of humanity. Even that she blamed on Parker for leading her astray.

Gloria set about the task of placing guilt where it belonged. "The crux of the problem," Gloria scolded, "is that you have separated yourself from your husband's interests. When you were lovers you had shared a common passion for the poor and suffering of the world. Then, you lost your compassion for the poor, leaving him to drift alone without your guidance. The fault is yours, not his. You must become involved in his work. Talk to him about it. Take notes. Make suggestions. Offer to help. Enjoy sex. Sex is the gift of God. Not perverted immoral sex, but the sex of mutual fulfillment."

As if a light had suddenly dawned, Gloria suggested that Parker's wife suffer the burden of the cross. "That," she instructed Constance Parker with the wrath of an angry prophet, "will increase your sense of humility."

The suggestion had not come easy to Gloria, for she found the spectacle of Christian pilgrims staggering through the narrow streets of Old Jerusalem, their backs bowed with the weight of a cross, to be a pageant of anti-Semitism. But there was no other choice. Christians didn't absorb Jewish guilt, not even the guilt of Gloria Goldensickle. The resurrection of Parker's wife required hard core Christian guilt. Hardly had the thought escaped Gloria's lips when Parker's wife was whisked away to the austere offices of a small missionary group in the Arab sector of the Old City and harnessed to a cross with a gaunt man with bulging eyes that burned with passion. The Mosad agent footed the bill. As always, Gloria had left little to chance.

The cross was heavy and her shoulders ached as they stumbled through the cobbled streets of the Old City. She had allowed herself a brief complaint to the gaunt man with whom she shared the burden of the cross. His bulging eyes had flared with anger as he snarled that her pain was less than Christ's, unless, of course, she wanted her hands pierced. And when she had uttered a cry of pain as her foot twisted on an uneven cobblestone, he had told her to stop sniveling.

"You're just like all of the other Christians," he sneered. "That is the trouble with Christians today. They lack conviction. Always sniveling about immorality, but never doing anything about it. Look around you," he had continued relentlessly, straining to turn his head under the burden of the cross. "These are the streets of pain. Christ bore his pain and you must do the same or burn in hell. The Jews know suffering. It is their penalty for killing Christ. I and my disciples are waiting for Armageddon. We live on crumbs and make the Israeli's nervous, but the Bible predicted Armageddon just as surely as it predicted the rebirth of Israel. The cowards wait across the river Jordan, hoping to watch the end of the world while they sip their tea. What fools."

Gloria's words pounded in her mind as the weight of the cross crushed her back. Gloria was right and so was the gaunt preacher who had chastised her for sniveling. She had been weak and filled with self-pity. Christ's suffering had been used as an excuse rather than as an inspiration. She would suffer sex much as she suffered the cross. And there, as she stumbled through the narrow streets of the Old City in a state of ecstasy that comes only from pain, she vowed to remain with Parker and become part of his life. Only that would ease her guilt and pave the way to rural Nebraska. It was God's will. Passing Arabs looked at her as if she were mad. Perhaps she was.

Her ordeal ended and salvation assured, Constance braced herself for the next item on the agenda, a seminar with Gloria's students. That was her share of the exchange program. She confessed a certain nervousness to Gloria, but Gloria, as always, had calmed her fears. "Just a bunch of ladies gabbing," she joked. "Talk about fundamentalist Christianity and feminism and how you have made a personal fusion between the two. Don't forget, Jews have the same problems that you do and they will benefit from your experience." Then, she added with a touch of humor, "There may be a few men there, but not to worry. They are just some of the girls."

Reassured by Gloria's humor and her faith confirmed by the ordeal of cross, Constance Parker found herself remarkably at ease. The seminar, in reality, was just another of her club meetings at the church. In fact, it was far better. Gloria's students were far more alert than the plump ladies seeking a respite from the boredom that assaulted them in the tedious hours that stretched between the luncheon martini and evening cocktails. They were also more tragic than the plump ladies. Sensuous and aggressive, they dreamed of a mythical world that combined professional fulfillment and marital bliss; a world of loving husbands who praised, helped and encouraged, all without sacrificing their masculinity. The plump ladies knew better. Only the gays, it seemed, were at peace with themselves.

Gloria, too, surveyed the audience. It was larger than she had expected and several of the faces were unfamiliar. Some of the boys, so to speak, were not girls. There were hecklers and, in all probability, there was an agent or two from the Mosad. She remained silent and prayed for the best.

Parker's wife spoke of her dreams, of her despair and of how, with Gloria's aid, she had found the path to a new beginning. She confessed that she had allowed herself to grow apart from her husband and placed her own spiritual development above his own. "That," she lamented, "had been a mistake. A common dedication to Christ," she intoned with the fundamentalist zeal of her uncle, the president of the small religious college, "was the bond that made it possible for a man and a woman to combine professional careers with the fulfillment that can only come from marriage." Tears filled her eyes as she recounted Parker's return to the church and the renewal of their sexual intimacy and how, because of her own insensitivity, they had once again drifted apart. This was a remarkable confession would have been impossible before her sufferance of the cross. But she had been born again in the truest sense of the word.

Emotions begot emotions. Gloria's students rejoiced with the message that their dreams were attainable. Yet, it was a subdued rejoicing. It was their first exposure to Christian prostelization and they found it disturbing. Did they have to accept Christ to achieve marital bliss?

Gloria, ever vigilant, jumped into the fray. "You see, my children, what honesty produces?" she effused. "It shows that the dream of a happy marriage that combines equality, sexuality, and professional fulfillment can only be achieved through religion. This is as true of Judaism and Islam as it is true of Christianity. All draw their power from God and his prophets.

"No Muslims, no terror," snickered a heckler, before fleeing the room. Then, having reached the safety of the corridor, he stuck his head through the door and shouted, "Shu, Shu, if it weren't for Christ you'd be a Jew."

"Our challenge is great," came the resounding voice of Gloria, "but we shall prevail. Our sisters in Cairo will soon march to demand their rights. They must know that we support them. We must join them."

"We will join you," shouted one of the gays overcome by emotion. "Gays and feminists must unite their forces. *Allah Akbar.*"

"Will you help us sister?" questioned Gloria, addressing herself to Constance Parker in a tone that brooked no refusal.

Parker's wife, speechless with emotion and not comprehending the full import of Gloria's question, had nodded her assent.

"She is a saint," screamed one of the gays. "With Jews and Christians united we shall free the world of the scourge of Islam."

"With Jews, Christians and Muslims, united we will lead the world to enlightenment," corrected Gloria, having seen the worried look on the face of her guest. Then, glowering at the offending gay, she added with severity. "Jews believe in tolerance. We are a non-violent people."

"Where have you been living?" shouted a particularly pale woman in the back of the room, a Peace Now badge clearly visible on her purse. "We have ceased to be a tolerant people. We are doing to the Palestinians what the Nazis did to us."

"Violence was forced upon us by the terrorists," shouted another in response.

"Interfaith harmony will be a difficult task," grimaced Gloria to herself as she struggled to regain order. "First Constance attempts to convert the class to Christianity, and now this madness."

* * * *

Gloria had taken Parker's wife to a quiet restaurant following the lecture and then dropped her at her hotel. Both were emotionally drained and they had talked little. Gloria had apologized for the flare up in the seminar. "These are very trying times," she sighed. "We are struggling to survive as a nation, and that often leads to violence. Only feminism can lead the way to peace. That is why your participation in the march is so important."

The wine had calmed the nerves of Constance Parker and nothing remained but exhaustion. She slept without dreaming and awoke with a start as the phone next to her bed sounded a warning call from Gloria. A quick breakfast and then off to the airport.

"You are a saint, my dear," Gloria effused as they nibbled a bagel and sipped stale coffee. "Your lecture has brought hope to their lives. With your gracious help, we will make the unity of Christian, Jewish and Muslim feminists a reality." With that, she launched into a detailed plan of just what she expected the help of Parker's wife to be. If Parker's wife had slept, Gloria Goldensickle had not.

Chapter 21

If Only They Knew

Parker was watching Egyptian television when she returned, indifferent but not hostile. She detected a hint of concern for her welfare, but that was not unnatural. They were still friends, if nothing else. Marriage seemed to be the problem. She was seductive, but not apologetic. Gloria would have demanded no less. He was responsive, but neither passionate nor punishing. Dutiful, perhaps. He didn't forgive her, but wanted life to go on. For the moment, that was enough.

Afterwards, sitting on the balcony, he had walked with her step-by-step over the cobblestones of the Old City and marveled in awed silence as she recounted her lecture on Christian feminism and the discussion that followed. Everything had poured from her mouth in a rush of emotion: the feminist march, the Israeli participation, the gays, the plump ladies, and her vows to become part of his life.

Parker had been concerned. Not for her welfare, but for his own. Things were far worse than he had imagined, but what was done was done. Now was the time for damage control. She had become Gloria's eye on Egypt. Now she would have to become his eye on Gloria. She, alone, knew Gloria's plans.

But how was this to be achieved? He couldn't order or intimidate her that would place her on the defensive. Nor could he withdraw from her as he had done so often in the past. She would sulk and become petulant. Perhaps she would bolt. That prospect, to be devoutly wished only a month earlier, now promised disaster. He had heard enough of Gloria to know that she would not be deterred from her assault on Cairo, wife or no wife.

There was but one answer. He would make Constance part of his life, his partner. That was what Gloria had ordered and that was what Gloria would get. She had played upon his wife's morbid guilt and had inspired false hopes that Christian feminism could fuse the purity of her childhood with the sexual ecstasy of their Wisconsin years. Parker was an expert on his wife's guilt, far more so than Gloria Goldensickle. He could also play the Nebraska card if need be. He had no intention of spending the rest of his life teaching in a Bible college on those desolate wind swept plains, but a few weeks in a rural setting might be just what he needed to decompress from the tensions of Cairo.

* * * *

"I was afraid that you would be terribly upset," she confessed.

"I was," he responded with a touch of reality. "But the way our marriage has been going, who could blame you? Religion is the heart of your life and the Holy Lands are the heart of your religion."

"Our religion," she corrected, secretly pleased by his recognition that he was part of their problem. "Do you think the march will cause trouble?"

"I don't know," he responded thoughtfully. "The person-to-person approach to peace is worth a try. Nothing else has worked. I'm not sure that a feminist march is the best way to go about it, but who knows?"

"Will it cause problems for your project?" she asked quietly. That, after all, had been his unspoken concern since Gloria had arrived on the scene.

"Not if I have time to adjust," he replied. "I would hate to have Cairo blow up before the project is finished. If its does, we might have to stay here for another year. That's the Boss's back up plan. It seems that the Embassy is willing to fund it."

"Aren't you being a little dramatic," she cringed. "A delegation of Israeli feminists and a handful of gays won't even be noticed in the march."

"Perhaps you're right," responded Parker. "Unless, of course, Muslim extremists attack the march. They don't like feminists, they don't like Israelis, and they don't like gays. One wave of an Israeli flag and all hell could break loose. They would hit the dainty skull caps first."

"But the police are everywhere. You can't even breathe without bumping into a cop or a security guard, and that doesn't count the secret police. That's one reason I hate this place."

"Why do they need so many police if they aren't worried?" asked Parker with his infuriating logic. "Besides, the police don't like feminists, gays or Israelis either."

His words crushed her with the weight of the cross. Their marriage could not survive another year in Cairo. She could not survive another year in Cairo. She was not sure that she could survive a few more weeks in Cairo. Gloria had not spoken of danger, merely sisterhood and peace. Was she aware of the danger?

"Do you want me to back out?" she asked, tears now welling in her eyes. Things had somehow gone terribly wrong.

"No," replied Parker after a long pause. "Things will happen one way or another. At least your involvement gives us time to adjust. Having an American church involved will also make things easier. The church will get the blame and we'll be lost in the shuffle."

"I can't involve the church," she pleaded. "That's not right."

"You've already involved the church," Parker replied gently. "The church has survived for 2000 years, and it will survive this. We will work things out."

The *we* had been his final ploy. It was the *we* of hope and the *we* of her dreams for a resurrected marriage. It was also the *we* of last chance.

*　　*　　*　　*

Parker's casual mention of his wife's trip to Smith and Mandy had been met with stony silence. "You know these damn Egyptians," Smith grumbled once the gravity of the news had sunk in. "Just the briefest mention of Israel and they turn sour. Things have gone too far to turn back. We can't have any screw ups."

"If only you knew," Parker thought to himself. Of course, they would have to know, just as Sheikh Yassin would have to know. Or would they? His wife was right. There were police everywhere, more police than she could possibly imagine. Egypt was a police state masquerading as an emerging democracy.

That was the crux of the problem. For all of the Minister of Interior's police and security forces, his grip on Egypt's streets was crumbling. The American occupation of Iraq had flooded Cairo's streets with demonstrators as had the Israeli slaughter of Palestinians. So had the American threats to Syria, Iran Hizbullah, and everyone else in the Middle East.

The Minister of Interior had been slow to respond to the anti-American demonstrations, fearing the wrath of his own people more than he feared the wrath of the United States. A wise man, he also doubted the loyalty of its own security forces. It was true that he had a half a million Egyptian troops armed by the

United States under his command, but were they half a million troops armed by the United States preparing to shout *"Allah Akbar?"* The feminist march could be the spark that led to chaos and especially a feminist march with an Israeli hue.

Who knew what the result would be? Perhaps Jake would get his wish and the Army would take over. More than likely, the jihadists, now regrouped, would seize the moment to pounce. It was happening in Iraq, Yemen, Palestine, Jordan, Syria, Algeria, and Saudi Arabia. Why should Egypt be any different? On the plus side, a jihadist riot that killed feminists and Israelis would force the United States to recognize that the Minister of Interior had lost control. With no other option in sight, the way would be paved for negotiations with the Brotherhood. That, of course, assumed that the Brotherhood was not involved in the mayhem.

Such were Parker's thoughts as he set about the task of calming the nerves of his co-conspirators. It was not Egypt that they worried about, but their careers. They were not poker players and had little taste for betting their futures on the turn of a card or the roll of the dice. That was Jake's life, not theirs. Smith said nothing but his expression said it all. "Why and the hell can't you keep your wife under control? Don't you know that this is serious business?"

Mandy seemed lost in her own thoughts. While Smith and Parker exchanged barbs, she was visualizing herself as a professor's wife. He would be a demanding lover, and she his confident and co-author. A brief smile played over her lips and then faded. "If you cheat on me I will cut off your balls," her lips moved inaudibly. The stare of their eyes shook her back to reality, and she sat up, startled. "Sorry," she mumbled without conviction. "I was trying to plot our next move."

"Not to worry," Parker soothed her as he accepted a second scotch from Smith and cast an appreciative eye on her legs. "It fits the pattern. Egyptians expect Americans to go to Israel. Especially religious ladies such as my wife. They would find it strange if she didn't visit the holy places. I've been there myself on several occasions and they don't have trouble with that. It's things that don't fit the pattern that set off the alarm bells."

"But what if there are more trips to Israel and more visits from Gloria Goldensickle?" pursued Mandy, mollified by his logic, but irritated by the mention of his wife. "I heard Gloria's lecture. It was heavy on feminism, but nothing to cause an international crisis."

"I asked our Embassy in Israel for a bio on her," offered Smith, "but there was little of interest. She is a feminist who teaches psychology at a minor Israeli college and writes op-ed pages for the papers urging peace through feminism and inter-faith contacts. The Israeli Foreign Office thinks she's a crackpot, and gives her a small grant from time-to-time just to keep her quiet. All in all, a minor player."

"I thought you people were big on inter-faith contacts," commented Parker, with a touch of levity. "Perhaps you should encourage her visits as cover for the whole operation. One more sideshow to divert attention from your negotiations with Sheikh Yassin. The more the better. Why not throw in the Israeli gays and the feminists? Just think of all of the points you will get in Washington. Even Jake will be happy. What better way to stick it to the Minister of Interior than flooding Cairo with Israeli feminists and gays."

Parker's tone was facetious, but honesty had been served. The cards were on the table. Smith and Mandy were intelligent people who could put two and two together. Smith was devious by nature and Mandy was aware of the feminist march. She had to be. Women's affairs were her territory. Both had the power to crush Gloria's visit to the church if they saw fit. The church listened to the Embassy. His wife had also been tamed and was unlikely to try another unilateral venture. Maybe things would work out after all.

He could have spelled it out for them, but that was premature. Perhaps Gloria's rambling about Israeli feminists descending on Cairo were little more than pipe-dreams. Smith, himself, had said that she was a minor player. No need to rock an already shaky boat. It wasn't dishonesty, for Parker was not dishonest. He simply wasn't an alarmist. His wife would keep him informed and there would be time for adjustment.

Parker looked at Smith expecting an irritated glower followed by an interrogation on precisely what had taken place in Jerusalem. The best strategy, he decided was to plead ignorance. He would fill him in as the situation developed. If worse came to worse, Smith could alert the U.S. Embassy in Tel Aviv and have them cancel the visit. The Israeli Foreign Office would be happy to oblige. The last thing they wanted was a massacre of Israeli feminists in Cairo. Gloria would be put under wraps and all would be well. For the moment, however, his job was to assure that the negotiations with the Brotherhood remain on track.

A warm glow filled Parker has he prepared for battle. He liked games and he welcomed the anticipation that preceded the turn of a card. How different he was from Jake, yet how similar. Both were gamblers willing to bet their futures on the turn of a card and both had made it pay. Perhaps that was because both were psychologists, intimidating their opponents into submission and bluffing when need be. Each had a solution for the jihadist threat and each was willing to pursue it to the bitter end, come what may.

"You're right," Smith responded to Parker's dismay. "Washington is on our back to promote inter-faith dialogue between the Egyptians and the Israelis. The Israelis want it and so does the Christian right. They think that they are going to convert the Muslim world and are sending a delegation to Cairo to force the issue. Jake gave me a direct order to get something started and this is the only blip in sight."

Mandy nodded in distaste. Yet another delegation of imbeciles to deal with. Smith would duck and she would be stuck with the honors. "You handle it," Jake would say. "You're good at these things and I can trust you not to screw it up."

"It might be risky," cautioned Parker, his glow deserting him. The situation was delicate. The Embassy's complicity in a feminist march that resulted in the killing of Israeli feminists would queer everything. Smith and Mandy would be shipped out of the country and Sheikh Yassin would run for cover. The march, itself, would make an interesting diversion, but the Embassy had to stand clear.

"Perhaps it would be better to wait and see how things develop." Parker cautioned. "The Embassy's involvement in the affair might prove embarrassing."

"No doubt," acknowledged Smith, "but we have to have something in place before this delegation of Evangelicals arrives, whenever that is. Maybe your wife could help out? Besides, your logic is impeccable. Inter-faith dialogue provides a perfect cover for negotiations with the Brotherhood. Maybe we can even arrange an informal side meeting between the head of the delegation and Sheikh Yassin."

"The Sheikh may not be so enthusiastic about the idea," warned Parker. "He is a champion of inter-faith cooperation, not the conversion of Muslims. The Brotherhood does not like Christian missionaries."

Chapter 22

Spreading the Word

Parker assumed that his wife's trip to Israel had been noticed by the Institute. He was not mistaken. It was the Nubian who, in his typical jovial manner, raised the issue.

"It seems that your romance with the pretty one is becoming serious," he smirked in a conspiratorial tone.

"How is that?" asked Parker, not sure of what to expect.

"Isn't it obvious?" chided the Nubian, good-naturedly. "No sooner does your wife leave for the airport than you rush to the apartment of the pretty one. Zahra is not pleased. As for me, I have always been curious about Israel. We have much to learn from them about democracy and development. You must find Israel fascinating, too."

Parker assessed the Nubian's remarks according to a formula that seldom failed him: the greater the danger, the less the subtlety. The Nubian, despite his humor, had been less subtle than usual.

"Your mind is too devious," Parker flattered the Nubian while ignoring his reference to Zahra. "I promised my wife a trip to the Holy Land before we left Egypt, and this was it. Hopefully, she was able to carry a cross through the streets of Jerusalem during the High Holy Days. She wanted me to come along, but the project is going well and I couldn't leave"

"But you are a Christian," pressed the Nubian intrigued by Parker's bizarre tale. "Don't you want to carry the cross?"

"To be sure," smiled Parker as he prepared to savor victory, "but the pretty one won't let me."

The Nubian smiled knowingly, and issued a stern warning, "Take care, my friend. I am a man of the world and understand these things. Zahra doesn't. She has committed herself to you and has no other place to turn. You are her life. The pretty one has spread rumors of your impending marriage and left her no room for maneuver."

The Nubian had stressed the word "life" leaving no room for ambiguity. Parker had none. The rumors of his impending marriage to Mandy were insane. She hadn't spread them, but who had? Never mind, the damage was done. Fears that he would be branded an Israeli spy faded only to be replaced by a looming disaster on the Zahra front. He descended to the secretary's office, fearing the inevitable.

※　　※　　※　　※

If the Nubian had tried to be subtle, Zahra made no such effort.

"Did your wife enjoy her trip?" she asked with mocking interest after an agonizingly long kiss that invited disaster.

"Very much," responded Parker, catching his breath and struggling to regain his composure. It wasn't the kiss per se, although her kisses usually left him in a state of turmoil, but the ever bolder explorations of her hand. He repeated the story of the cross, but she had little interest in the affairs of his wife. Constance Parker's marriage was doomed. It was known to all. Had she not arranged for a return ticket to the States?

"Why didn't you join her?" asked Zahra with bitterness. "I would have preferred that to your vacation with the pretty one. I do not like her."

"We're merely friends," soothed Parker, "It is your beauty that has captured my soul."

"And what good is my beauty?" snapped Zahra, her bitterness deepening. "I cry all night while the pretty one enjoys your caresses. I cannot lose you, Scott. You are my life." Sensing the approach of the secretary, she whispered, "Please do not marry her, Scott. I know that you need a woman, but please do not marry her. It will work out, Scott. I have a plan."

The clicking of the secretary's heels provided Parker with a reprieve, but he knew that it was just temporary. The thought of Zahra's plan made him shudder. Every step they took was followed by a thousand peering eyes. Any plan was madness. He wanted to run, but he couldn't. She was his contact with Sheikh Yassin and God knows what would happen to the negotiations between the Brotherhood and the Embassy if she made a scene. He didn't have to buy into her plan, but he knew better. Visions of this most erotic of jinn had haunted his dreams since puberty, and now he had found her. But, was she a good jinn who would lead him from the physical world to the spiritual world through the *barzakh* (intermediate world) or a bad jinn allied with the devil? No matter, he had fallen under her spell and retreat was impossible.

Zahra embraced the secretary and, after a flurry of whispers, turned to Parker and asked, "Will your wife be joining the feminist march?"

"I don't know," replied Parker thoughtfully. "She may have toyed with the idea, but I don't think that she is the marching type. Anyway, I will ask her."

"Ask the pretty one, too," Zahra glowered, and then left the room at the heels of the secretary. Parker prayed that the question wasn't part of her plan.

If Zahra knew of the march, Parker reasoned, Sheikh Yassin also knew. In all probability, the question had come from the Sheikh. The march was sensitive. The Muslim Brothers were conservative and hostile to the feminist movement, but not fanatics. They occasionally ran a woman for the parliament and their female representatives, suitably robed but without veils, spoke elegantly of Islamic equality and the role of the woman as the core of the family. It was all quite general, but contained little of the vitriolic sadism of the jihadists. The march, however, could be incendiary. With Israeli participation, disaster was a foregone conclusion. Even a hint of Brotherhood's involvement would shatter hopes of a deal with the Embassy.

The Sheikh had to be warned if he were to keep his troops under control, but how? Should he drop hints to Zahra or wait for the promised second meeting? Hints were easy but subtlety seldom survived reinterpretation, especially with Zahra. Time was of the essence and his American instincts were to lay his cards on the table and let the chips fall where they may. But that was not the Egyptian way. Subtly ruled. Enemies were everywhere and the stakes were high. No one was to be trusted, even closest of friends. No one understood the venality of human nature better than the Egyptians. He decided to wait.

* * * *

The Sheikh had, indeed, asked the question. He well understood the significance of the demonstration. A disaster, if such there were, had to be pinned on the Minister of Interior and the jihadists. But what was the level of American involvement? Had the Embassy financed it? Were Americans going to participate? Perhaps American participation would be useful. Jihadists burning Old Glory while the Minister of Interior fiddled would make wonderful press. The truce would be shattered. Whatever the case, it was vital that the Embassy be convinced that the Muslim Brotherhood was not involved. Sheikh Yassin knew that there would be agents provocateurs. The Minister of Interior would try to frame the Brotherhood, and Sheikh Hassan would help by planting Brotherhood literature. It was essential that the Embassy be warned of the Minister of Interior's trap. Thus it was that in their Friday chat at his son's house, he asked Zahra to arrange a second visit with Parker.

The question was, what kind of visit would it be: a gaudy pilgrimage to the mosque, or a clandestine tête-à-tête in his country villa? It was not a question of secrecy, for secrecy had become impossible. He and Parker were watched and the servants were venal. No, it was a question of strategy. A visit to the mosque would tantalize the crowds and divert attention from Zahra's rumored infidelities. It had been two weeks since the last episode in the soap opera and the rabble were becoming restive.

But what message would it send to the Minister of Interior, Sheikh Hassan, and his other adversaries? They would be curious but confused, perhaps interpreting Parker's second visit to the mosque as a bluff or, even better, as a sign that negotiations between the Embassy and the Brotherhood were going poorly. A clandestine meeting, by contrast, brooked no ambiguity. He knew their minds well. Parker's first visit had been the circus. A second and clandestine meeting was sinister and spoke of plots being finalized. The Minister of Interior would become alarmed and ponder a preemptive strike against the Brotherhood, a most tempting strategy in the run up to the elections. People would fear violence and avoid the polling booths. No problem. The police would cast their votes for them.

The Sheikh opted for the mosque. The rabble would have another circus and his adversaries would reach the conclusion that conversations between Sheikh Yassin and the Americans had yet to reach threatening proportions. The meeting with Parker would be staged to convey that impression. Perhaps he would even use the meeting to bait Mizjaji into attacking the feminist march while simultaneously assuring the Americans that the Brotherhood would not be involved. "Yes," nodded the Sheikh to himself as he continued to stroke his beard. "A circus it will be. But the real circus is yet to come."

The Sheikh's confidence was not without reservation. It was possible that the march would pass unnoticed. The police would be present in force and the jihadists would honor their truce with the government and refrain from involvement.

They were preparing for the final battle and were unlikely to be diverted. With the Brotherhood on the sidelines, everything depended on Mizjaji and the rabble, but they were unlikely to challenge the police. That was not the way of shadow dwellers. There would be no circus at all! "You see," the Minister of Interior would mock the Americans, "everything is under control. Egypt is a peaceful country dedicated to human rights and democracy."

The time had come for greater frankness, but even that was difficult. What confidence could he place in Parker? He was an enigma. He was clearly tied to the Embassy, yet had rashly become involved with Zahra. Very undiplomatic. It was also very unlike an operative of the CIA. Zahra was too visible and too insignificant to be of concern to them. Perhaps Parker was merely an innocent scholar who had been lured by Zahra's haunting beauty into a vortex of intrigue from which there was no exit. The Sheikh had studied in the States and had been stunned to find that most Americans were simple people who really were what they seemed to be. But this explanation was also flawed. As a leading expert on Egyptian society, Parker knew the risks of becoming involved with Zahra. It was a death warrant. The haunting beauty of Zahra, moreover, had not kept him from the bed of the pretty one. Then why did he do it? The Sheikh fought his fears of a grand conspiracy. Yet, what other explanation was there. The *kawagas* were clever people.

* * * *

Parker's second journey through the twisting alleys of Boulaq was uneventful, eerily uneventful. Rare was a shadow without peering eyes, and Boulaq was a place of many shadows. Sheikh Yassin was warm and gracious. They talked of everything and nothing, each waiting for the other to commit a fatal confidence. The Sheikh marveled at Parker's good health and prayed that it remained that way. It was standard fare, but perhaps also a warning. He also prayed for the success of the project, a subtle reference to Zahra and the need for Parker's early departure. Just to be on the safe side, the Sheikh expressed his hope that Parker would be spared the pain of an Egyptian summer that routinely saw temperatures soar above the 120 degree mark.

Parker stressed America's dedication to human rights and noted a growing acceptance of moderate Islamic currents. The Brotherhood could not be mentioned by name. The Sheikh responded that Islam was the most tolerant of religions and actively sought the equality of all people within an Islamic framework.

Was that a sign that the Brotherhood would accept the march? Too vague. Parker decided to press the issue.

"The Egyptian government accuses the Brotherhood of wanting to set back the clock and force women to live in seclusion," he said softly.

"The government says many things," replied the Sheikh, seemingly relieved that the discussion had become focused. "It is they, not we, who are the threat to human rights in this country." Then, as if an after thought, he added. "Some of the sisters may even march in your feminist parade. Their foremost goal is eradicating Egypt from the scourge of female genital mutilation. It is a practice most offensive to the Glorious Koran. It is an African sickness that has nothing to do with Islam."

Parker nodded approvingly.

"And your wife's trip," the Sheikh asked, rising to indicate the end of the interview, "did it go well?" Parker repeated the story of the cross which Sheikh Yassin had obviously heard from Zahra. Pushing all of his chips in the pot, he recounted the lecture and the treats of Israeli participation in the march.

"We are not troubled by provocateurs," smiled the sheikh. "We know the Israeli game. They want to make trouble between us and your government. It won't happen."

Parker was elated. The Sheikh had gone all in. He wanted a deal with the Embassy.

The Sheikh was also elated. Parker had given him the bait he needed to send Mizjaji's thugs surging into the parade, knives at the ready.

Chapter 23

Setting the Date

Curiously, no one seemed to know the exact date of the march. The Minister of Interior wanted it that way. He knew that he couldn't stop the march. The Egyptian government, itself, had hosted an international conference on women's health to demonstrate its concern for human rights. The Americans had been pleased, openly praising the Egyptian government for its humanity. The United States likes its puppets to be big on human rights.

There were also the more practical issues. Too many important wives and daughters were involved in the march, few of whom cared much for the Minister of Interior. They would march without a permit and defy the police to arrest them. The students would pour into the streets in support of the march and all hell would break loose. Elections also loomed. A riot just weeks before the elections would cause an uproar in the international press and he would be sacked as the scapegoat. He had asked Egypt's President to delay the march until after the elections, but his quest had been rejected.

"It wouldn't look good," the Egyptian President had cautioned. "The international press is gathering for the elections and would smell blood. Democracies do not cancel feminist marches in the run-up to elections. Let there be a march; an orderly democratic march that puts the world at ease."

The President's tone had been soft, but his message threatening. There was to be a march, and it was to be a peaceful march, or else. The best the Minister of Interior could do was keep people guessing. He had to keep them off guard and prevent them from marshaling their forces. He would also set up road blocks to keep the Brotherhood from flooding streets with its supporters and turning the march into an election rally, or worse. But when, precisely, would the march take place?

The organizers had preferred an early date, perhaps mid-March. The weather would be cool and the flies less numerous. The occasional shower would mean less dust. The Minister of Interior had stalled, pleading the need for more time to organize adequate protection for the marchers. They could not argue, for the most innocent of demonstrations in Egypt could turn violent without warning.

It was the Minister of Interior's struggle to balance the march and the elections that triggered his genius for survival. "We will have the march on election Sunday," proclaimed the Minister of Interior to an appreciative adjutant. "The press and everyone else will be preoccupied with the elections and the march will go unnoticed. The Christians (Copts) will be at church and that should ease chances of a religious riot. Far better," continued the Minister of Interior, "both the elections and the march that will take place in the middle of Ramadan, our beloved month of fasting and redemption. Fasting by day and feasting by night, most Muslims will be too exhausted too worry about a bunch of lesbians and liberals plowing through the streets. With God's blessing, a spring sandstorm will send clouds of biting sand swirling through the streets of Cairo, choking those foolish enough to venture out without cause. Yes," the Minister of Interior smiled with self-satisfaction, "the ladies will have their march. They will have their march and I will have my election."

His thoughts then turned to the jihadists and the Brotherhood. Just to be on the safe side, he would fire a warning shot over the bow of Hassan and the other jihadist leaders. Perhaps a few minor arrests to please the Americans. Nothing serious enough to endanger the truce. Just enough to convey the message that he was serious about having a peaceful march, dead serious. Perhaps he would round up Mizjaji and a few of the other street sheikhs. They were after all, jihadists. Sheikh Hassan would be pleased and say nothing. It was these violent jihadist thugs who threatened the truce, not he. If the Brotherhood caused trouble, so much the better. The world will applaud while I crush them. "Who knows?" the Minister of Interior smiled magnanimously at his adjutant. "I may even ask the Americans for more aid to complete the job. It is really amazing how a country with so much power can know so little about the Middle East."

"Ramadan is a very emotional month for Muslims," worried the adjutant. "There could be riots and violence. The security forces will be preoccupied with assuring a government victory in the elections. If the march erupts into violence there will be no security forces to control the carnage. Only screams of agony smothered by shrieks of *Allah Akbar*." But he worried in silence. His role was to applaud and to see that the Minister's orders were executed. Nothing more.

"You cannot foresee difficulties with my plan?" challenged the Minister of Interior, forcing his adjutant to applaud while muttering inanities.

"A sandstorm might dampen voter turn out," offered the adjutant meekly.

The Minister of Interior glowered at his adjutant with deserved contempt. "That will make it easier for you to stuff the ballot boxes, will it not my friend? That is, of course, unless your men fear a little sand."

The adjutant averted his eyes, secretly praying for riots and violence. Perhaps he would be the next Minister of Interior, although that was unlikely. The President's cousin aspired for the position.

* * * *

Sheikh Yassin pondered the Minister of Interior's decision and begrudgingly acknowledged his cunning. The feminist march would go unnoticed in the circus of elections. The official media would praise the government and the opposition papers would scream fraud. One way or another, the feminist march would be relegated to the back pages of the newspapers.

Sheikh Yassin also knew that the Minister of Interior would attempt to divert the attention from the march by solemnly swearing that the security forces would not intimidate voters. That, of itself, would focus attention on the polling booths. Foreign reporters would be escorted to ideal precincts replete with opposition posters and fiery speeches denouncing the regime. Their duty done, they would rush back to their hotels for pool side cocktails. The Minister of Interior would assure that the barmaids were more attentive than usual.

Those foreign reporters courageous enough to penetrate rural Egypt, and there were some, would be stopped by security guards and detained for having flawed identity papers. It would be a routine task, for the identity papers of all foreign reporters were routinely issued with flaws. They couldn't speak Arabic, so how would they know? They would sit out the day in a rural jail, making empty threats to mindless guards who spoke no English. There would be no spectators to witness the Brotherhood's supporters being bludgeoned with rifle butts, nor would the world press describe how the police herded hapless peasants into the polling booths, their ballots pre-marked. If Egyptian reporters knew, they would be too terrified to tell. Their punishment would be far more severe than a day of inconvenience.

The Minister of Interior's adjutant, of course, was right. All of Egypt's security forces would be preoccupied with the election. They had to be. The regime's survival was at stake. The Brotherhood's support was swelling and the public was hostile. Election violence was inevitable.

Far worse, the Muslim Brotherhood didn't have to win the elections in order to launch Egypt into a spiral of instability. A strong showing by the Brotherhood would be a signal to the Egyptian public that a government that routinely won more than 90% of the vote was losing its grip. Sensing change, they would desert the ruling party like rats deserting a sinking ship. *Allah Akbar.* It was merely a matter of when and who. When would the regime collapse, and who would take over? Would it be the Muslim Brotherhood or would it be the jihadists? Perhaps the Americans would arrange a coup, but to what avail. A few years of martial law while the masses seethed, and then the explosion, the inevitable explosion.

The Minister of Interior attempted to explain all of this to Jake, but without success. "Once Egyptians smell a sign of weakness," he warned, "all hell will break loose. Egypt has never had a fair election and it sure as hell won't happen if the Brotherhood takes over."

Jake was unmoved and kept pressing the Minister of Interior to allow for a more democratic election. "The opposition doesn't have to win, mind you," he scolded the Minister of Interior, "but it has to receive enough votes to convince the American public that the administration's democratic initiative is moving forward, not that anyone but a few intellectuals gives a damn." Jake had more or less bought into Mandy's plan, but the image of 300 million Muslim Brothers plotting global revolution still haunted his dreams. If he let them take power, would a coup be able to unseat them? He had to go slow and see more cards before he went all in.

"When you rule by force, you rule by force," the Minister of Interior screamed. "Any sign of weakness is dangerous. Even your friends will turn on you."

The Minister of Interior hadn't screamed. It just seemed that way to Jake, and he bristled. "Power," he lectured the Minister of Interior, "is the ability to make suckers think that they have a chance. That's how you keep them in the game. Clubbing supporters of the Brotherhood is a sign of weakness. They get pissed and start supporting the jihadists. That is when you lose. You win the pot, but the pot is empty. All the money is on the sidelines waiting for you to collapse. What will it be, Your Excellency, reasonable elections that keep the Muslim Brotherhood in the game, or a resurgence of jihadist violence? They are using your asinine truce to rebuild their strength and the CIA says that they are almost there."

The Minister of Interior left the Embassy in a foul mood. Jake, for all intents and purposes, had issued an ultimatum. Attack the jihadists or the Embassy would seek new alternatives. Jake's demand for a somewhat fairer election was merely a ploy. The US had never given a damn about elections and they didn't care now. A mild slap on the wrist at best, and life went on. Now it seemed that Jake would use the elections as a pretext for dumping the regime, but how?

* * * *

Parker learned of the struggle between Jake and the Minister of Interior from Mandy and mentioned it as passing gossip to Zahra, confident that it would reach Sheikh Yassin within minutes. Parker exploited his role of intermediary to the fullest, rationing information to the combatants in a manner that served his purposes, never giving something without receiving better in return. That, too, had become part of his strategy. People only believe what they have to pay for. He traded the Embassy to Zahra and he traded Sheikh Yassin to Mandy. Each pressed him for more information, often forcing him to blend fact with interpretation. It was from Zahra that he learned of the murky world of the jihadists and Mizjaji, a world that he had only guessed at. The reality made him cringe, perhaps having second doubts about Sheikh Yassin, himself. The Wisp, too, had entered the game, feigning friendship with Parker in a frantic effort to gain information for the Minister of Interior. He begged Parker for news of his scholarship to the US, but that was merely a ploy to lure the *kawaga* to his doom. As always, it was the Nubian who alerted him to the danger.

"My, my, you live a charmed life, my friend," smirked the fat one in their daily game of mental gymnastics. "The Embassy, the Sheikh, the Israelis, the Boss. Everyone is interested in your affairs. Even the Minister of Interior is following your adventures," he added quietly, cutting his eyes to the vacant desk of the Wisp. "It seems that the jihadists are the only ones left out, and they tried to kill you." The Nubian saw the flash of worry in Parker's face, and erupted in another burst of laughter, slapping Parker on the knee. "Just joking, my friend," he smirked, knowing that he had Parker by the balls. "These things happen all the time in Boulaq. Had they wanted to kill you, you would have been dead! By God, you lead a charmed life."

The Wisp's link to the Minister of Interior was the final piece of the puzzle. Parker bided his time, waiting to see what the Wisp had to offer. He replied to the Wisp's inquiries about a fellowship with optimism, but lamented that he had heard nothing. The Wisp got the message and, over glass of tea, suggested in the greatest of confidence that the Nubian was not to be trusted. "His supposed friendship is guiding you into great danger," he lisped, waiting expectantly for Parker to take the bait.

Parker remained passive, weighing the remarks, but saying nothing. The pieces were coming together, but gossip about the Nubian was not what he wanted from the Wisp. He wanted information about the Minister of Interior and his plans for the march. Mandy could provide the coveted fellowship if need be, but only for a price.

Nevertheless, Parker pondered the revelation. The possibility of the Nubian's duplicity had not escaped him. For all of his good humor, the Nubian remained an enigma. His bits of gossip and innuendo had guided Parker along his path with subliminal nudges, always allowing the American to believe that he was the master of his own destiny. At every juncture it had been the Nubian who had pointed the way. It was he who had alerted Parker to Zahra's subtle flirtations, blatant in Egyptian eyes but imperceptible to an American accustomed to dodging sexual come-ons so conspicuous that they threaten to spoil the game. Where was the chase? It was the Nubian who had exposed Zahra's vulnerabilities with his raucous imitation of a female orgasm. It was he who pointed out Zahra's link with the Sheikh, just as it was he who had warned of her jealousies. The list was endless. It was the Nubian who had cautioned Parker that he was being watched and it was he who had eased his fears about his wife's trip to Israel.

There were wheels within in wheels and games within games. Mind games that delighted. Mind games that were a guise for a more sinister game of which Parker was unaware. It was Egypt's favorite game, the feared *kawaga* being led to his doom by the wily Egyptian. It was the stuff of Egyptian fairy tales. By why? To what end?

There could only be two explanations for the Nubian's behavior. Either he was the pawn of one of the power brokers, or he was a survivor. Parker opted for the latter explanation. The Nubian was a survivor. While others plotted and cleft, the Nubian used humor to nudge his adversaries to their doom. He laughed with them and he laughed at them, flattering them as he poured gasoline on their smoldering hatreds. Each believed him to by a loyal supporter, a buffoon to be promoted for his servility and kept alive for his entertainment value.

The error was theirs. It was he who would have the last laugh, tears of mirth pouring from his eyes as his belly heaved with delight. And he, Parker, had been a godsend. With a little luck, they would all be burned. The Boss, the Minister of

Interior, Sheikh Hassan, the Wisp, the Embassy, Sheikh Yassin and Zahra, the Goddess whom Sheikh Yassin had so cleverly placed in the very heart of the liberal Institute. Only the Nubian would be left. Who knew how high he could go? A figment of Parker's imagination? Not so. An earlier Egyptian president had uttered these most immortal of words, "We are all survivors."

It was in the middle of these speculations that Parker cautioned himself against sinking into the Arab trap of seeing a conspiracy at every turn. The unaccountable was the will of God. Everything else was a plot to be dissected and punished. Why did the Nubian's mind games have to be a plot? Why couldn't they be an end in themselves, a glorious chess match. The joy of victory. The vicarious thrill of accompanying Parker from the arms of Zahra to the bed of the pretty one. What a marvelous fantasy for a super intelligent individual fated to remain a researcher while others with *wasta* (connections) moved to the fore. The Nubian was from a poor family and had few connections. Parker's world was a world he could only dream of, a world of Embassy parties, beautiful women, secret sessions with Sheikh Yassin, and unknown Israeli connections. He had confessed that he lived through Parker, this fat, bald, giant, his Swedish wife fatter than he. For the briefest of moments, he was the puppeteer, guiding Parker from one adventure to another, a feast of delights all without cost or fear.

Had Parker not played the same game, using the Nubian to pursue his quest for the soul of Egypt? They both knew that the game was fantasy, but Parker had violated the rules and allowed himself to become enmeshed in a torrent of events beyond his control. There was time to flee, but he couldn't. He had gone all in. If he quit, he would lose everything: the project, fame, the opportunity to shape the course of events in the Middle East, the goddess of the Nile, but above all, his search for the soul Egypt, a search that now appeared within his grasp.

Chapter 24

The Plot Thickens

The game had now begun. The Minister of Interior had placed his bet. All of his chips were on the elections. The feminist march would be a diversion covered by a handful of traffic police. The remaining security forces would surround the polling places, clubs in hand, and pistols at the ready. The decision was a closely guarded secret, but there were no secrets in Egypt. How many members of the security forces were Muslim Brothers? God only knew. The jihadists lurked. The Americans, at least, would be kept in ignorance. That was the important thing. He couldn't have Jake micro-managing his security arrangements.

The others followed suit, plotting their strategy. Sheikh Hassan convinced the prison sheikhs to boycott both the elections and the march. They needed a few more months before they were ready to strike. They were almost ready, but not yet. Let the Minister of Interior and the Brotherhood slug it out. The jihadists would bide their time while their opponents destroyed each other. A lack of patience had been their fatal flaw during the 1990's when they had a chance to seize power. They could not fail again. Unsaid, but very much on Sheikh Hassan's mind, were his secret conversations with the global jihadist leadership. The battle was not just for Egypt. It was for the Middle East. It would be the larger battle that determined the timing of his attack. Egypt was the key, for where else could you find so many Americans with so little protection?

The prison sheikhs had agreed. They understood that the elections and the march were petty diversions from the final battle. They couldn't tip their hand or waste vital resources by challenging the Minister of Interior at the polling booths. Let the Brotherhood get bloodied up. They also had little interest in the march. Killing Muslim feminists was not in line with the jihadists' new image of love and hope. They would take care of the feminists when the time came.

Sheikh Hassan and the other prison sheikhs had learned patience in prison. Passion had given way to planning, but patience was difficult for those who had not suffered the horrors of Egypt's prisons. They had not suffered the days of interrogation without sleep, the maggots, the lash of the whip, the blows of the club, the sickening stench of burning flesh as the interrogator's cigarette pressed deeper into the flesh or, most of all, the fear of death without bidding farewell to your children.

The younger jihadists, like the younger members of the Brotherhood, had yet to learn patience. Their faith had yet to be tested and they chaffed under the restrictions of the truce. A few, their numbers still small, had violated it. Could they resist the temptation to assault the march?

Then, there were the Mizjajis of the Islamic world. These rabble who masqueraded as jihadists while doing the work of the devil. They could not be allowed to shatter the grand plan of which they knew nothing.

* * * *

Sheikh Yassin weighed the news with care. His task was clear: unleash Mizjaji while keeping the Brotherhood under control. If there were a confrontation between the security forces and the Brotherhood, it would come at the polling station and not during the march. Let the world see Egyptian democracy in action. Simple peasants clubbed into submission by the security police as they attempted to vote. Indeed, the Sheikh had selected the sites for the confrontation in advance. The international media would be alerted at the proper time. Escorts would be provided. His men in the security services would man the road blocks erected to check their identity papers. There would be no problems.

The question was timing. How was he to leak word of the Israeli involvement to Mizjaji without alerting the Minister of Interior? It would be tricky. Some of Mizjaji's men were the Minister's spies. For the moment, only he and Parker knew of Gloria's plan. It was their little secret. At least he had received that impression from Parker. For the briefest of moments he had toyed with the idea of leaking the news to the Minister of Interior on the day before the elections. The Minister's plan would be thrown in to chaos and he would be forced to split his forces at the last minute. If God willed, he would lose control of both the march and the elections. Wonderful thought though it was, the Sheikh rejected it. The Minister of Interior would simply cancel the march. It would be an embarrassment, to be sure, but little more. The moment would be lost.

There was no choice. Mizjaji would be informed of the Israeli involvement at the last possible minute. Not directly, of course, for direct news is viewed with suspicion in the Middle East. It was for occasions like this that Sheikh Yassin had allowed Mizjaji's spy to sit on his council. Not the inner circle, of course, but close enough to report what the Sheikh wanted him to report. For the moment, there was no rush. The angel of death, as Mizjaji increasingly referred to himself, would be feasting on the news that the security forces would be deployed elsewhere.

And so Mizjaji was. Confident that the march would be unguarded, Mizjaji drew up minute plans for the pillage of the plush buildings that lie along its route. None were to be spared. Gold, jewels and dollars would fill Ali Baba's cave as never before. They would be his Aladdin's lamp, enabling him to buy what he craved most in the world: power.

Sheikh Hassan's fears that Mizjaji would violate his orders and attack the march were well founded. Intellectuals like he had paved the way to revolution only to perish in a swirl of violence and betrayal. In their wake came the street sheikhs. Functional illiterates, few of whom had ever read the Glorious Koran. Each spouted Islamic slogans and escalated violence in the hope of forcing others to accept his authority as the grand potentate. He, alone would speak in the name of God. It was this rabble who had spawned more than 150,000 deaths in Algeria. It was now they who threatened Sheikh Hassan's dreams of an Islamic paradise free of sin, a paradise so pure that even song would be eliminated. He had warned the Minister of Interior of Mizjaji's threat, but the Minister had not listened. In his mind, Mizjaji was a simple thug. He could have him shot at will, but to what avail? Boulaq produced an inexhaustible supply of thugs and thieves, each more vicious than the other. At least Mizjaji kept his people under control.

It was the lust for power that drove Mizjaji. Islam was his excuse. He would rule Cairo as he ruled his mob, those pathetic misfits that cowered with fear in his presence. He assigned them all names. Some were named after movie stars such as Omar Sharif. Others were mythical heroes such as Attar or famous personages such as Omar Khayam. Mizjaji, alone, was permitted religious titles.

The names were a ruse to confuse the police, not that they cared much what happened in Boulaq. But they were so much more than that. For Mizjaji's rabble, they were a rebirth. They had become their namesakes. The scum of the earth had become its rulers. They swaggered as cash jingled in their pockets. Their belts glistened with weapons. Only Mizjaji dressed in the rags of piety, a scraggly beard hiding a weak chin and his mutant arm dangling helplessly at his side. Mizjaji was their savior and their guide. It was he who had given them rebirth, and they referred to him as the *emir al mu'ma'neen*, the prince of believers. This, of itself, was a sacrilege, for only the most illustrious of Muslim luminaries dare wear the title of prince of believers.

Mizjaji dared, issuing *fatwas* (religious decrees) justifying rape, pillage and plunder in the name of Islam. All were fit punishments for the infidel, and all but Mizjaji's mob were infidels. He imposed tests of faith on his disciples. Some were forced to carry out daring robberies. Others were ordered to assassinate rival street sheikhs. More than one of Mizjaji's disciples had killed a family member suspected collaboration with the police. Death was the penalty for suspected treason, often no more than a casual conversation with a rival sheikh. Mizjaji was the judge and jury. Rumors of Mizjaji's temporary marriages abounded, daughters and sisters hurriedly returned to the remote villages from which they had come. But none possessed the beauty of the goddess Zahra. When he had become the paramount jihadist Sheikh, he would claim her as his bride. It would be he and not Sheikh Yassin who controlled the goddess of the Nile.

Yet, all was not well in the world of Mizjaji. It was not easy being the prince of believers. Rival street sheikhs resented his growing popularity. Each reigned supreme in his own slum, petty kingdoms in which others feared to tread. When their paths crossed, which was often, the police counted the corpses. It was victory in these wars that had established Mizjaji's *baraka*, that special sign of God's blessing that separates prophets from ordinary individuals. He was the chosen one, the master of gutter warfare, the object of emulation, the prince of believers, and the angel of death. Others could not match his cunning or sadistic brutality. As his power grew, the thugs of defeated gangs gravitated to his congregation and his kingdom expanded.

War, however, was dangerous. God giveth and God taketh away. A defeat would shatter his *baraka*. It would be a sign to all that he had fallen from grace. Doubts would erode his authority. Rival sheiks would become bold and his lieutenants ambitious. The swine. He needed something beyond gutter wars. He needed a war to end all wars. He needed a grand victory that would set him apart from his rivals and enshrine his *baraka* in myth. Only with such a victory could he challenge the power of Sheikh Yassin and Sheikh Hassan. There would be an Islamic state in Egypt. It was fated. He could see it in the stars and feel it in his bones. It was just a matter of time. But who would rule, he or they?

Mizjaji was semi-illiterate, but shrewd, very shrewd. He knew the dangers that confronted him and he knew the weaknesses of his foes. Yassin would bide his time and crush him when the Brotherhood seized power, but who knew when that time would come? The big event was always *bukra* (tomorrow.). The masses had too many *bukras* and were losing faith.

He also knew that Sheikh Hassan could not play the waiting game. It was he who had ordered the truce and forced order in the ranks of the jihadists while they prepared for the final battle. Only the street sheikhs had defied his will. It was their violence that alarmed the Americans and threatened Sheikh Hassan's truce with the Minister of Interior. He suspected Sheikh Hassan of plotting with the Minister of Interior to eliminate him. Paranoia? Hardly. It was that sixth sense that comes only to the blessed. It is the secret of their survival.

Thus, the march loomed large in Mizjaji's mind. It would be a pageant of violence and pillage that shattered the truce and threw Cairo into chaos. He would let the other sheikhs loot while he slaughtered the infidels. They would, of course, be required to give him half of their take. That was the price for his carefully crafted surveys of the buildings to be looted. Only he knew where the treasures lie and how to reach it. The truce would be shattered and a disgraced Minister of Interior would unleash the security forces on the jihadists and Brotherhood alike in a desperate move to save his job. Folly, for the American's would have his scalp. The ruling party would win its election but lose the war. Only he, secure in the gutter, would survive.

But first, he had to organize the street sheikhs. They would descend on the feminist march like locust, destroying all in sight. But how to organize them? Fear ran deep. There had been too many double-crosses in the past. Would they come? Would they submit to his authority? Would they obey? He toyed will a meeting: a grand council of street sheiks with him as the God Father. But meetings were dangerous. There would be spies. The Minister of Interior would be alerted. Sheikh Hassan would pounce. Sheikh Yassin would block the alleys.

No, there could be no meeting. Far better to incite envy and greed. How? Simple. He would leak rumors to the other street sheikhs that he planned to use the feminist march as cover for a grand heist. They would worry about the police, but he would spread the word that there would be no police. They would be tied up with the election. A simple warning to his disciples to keep mum would do the trick. He knew that the other street sheikhs would come. They would come to reap and they would come because they had no choice. They couldn't leave the march open to him. His coffers would be full and his men flush. His name would be whispered in tones of awe among the rabble of Cairo's twenty million tortured souls. They had to pillage or lose the support of their followers. They couldn't allow him to become the paramount sheikh; the thug of thugs. Their survival depended upon it.

Yes, rumors were the way to go, but not too soon. The police also had spies. Only the final hours before dawn would do. Cell phones would buzz. Some of his disciples would boast to friends. Others would alert cousins thrice removed of gains to be had. But phones weren't necessary. Rumors were the soul of the slum, soaring with the breeze and penetrating the most wretched of hovels. A few minutes would do. The rabble would come in droves. Not just the street thugs; but gnarled hags and crippled beggars. The blind would probe, picking pockets along the way. Yes they would come, all in search of a gift from God that would enable them to survive for another day. But nothing would be said about killing feminists. Crime didn't worry the police, politics did.

* * * *

Gloria Goldensickle was irritated by the timing of the march. Her troops were at the ready. It would take all of her energy to keep them at fever pitch for a few more weeks. They had all read gory reports of Israeli tourists being murdered in Egypt. It didn't happen often, but it did happen and they were skittish. Fear of election violence wouldn't make things any easier. Gloria, herself, didn't fear violence. Indeed, she welcomed it. Perhaps a little violence was just what the doctor ordered to publicize the plight of women. Not serious violence, of course. Just well publicized jostling, an occasional bruise or two, perhaps a broken arm. Nothing more. She couldn't admit that to herself, but made a note to pack a generous supply of Israeli flags and banners. But now, all would be lost in the swirl of the elections. That was, unless she could persuade some friendly reporters that covering the feminist march would be worth their while.

Gloria had other problems as well. The gays were becoming a nuisance, stopping by her office on a daily basis to get the latest information and offering suggestions for lodging and transportation. That was not the problem. She felt kindly toward her gay students and welcomed their participation. That was, until the word coordination had crept into their conversations. It was an ominous word that suggested that the gay contingent would be far more than a hand full of flawed males lost in a sea of feminists. Israeli gays had already hosted several gay marches in Israel and she didn't want them upstaging the feminists in Cairo.

The Egyptians accepted feminists as a necessary evil foisted upon them by the Americans. They didn't accept gays. Gays were persecuted in gaudy show trials.

Yet another soap opera to titillate that masses and portray a corrupt government as the guardian of morality. Islam, much like Christianity and Judaism, its sister faiths, denounced homosexuality as an abomination. And yet, Muslim societies had always been tolerant of gays. The seclusion of women demanded no less. Hypocrites all, the very hint of a gay presence would provide an excuse for the cancellation of the march. It also posed the threat of greater violence than she could accept. Real violence, not just show violence.

Such were Gloria's thoughts as she arrived in Cairo for a repeat engagement at the church. It would be her final visit before the march itself. It would be her final chance to go over her plans with Parker's wife. Not all of the plans, just those plans that required her cooperation. Constance Parker was to sponsor a seminar on interfaith solidarity the day before the march. It would be their cover. Many of the Israeli marchers would come a day or two early to visit the pyramids and museums. Nothing out of the ordinary. Israelis were big on museums and the Americans were big on interfaith meetings. The church would be the staging point for the Israelis and their refuge should things go terribly wrong. Gloria hadn't said this per se, but suggested that they all return to the church to assess the success of the march. No need to mention the possibility of violence to Parker's wife. It would be Gloria's little secret.

✻   ✻   ✻   ✻

Jake found the timing of the march to be bizarre, but not of particular concern. The elections were the main attraction. Cairo had so many police there were surely enough to go around. He smiled when Mandy mentioned the interfaith conference. It would look good on his record and piss off the Minister of Interior. "Cover this thing," he had said to Mandy, with a fatherly smile. He knew that she resented being stuck with teas and garden parties, but that was the nature of the beast. Males couldn't do it. Besides, he suspected that she was a closet feminist.

Chapter 25

An Evening in Paris

"Ah, my friend," said the Nubian with a touch of envy, "you are the eye of the storm. You are the only one who talks to everyone. You talk to Sheikh Yassin and you talk to the Embassy. You are friends with the Boss. You are the lover of Zahra and the pretty one. Your wife is an Israeli agent and the Wisp is your link to the Minister of Interior. You are a very clever man, my friend. No wonder they sent you here." With a wink and uproarious laugh he added, "Someone is bound to kill you!"

"You forgot the jihadists," responded Parker, unwilling to give the Nubian his due.

"Ah, but I didn't, my friend. Hardly a day passes that you do not pause to exchange a few words with Ahmed the bootblack. Or are you really that concerned with polishing shoes that will be covered with dust before you have taken three steps?"

"Bah," responded Parker, "the man is an illiterate. We discuss the weather and nothing more."

The Nubian was not to be dissuaded. He could sense that Parker had become worried, very worried. Parker had cause to be worried. Was the butagaz attack not premeditated? Had the macabre humor of the Nubian not confirmed his fears? Had Ahmed the shoeshine man not warned of hot weather ahead, very hot weather? Had Mandy not clung to him in the aftermath of passion and pleaded with him to be careful? Had the CIA picked up something? He wanted to ask, but couldn't. That would force her to break protocol. If she refused, their relationship would cool. If she complied, he would be committed to a deeper relationship, a much deeper relationship.

He fought against his fears, rational explanations giving way to confusion as the storm tightened around him, winds lashing him from every side. The Wisp hinted that the Minister of Interior was displeased by his visits with Sheikh Yassin. His wife revealed that the church would be the staging ground for the Israelis. Mandy began speaking openly of marriage and Zahra vowed that she would rather die rather than lose him. Generals had become increasingly prominent at Jake's special gatherings and Smith seemed to be losing his nerve. As if that were not enough, close friends of the Boss were arrested for civil rights activities. Would the Boss be next? The project would be lost without him, for nothing in Egypt succeeds without a powerful patron. Sleep became difficult. His dreams were tormented by bucolic scenes of life in rural Nebraska.

He needed time to stand back and evaluate. Time away from Cairo. Time away from his wife, Zahra, Mandy and, above all, time away from the Nubian. He searched his briefcase for the letter inviting him to present the results of the project at a conference in Paris. He had delayed, fearing he'd lose track of events in Cairo. Besides, the results of the project were not final. No matter, he could give a progress report. Everything was in line. He had already been to two conferences and the Boss had asked him to make it a third. The Boss had planned to go himself, but his stomach wouldn't allow it. He would have peace, total peace. His wife would be tied up with the impending visit of Gloria Goldensickle, and Mandy was committed to escorting visiting Congressmen and their special friends down the Nile. Zahra had reluctantly agreed to spend time with an ailing aunt. Anyway, how could one turn down a free trip to Paris? He hadn't gone totally bonkers. He sent his acceptance. The winds abated.

*   *   *   *

"Ah, my forlorn friend," consoled the Nubian with obvious pleasure, "his true love has deserted him. She has gone to see her auntie. No doubt Sheikh Yassin has sent her away for safe keeping, far away."

"For the best," responded Parker, "her grandfather is a wise man."

The Nubian smiled indulgently at Parker's nonchalance. Then, unable to restrain the tears of laughter that streamed from his enormous eyes, he asked mockingly, "You know where her auntie lives, of course?"

Parker, afraid to ask, shrugged his shoulders in a gesture of disinterest. "It doesn't matter. I'm not the type to scale castle walls in search of love."

"No need!" bellowed the fat man in glee. "She is in Paris. The family has a compound there. All of Egypt's powerful families do. Either Paris or London. My you are a clever man, my friend. I have never met anyone quite like you. You think of everything. No wonder the Americans rule the world. It is their destiny."

"America rules the world because you people are lost in your conspiracies," chided Parker.

"Ah, but it is not a conspiracy," glowed the Nubian. "She knew the dates of the conference and she knew that you would be attending. The Boss accepted the invitation in your name weeks ago. Didn't he mention it to you? How forgetful he is. But that's the way Egyptian bosses operate. Why, she even knows your hotel. The Meridian by the Bois de Boulogne, isn't it? The Arabs love it. Her very presence among the sex crazed Gulf Arabs will cause a riot. Never mind, the Bois was designed for lovers. Miles of empty lanes, shaded nooks and Brazilian transvestites. The invitation and all of the details were on the Boss's desk. If I could see it, you know that she could see it. She has the run of the Boss's office, this gazelle, his office and the office of every other dirty old man in the place. Oh, how she fills their dreams with pleasure. She will do more for you. Oh, how she will delight you, my friend. Believe me, I have known all types of women: American, French, German, and Arab. Zahra is more than a woman. She is a goddess, a jinn."

"But, ah," interjected Parker in an effort to blunt the Nubian's euphoria, "have you ever made love to an Israeli?"

"Bah," scoffed the Nubian, "the Israelis are a race dominated by females. They castrate their men and pickle their testicles. Can you imagine making love to that Israeli spy that your wife keeps bringing to the church?"

Parker visualized Gloria arranging the pickled testicles of her former husbands on the hearth and began to laugh. Perhaps that was the reason why so many Jewish men married Christians. They wanted sex rather than chicken soup. His mind always wandered in moments of stress. It was a psychological mechanism that restored his sense of balance.

The Nubian's voice jarred him back to reality. "You will see my friend, none can compare to Egyptian women. They are bred to bring pleasure. You will divorce your wife and forget the pretty one. Zahra will consume your soul."

His balance restored and unwilling to concede victory, Parker looked the Nubian in the eye and whispered, "I hope so."

Parker won the point. It would be he who enjoyed the sensuous pleasures of Zahra.

"Be careful, my friend," warned the Nubian, his voice now devoid of humor. "Your every move in Paris will be watched."

*   *   *   *

Parker arrived in Paris early in the afternoon, checked into the Meridian, and then walked the half block to the metro station on the far end of the Champs Elysees. He peered around, half suspecting to see covert eyes following his every move, but soon gave up the venture. Paris was bursting with Arabs. They were cab drivers, sidewalk hawkers, street workers, business men, students, and oil sheikhs dripping in wealth, their veiled wives being fitted for the latest in Paris gowns, fringes of chartreuse or burgundy flashing beneath their somber robes. If he were being followed, so be it. If Zahra had planned some mad venture, that was her problem, not his. He had no intention of winding up in the bottom of the Seine. Anyway, the very thought of a rendezvous was absurd. The Nubian had gotten into his head with his mind games.

It had been a long day, and he thought better of the metro. Better to stroll through the Bois, enjoy an elegant seafood dinner at the corner restaurant, and then turn in for an early evening. He'd watch some French TV replete with naked breasts and then go to bed. He wound his way through the underpasses linking the Champs Elysees to the island fountain and the Bois beyond. The air was brisk, clearing his mind and strengthening his resolve to expedite the project and be done with Cairo. He strolled the lanes of the Bois until the shadows of evening gave the tangled hideaways a sinister aura. The Bois was dangerous at night.

It was a subdued Parker that made his way to the seafood feast that he had anticipated with such pleasure. Had he really expected Zahra to motion to him from behind a bush, a common whore with blanket in hand? Absurd. More likely, a discreet telephone call would direct him to an obscure address in a remote part of the city.

The maitre d' sat him at a small table overlooking the avenue, the warmth of the nearby fireplace conspiring with the wine to transform the dancing lights of the street into exotic shapes. He held his glass to the window and the shapes became phantoms. Beautiful phantoms, jinn, each more beautiful than the others, dancing and intermingling, their naked breasts inviting him to join them as they disappeared into the shadows. The waiter refilled his glass, and the jinn reappeared, weaving an arch crowned by the most beautiful woman he had ever seen. It was Zahra, naked and seductive. She beckoned and he followed.

"May I bring you another bottle of wine?" the waiter asked.

"No!" cringed Parker, still lucid, and made his way to the hotel.

"You have a call," said the lovely Lebanese clerk, her eyes dancing with a knowing humor. Or was she Egyptian? No matter, the Gulf Arabs who frequented the Meridian liked lovely clerks with dancing eyes.

He took the paper and made his way to his room. There was no name, merely a chain of numbers. He placed the paper on the table, hoping that a shower would clear his head. "No, no," screamed the phantoms, "call now. She is waiting for you." Parker obeyed, his heart pounding as he dialed the number. He would refuse the invitation. He had to refuse.

"Dr. Parker," came the deep male voice. "We are so happy that you have arrived safely. Could you kindly join us for breakfast?"

Parker recalled accepting the breakfast invitation, but little more. Phantoms swirled in his head as he collapsed on the bed. A thousand Zahras beckoned him to follow. There was no need for French TV.

* * * *

There was a gentle tapping at the door. A swirl of perfume rushed by him. What devious means had she employed to reach his room? He could only guess. It didn't matter. She was beside him, her clothes dissolving into the air as she dissolved into his arms. There was no time for talk. How long would they have before disaster struck? Seconds? An eternity. A blinding explosion of passion, and then what? She had left him no choice. They were together, compromised. He would force her to reveal the soul of Egypt. If they died in a lovers pact, so be it. He was as insane as she.

And now they were on the bed, lips fused, his trembling hands discovering the glorious breasts that he had only been allowed to grope from beyond her robes. How silly Western women were to bear all, robbing their lovers of the thrill of discovery and conquest. Where was the game? Sex devoid of intellect was animal husbandry. It was the game that separated man from beast. Even now, in the dusk of the room he could only guess at the magnitude of her beauty, his tongue exploring the contours of her body, his teeth sinking into the soft skin of her nipples, his fingers unleashing the fragrant pleasures of her soul. She, more curious than he, denied herself nothing.

"Have I pleased you?" whispered Zahra, clinging to him much as Mandy clung to him and his wife had clung to him in days gone by.

"More pleasure than I have ever known," replied Parker. "More pleasure than I could ever have imagined." It was the stuff of dreams: the warmth, the tenderness, the submissiveness, the desire to be conquered, the spontaneity, the inventiveness, the temptation to deviance. He had immersed himself in it all, again and again until he could immerse no more.

Yes, she had brought him pleasure. Pleasure beyond description. But, it was a pleasure troubled by doubt. Had he brought her pleasure? Could he bring her pleasure? Did it really matter? Ah, but it mattered. It mattered to Egyptian men. How else could they prove their manliness? How else could they be sure that their wives wouldn't stray in an insane desire for fulfillment? Cuckolds, one and all. How many times had the Nubian regaled him with stories of husbands driven to drugs and madness by their inability to please wives mutilated by the knife, his voice just audible enough to be heard by the general's wife? Was that not the hidden theme of Egyptian soap operas? What a wonderful irony. The passions of the womb inflamed by the very mutilations designed to quell them?

It mattered to Parker. For the same reasons? Perhaps, but it was so much more. It was a game, a challenge. Submission was not conquest. Conquest was total domination, psychological as well as physical. One without the other was a mirage. Had the Egyptians not proven that over the centuries, each new wave of *kawagas* falling prey to their seemingly placid docility? Sexual conquest was the most difficult of all. Penetration was the easy part. It was the rest that counted. The anticipation, the explosion of passion and the glorious peace of fulfillment. Was he demanding enough? Cruel enough? How often had the Nubian preached the need for sexual violence? "Egyptian women craved force," he leered as Zahra had left the bullpen. "What else can they feel? They taunt their men until they become violent. It is their revenge."

Parker had looked at him as if he were mad. "Any fool can rape a woman," he sneered. "One rules by compassion and guile. Force is a condiment to be used sparingly."

"Do you really believe that crap?" taunted the Nubian. "You pretend to be holier than thou, but is your society really any different? Everything is sexual exploitation. Your movies and videos glorify violence against women, even your music. It's the same in Israel. You read the Israeli papers don't you? They are always complaining about wife abuse."

"You don't understand our society," snapped Parker.

"You don't understand ours," countered the Nubian. "Don't forget that she is an Egyptian lady. It would be a shame if she lost her awe of the *kawagas*. Awe is the key to your rule of the Middle East."

How could he know if he had conquered? What was the measure of such things? The Nubian had assured him that Sheikh Yassin would not allow such barbaric practices, but how did the Nubian know? For that matter, how did the Sheikh know? It was the grandmothers who perpetrated this hideous act in a fit of misguided compassion. Mutilated daughters were more marriageable and Egyptian society demanded marriage. He relived the scene a thousand times. The signs were there: the sighs, the trembling, the cries for pain, the self-flagellation of her breasts so brutal that it threatened mutilation, the tears, the frantic laughter, and the raucous hiss that the Nubian had imitated so eloquently.

He knew that he had conquered. Yet, the words of the Nubian remained embedded in his subconscious. "You don't understand our culture. Don't forget that she is an Egyptian lady. Don't disappoint her. Don't be fooled. We have been trained to deceive *kawagas*. It is in our blood. We are actors, one and all. It is our glory. Our survival depends upon it."

"No," Parker smiled to himself, "it was real. So gloriously real that there was no turning back."

She had appeared in a dream and left in a dream. "A demain," she had whispered, "Je t'aime." Tomorrow or good bye? Which was it? Perhaps it was a dream. He prayed that it was a dream. He searched the room for signs of her presence. They were everywhere. The scent of her perfume, the empty wine glasses, the intimate garment neglected as the bewitching hour approached. If only it could have been a dream. But it wasn't. Stolen seconds had become stolen hours. Pretend had become reality, a reality more glorious than the Nubian's wildest fantasies.

Chapter 26

Did Anyone Know?

The evening in Paris had changed nothing and it had changed everything. The tensions that had dissolved as Parker boarded the flight to Paris returned in force as his plane circled Cairo, its glorious pyramids looming in the evening dusk. The march had gained its own momentum, inexorable, fated and doomed. No one could back out because they were all in. To withdraw was to lose. The only hope of victory was to watch the cards unfold. So, they watched, and watched, and watched.

Had they been seen? Parker had suppressed the question in Paris, but now it assaulted him in his dreams and at the turn of every corner. Again, questions begot questions. Had she wanted them to be seen? How could she win without them being seen?

* * * *

"Have you followed your heart?" asked the Sheikh with the special gentleness that he reserved for his granddaughter. Beyond speech, she avoided his eyes and nodded her head in the affirmative. The Sheikh had anticipated the revelation and received the news with equanimity. He had ordered her to follow her heart and the conclusion had been foreordained.

"It was God's will," he consoled her, his voice compassionate and devoid of blame or disappointment. "People must serve God according to their abilities.

Some give of their money and their skills. Others give of their lives. All are honored in paradise. You have served God well and you will reside in heaven whatever your persecution on earth."

Zahra dismissed, the Sheikh prayed for guidance. He had subconsciously hoped that they wouldn't return from Paris; that Parker would whisk her away to the States and the matter would resolve itself with time. But they had returned. She first, and then he. It was God's will. They had a role to play, but what role?

The more he prayed the clearer God's will had become. God had arranged the meeting in Paris to inflame the melodrama until it reached a feverish pitch on the eve of the march. Cairo would not have done. They would have been observed and all would have been lost; she attacked by crazed madmen and Parker assassinated. Had they been seen in Paris? Irrelevant. Any fool could put two and two together, and his adversaries were not fools. Rumors would swirl and God would be served. Alas, any pretense of Zahra's purity had disappeared.

The Sheikh's thoughts were interrupted by the gentle cough of his son. The Sheikh beckoned him to enter and for a moment they sat in silence. There was no need for words. The son's face was ashen. He knew the situation well. To serve God was to suffer and sacrifice. The son's voice trembled with emotion when finally he spoke, "Can you save her, my father?"

"What would you have me do, my son?" asked the Sheikh with a sorrow that challenged the depths of his faith? Could he really transform the rabid superstitions of the masses into enlightened Islamic rule that would honor the Prophet Mohammed? He had his doubts, but his faith remained unshakable. God alone would decide. What he did know was that there was no other choice. Nationalist thugs had slaughtered in the name of secularism and the jihadists had slaughtered in the name of Islam. The present regime served only itself and the Americans. His mission was to guide Egypt toward a moderate Islamic government. Failure would mean civil war in Egypt and carnage in the region. God had ordered him to try. His meetings with Parker suggested that the Americans were supportive.

The son remained silent, his question unanswered. The call to prayer beckoned from a nearby mosque, and Sheikh Yassin excused himself, patting his son on the shoulder as he whispered, "God will provide." He then kneeled on his prayer rug and prayed for guidance.

* * * *

His prayer over, he made a phone call. Hushed words were exchanged and he sent for his granddaughter. He spoke softly. "God has ordered that you marry Ali al-Nimr. He is one of the most powerful men in Egypt and he will soon, God willing, become the Minister of Interior. You will help him make peace with the Brotherhood and prepare the way for a moral society."

Zahra did not speak. Ali Al-Nimr was thirty years her senior, perhaps more. His youngest daughter had been her friend in college.

"He cannot marry me," replied Zahra, when the shock of her grandfather's words had abated. "It is known that I have given myself to a man without marriage."

"What is known," corrected the Sheikh, "is that you will soon be a divorced woman. Divorced women are much prized in our society." There was little need for elaboration.

She looked at him speechless, uncomprehending, as if she were locked in a ghastly nightmare from which there was no exit.

"You will marry the American in a few hours. The divorce will follow."

"It is forbidden for a Muslim woman to marry a Christian," protested Zahra.

"He will convert," smiled the Sheikh reassuringly.

"But he is already married," stammered Zahra in disbelief. "He cannot marry me."

"A mere formality," smiled the Sheikh. "Muslims are permitted four wives."

A great sadness seized Zahra as she grasped the inevitability of her fate. Thoughts of suicide raced through her mind, but soon vanished. That was the stuff of Western soap operas. Eastern women were more realistic. Their decisions had been dictated by their fathers since birth. What to wear, what to study, what job to take. All was prearranged. They would also have the final say on marriage. Protest was futile. Where was a woman to go? Perhaps it was for the best. How often had Muslim theologians preached the absurdity of allowing children to select their mates in the heat of passion? Was the West not a tragic landscape of shattered marriages and broken homes?

Zahra knew and she accepted. She had rebelled in college and attempted to become Western, but what had her rebellion wrought? She had acquired the veneer of Westernization but nothing more. An outcast in her own society, she faced a future of loneliness and despair. Friends that once envied her now tormented her with smiling infants.

"Will you spare him?" she asked, through her sobs.

"I will try, my pretty one," promised the Sheikh, but nothing more. He had reserved the phrase my pretty one for her alone, but now even that had become an abomination. It would be the pretty one at the Embassy that became Parker's wife and bore his children.

"To serve God is to sacrifice," continued the Sheikh in gentle admonition. "We must each play the role assigned to us. That is the true source of joy and forgiveness. God has provided you with a husband, money and power. *Allah Akbar.* Use your blessings to serve God." It was not a passion play, but a direct order.

His words did not ease her weeping, but gradually penetrated an agile mind desperately clinging to the dream of love. Money and power would enable her to travel. Her father's business connections in the US would provide the excuse. Her husband would be too old to care. Parker would have time to divorce his wife. Madness? Perhaps. But was it a greater madness than the nightmare swirling around her? But how much time would she have? The invasion of the meat and the fat had already begun. For the moment it had enhanced her beauty, but for how long?

* * * *

Parker made his way to the Institute much as he had always made his way to the Institute, marveling at the grand old houses of Zamalek and cringing at the cement monstrosities that encroached on their once glorious gardens. Then, crossing the bridge with its breathtaking view of the Nile, he made the harrowing dash across the six lane highway that hugs the river, navigated the pitted sidewalks of Boulaq, and paused for his ritual shoeshine. Ahmed took more time than usual with his shoeshine and warned of an approaching sandstorm. His mood was gloomy, perhaps sinister. Parker was appreciative of the reprieve and made no effort to comprehend the cripple's gibberish. He lacked the courage to enter the Institute just as he had lacked the courage to take the bus. A taxi would have been more secure, but that would have broken his routine and raised eyebrows. He could hear the tongues wag.

"The *kawaga* is taking a taxi these days."

"I wonder why? The weather is beautiful and he prefers to walk."

"Perhaps something has happened?"

"You know it had to, his affair with Zahra and all."

"I will check with the general's wife. She knows everything."

That would only be the beginning. Conspiracies would swirl faster than the dust of Galal Street, each outdoing the other in a race against reality. But what could these small minds grasp of the intrigue that swirled around them or the reality of Zahra.

Such, at least, were the thoughts of a man who would discover the soul of Egypt. He found himself singing hymns much as he had sung hymns as a lad with stick in hand streaking past the cemetery that flanked the road to his friend's house. By the time he reached the Institute, hymns had given way to the 23rd Psalm.

Parker took solace in the fact that it would soon be over. His project was drawing to a close and the eve of the march was approaching. His role in the drama was coming to an end. Exit stage left; descend into oblivion, never to return, never again to hold the goddess Zahra in his arms.

Zahra! The thought of her name shocked him back to reality. Within minutes he would face her and learn the truth. Had they been discovered? Did Sheikh Yassin know? Above all, had she shared an ecstasy so intense that it was beyond description? He recalled the phantoms and the passion, but little else.

He took the stairs rather than the elevator, and then, seeing the Boss's door open, joined him for coffee. Anything to delay the inevitable. The Boss congratulated him on the success of the project, but nothing more. The soft leather chairs that surrounded the Boss's massive desk were soon filled with the typical array of supplicants and conspirators, reducing Parker to an irrelevant curiosity. He tried to listen to the conversations that he had long found so intriguing, but could not. He had to see her and face his responsibilities however painful they might be. It was the Christian thing to do. He entered the secretary's office. She left on cue, but no Zahra. He ascended to the bullpen, finding only the Nubian and his endless mind games.

The Nubian, as always, was the first to weigh in. "Welcome back my friend," he exuded, his eyes sparkling with hilarity. "Oh, how we have missed you. The suspense has been insufferable, the rumors intolerable. I live through you, my friend, all the joy and none of the pain. I hope that she did not disappoint."

"I didn't know that you lusted after the pretty one," countered Parker, with a mocking smile. "I thought Western women bored you." Denial was his only option. To confess was to lose all. Face would be lost and families humiliated. Enemies would pounce and friends flee. Feuds would erupt and daughters would be slaughtered to save the family name. Zahra's life would be in jeopardy. Denial fooled no one, but forced madmen to hold their fire. Realities changed and amends were made behind the scene. That too was a game, a deadly game.

"Ah, but she was radiant when she arrived at the office," continued the Nubian with malice. "Men can hide their emotions. Women cannot."

The Nubian's counterattack was flawed by a moment of indecision. Mandy's absence from Cairo had been noted by his informants and its significance weighed. The *kawaga* was clever, but was he clever enough to use the pretty one as cover for his tryst with Zahra, deceiving both while he serviced both? He knew that he had lost the round.

"Zahra's joy was the thrill of seeing you after a long absence," mocked Parker, now confident that the Nubian was unsure of what had happened in Paris. "We all know that Zahra finds you irresistible." There had been rumors about Paris to be sure, but nothing more. The Nubian had been probing, hoping desperately for a slip of the tongue. If he were unsure, perhaps others were unsure as well. That was all that he could hope for. It would buy him some time, maybe enough time to escape. But first, he had to see Zahra.

Parker said nothing more, remaining passive and unresponsive. Without satisfaction, the Nubian would turn to other subjects. If Zahra were there, she would make a sign. Perhaps it would be a fleeting entrance to deliver yet another unneeded folder to the desk of the general's wife. Or, perhaps, the secretary would summon him to fill out yet another form, only to depart with the entrance of Zahra. But no one came. Not Zahra, and not the secretary. No one came! Not even the Wisp or the general's wife.

"Not to worry," smiled the Nubian with a rare touch of compassion. "She works irregularly, often missing days at a time. That is the prerogative of the rich and famous. She may not even be in Cairo. She passed by once, but not finding you, fled. No one has seen her since that time. Please understand, her life is in danger and the Sheikh has decreed that she will not participate in the march."

Chapter 27

Wedding Bells

Even as a youth, Sheikh Yassin had believed that his life was divinely guided. He questioned often and prayed for understanding, but he never doubted. He followed his instincts believing that they were the will of God. Now, on the eve of the greatest battle of his life, he could only marvel at God's wisdom. He had worried over the trip to Paris, but without it, how could he have forced the *kawaga* to convert to Islam and marry his granddaughter? Without the divorce, how could he have arranged her marriage to the prospective Minister of Interior? That, too, was part of God's plan, for the world was not going to change in a minute. Muslims needed time to repent and prepare the way. The new Minister of Interior, his soon to be son-in-law, was sent to facilitate the transition. God's hand was to be seen at every turn. It was to be seen in his decision to allow his son to become a member of the ruling party and a successful banker and in Zahra's college experiments. Everything was preordained. Nothing of significance happened by chance. So it was that this most beautiful of women would marry this most lecherous of knaves.

But that, too, was preordained. The governments of the Arab world were so rotten that an honest man could not function effectively. How were saints to take bribes, fill the government with incompetent relatives, organize death squads, and pander to ignorance and superstition? His new son-in-law was well versed in all. He was a perfect chameleon, a former general who preached democracy and secular reform while accepting grants from the Americans and taking bribes from the government. His lechery and dubious wealth were merely reflections of his power. He dined with the Egyptian president and figured high on Jake's plan for a coup.

For all of his talents, this marvelous chameleon had one fatal flaw, a conscience! Islam had been imprinted on his soul as a youth. He had strayed as a student and strayed farther as a young man. He pretended to be secular and drank openly in the night clubs of Cairo. Yet, the seed of Islam remained imbedded in his soul, depriving him of the pleasures of his labor. The search for inner peace led him to Sheikh Yassin, a worldly man who had himself been tempted by the lure of the West. They had talked of the past and politics, but most of all they talked about salvation. There had been no deal with the devil, but merely an exchange of ideas. Sheikh Yassin knew of Ali's political aspirations and suggested that his attendance at Friday prayers would be a political asset. It would be a sign that he, like most Muslims, was struggling with the cruel choice between westernization and faith. The thought was not new, but Honest Ali, as his friends called him, had rejected it, fearing that it would compromise his secular persona.

That, however, had changed with Sheikh Yassin's suggestion that Ali's presence at Friday prayers would enable the Brotherhood to support his political ambitions. In the end, he had come away as a closet Brother, an ace in the hold to be used at the appropriated moment. There had been no mention of drink or other moral issues. That was all part of the charade. He caroused and preached secular reform while the Brotherhood looked askance at his actions but said nothing. In the meantime, 20% of Honest Ali's ill gotten gains had found their way into Sheikh Yassin's coffers, more if need be. Doomed to an eternity in hell, Ali was more than willing to pay for the inner peace that comes with the certain knowledge of salvation. It was also the most pleasant of arrangements. He had purchased salvation and the license to sin for a fraction of his wealth. He would come when God called, and he came willingly when Sheikh Yassin requested him to marry his granddaughter. It was a pleasure to serve God. *Allah Akbar.*

"Yes," Sheikh Yassin mused, "his new-son-in law was just the man to replace the Minister of Interior. Ali would please the Americans by slaughtering jihadists and mumbling inanities about democracy and human rights. Government owned factories would be dismantled and a flood of imports from the United States would drive local producers to bankruptcy. Unemployment would skyrocket, but capitalism would be served. That was how one dealt with the Americans. Kill jihadists, flood the market with American imports, bow to Israel, and mumble inanities about a democracy that they didn't want. What the Americans wanted, the Americans would get. Honest Ali would be their man."

Of course, there would be neither democracy nor responsible government. Why would the Brotherhood want a secular government to succeed? To the contrary. It would be Ali's role to destroy the liberals. He was to prove to one and all that they were as venal and incompetent as the heirs of Nasser who would invite them to share power once Sheikh Yassin had disposed of the Minister of Interior. When would that time be? Why after the march, of course.

The power brokers would have no choice. They would need an alliance with the liberals to hold off the Brotherhood in the chaos that followed. A few liberals would be appointed to high profile positions, but they, like Ali, would be selected with care. The task would not be difficult. A few reformers were honest, but they were aberrations. Most would suck up bribes with the rapaciousness of jackals. It would soon be they who careened through Cairo with cell phones glued to their ears, their gaudy Mercedes spewing dust and body parts in their wake.

Would Ali succeed in destroying the liberals? Of course he would. It was God's plan. How wonderful things would be. Bribes would flow and inflation would soar. Not to worry. Zahra would dominate the society pages and Ali would advise a frightened President to raise the price of bread. Riots would follow, but Ali would crush them just as he would crush the jihadists. "Who knows," the Sheikh mused, "the ruling party might be so pleased with Ali that they would invite him to be president. He was, after all, an ex-general, the prime requirement for the presidency. The swelling lines of poor and unemployed would flood to the clinics, schools and soup kitchens maintained by the Brotherhood. God is the solution! Enjoy your soup."

Through it all, Ali would guild the coffers of the Brotherhood and slip its members into governmental positions at all levels. They would be ideal public servants, learning their trade as they bided their time. That was the trouble in Iran. The fundamentalists had taken over before they knew how to govern and made a mess of things. The Embassy would be nervous, but Ali would console them. "See how docile they are," he would whisper to the Ambassador, "They take their pay and make us look religious. A few bars are closed, the Israelis are chided for slaughtering Palestinian children, and some books are burned. Unfortunate, perhaps, but that's the price of doing business. We have to make them look good. The streets are quiet, the jihadists are in retreat, the rich are getting richer and American companies dominate the economy. Better the Brotherhood than the jihadists," he would warn the Ambassador. "It will be one or the other."

While Ali soothed the Americans, the Brotherhood would strengthen its grip on the Egypt. It would be they who had a strangle hold on the student organizations, the professional syndicates and the slums. Beards, that ubiquitous symbol of manhood and submission to God, would proliferate in the security forces, sending an ominous warning to those who pondered an attack on the Brotherhood. And when Ali's job was done and he had whisked Zahra away to his European estate, the Brotherhood would rule Egypt. The Americans would accept the inevitable. What choice would they have?

But first, the march had to succeed. The government had to be disgraced and the present Minister of Interior destroyed. Sheikh Yassin's job was to keep the Brotherhood focused on the elections while Mizjaji shattered the truce by launching a holy war, a *jihad*, on the marchers. *Allah Akbar*. God had foreseen everything. He had created Mizjaji precisely for this role. How else to better disgrace the jihadists and accomplish the goals of the march? Would Muslims die? Probably, but that was God's decision.

Now, as the plan unfolded, the Sheikh knew an inner peace reserved only for the purist of the faith. He had questioned, but he had obeyed. It was the test of his intelligence that his faith had overcome his doubts. It had all been so obvious. Why had he not seen it from the beginning? And so Sheikh Yassin carried out God's will. Parker was summoned to the mosque and final marital arrangements were made with the prospective Minister of Interior. This accomplished, he announced a special sermon to discuss startling new developments. Would the masses come? One did not miss the special sermons of Sheikh Yassin. He would discuss the elections and the march. Most importantly, he would discuss the situation with Zahra. He had not said as much, but one knew the hints. His agents had filled in the gaps. Let the circus begin.

* * * *

"Ah, my friend," glowed the Nubian, "you are blessed."

Parker cringed, but said nothing. Glad tidings from the Nubian usually turned out to be a disaster.

"The Sheikh would appreciate an interview with you. Is tomorrow afternoon suitable?"

"Did the Sheikh say what he wanted to talk about?" queried Parker with sarcasm.

"How am I to say, my friend?" responded the Nubian. "My cousin is a member of the Brotherhood and asked me to convey the message. You know how things are in our society. Everybody is the cousin of somebody." Then, shrugging his shoulders in mock seriousness, he ventured, "Perhaps the Sheikh has agreed to give you Zahra's hand in marriage."

Parker remained stoic. The Nubian contemplated his huge belly, and then nodded his head slowly in disappointment. "No. Probably not. You are not a Muslim are you? It's a pity. Paradise is reserved for believers. You could convert you know?"

Parker waited for the burst of laughter, but it did not come. The Nubian had delivered the message and awaited his response.

"Nothing pleases me more than meeting with the Sheikh," responded Parker, summoning up what remained of his courage. The invitation was an order and there was no escape. His only hope was that the Sheikh wanted to maintain contact with the Embassy or needed information on the march. Barring this, there was no reason for Sheikh Yassin to keep him alive.

* * * *

The Nubian's jest of marriage and conversion weighed heavily on Parker's mind as he made his way to the reception at Mandy's elegant flat overlooking the broad sweep of the Nile. The reception was tense. Mandy pouted and accused him of meeting Zahra in Paris. Did she know? Probably just a guess? Smith was nervous, and Jake, wearing a poker face, probed for hints of things to come.

"It seems that you are the center of the storm, Dr. Parker," said Jake with a mixture of curiosity and the begrudging respect that the less educated accord to those with higher degrees. "Have you been in touch with the Sheikh recently?"

"We have a meeting tomorrow." replied Parker

Smith and Mandy exchanged a worried glance. He hadn't mentioned a visit to the Sheikh.

"Very unexpected," continued Parker. "The invitation came as I was leaving the office."

There was another exchange of glances between Smith and Mandy as worries about Parker's duplicity gave way to worries about the Sheikh's message.

"Damn, man," exploded Jake in exasperation, sensing Parker's reluctance to speculate on the meeting, "I thought you were one of the few people around here with some balls."

"He didn't mention the purpose of the meeting," responded Parker with studied seriousness. "The Sheikh has great admiration for your direct approach to diplomacy, Mr. Ambassador. I presume that he wants you to keep a close eye on the elections and the feminist march. He fears that the Minister of Interior will use both to destroy the Brotherhood and strengthen his truce with the jihadists. I will contact Smith as soon as I return from the meeting."

It was clear from his expression that Jake had taken the bait. Sheikh Yassin would be pleased. Pleased enough to keep Parker alive for a few more weeks? He could only pray.

"Screw Smith," snarled Jake. "I will be at the Embassy."

Smith stayed for a while after the others had left. Parker spent the night. Things were moving in the right direction, but there was little cheer. Smith, a sensitive man, had been hurt by Jake's comments, and Mandy was upset at having been placed in charge of the feminist march.

"Make sure there are no screw-ups," Jake had ordered her curtly on his way out of the door. "I don't know what the Minister of Interior has in mind, but I do know that the s.o.b is desperate. Thank God that your friend has his ear to the ground."

"Do I get an 'A' for having good friends?" she smiled, chiding him for ignoring her role in the matter. It was a weak smile, for the thought of observing the march terrified her. The mere presence of Gloria Goldensickle spelled doom, not to mention Parker's oblique warning of Israeli gays. "Make sure there are no screw-ups," he had said. How and the hell was she to make sure that there were no screw-ups? The whole thing was a screw up. If she hadn't fallen in love with Parker, she wouldn't be in this mess.

But she had, and that evening they clung to each other with a haunting fear that this evening could be their last.

* * * *

"So kind of you to come," smiled the Sheikh, as if Parker had responded to an invitation for tea. "It has been a long time since I have had the pleasure of your company and we have so much to talk about."

"A sadistic cat and mouse game," worried Parker, "or was the Sheikh in a conciliatory mood?"

"How are your friends at the Embassy?" continued the Sheikh. "I hope that they are well."

"Quite well," responded Parker, "but very concerned about the elections and the feminist march. The Ambassador has ordered his staff to pay close attention to both."

"Please give the Ambassador my warmest appreciation, Dr. Parker," glowed the Sheikh. "I am pleased that he shares our worries. Observation by the Embassy will be most welcome. We can provide them with guides if that would be helpful.

Nothing formal of course, but we have friends in the secular community who are very familiar with these things."

"I will convey your message to the Ambassador," responded Parker. "He has asked me to meet with him after our visit. How shall I contact you if he would like your assistance?"

"We will find a way, Dr. Parker. You will be at the Institute tomorrow, will you not?"

Parked said that he would be there for most of the day, allowing himself an inaudible sigh of relief. At least he would be alive long enough to convey the Sheikh's message to Jake.

A long and awkward pause ensued, and for a fleeting moment, Parker dared to hope that the Sheikh didn't know about Paris. In the past, such pauses had signaled the end of the interview as both sides struggled to find a polite way to go about their business. In the end, the Sheikh would rise and apologize for having an urgent appointment. He waited for Sheikh Yassin to rise.

But he didn't rise. Rather, he looked at Parker with great sadness and asked in a tone that bordered on the apologetic. "Could you help me with a small problem, Dr. Parker?"

"Whatever is required," responded Parker, praying that cooperation with the prosecution would gain a reprieve.

"It seems that vicious and unfortunate rumors have circulated concerning you and my granddaughter," the Sheikh lamented. "Fortunately, you understand our culture and the problems that these rumors pose for her. They make it impossible for her to marry and her father is distraught. Personally, I find them to be the work of those who are attempting to destroy me and my efforts to work out an accommodation with the Embassy. There are also those who would have me kill her to save the honor of the family and the integrity of the Brotherhood. Barbarians, Dr. Parker, Barbarians!"

Parker remained silent, attentive.

"But there is a solution Dr. Parker," Sheikh Yassin continued as if they were discussing an abstract point of religion. "It is in your power to save her life and forge greater cooperation between the Brotherhood and the Embassy. Alas, your role will require great courage."

"I would willingly sacrifice my life for the honor of your granddaughter," responded Parker. He spoke solemnly as befits one waiting for the judge to pronounce his sentence.

"I wish you a long life," replied the Sheikh, relieved that Parker was proving cooperative. "There are, however, certain formalities that must be attended to. Nothing, of course, that can't be undone at the appropriate moment."

"I am at your disposal," responded Parker stoically. The Nubian had given him a general idea of the script. All that remained were the details.

"I would be honored if you would marry my granddaughter," continued the Sheikh with a graciousness that reflected a growing affection for the American. "Unfortunately, it will not be a long marriage. Perhaps a minute or two. The divorce will quell the rumors and she will be free to marry a groom of her choosing. Strange customs we have, don't you agree, Dr. Parker? A divorced woman bears none of the scars of a virgin. Indeed, this very day she will marry one of the most prominent politicians in Egypt."

Parker had not foreseen the news of Zahra's impending marriage, and he struggled to suppress his anger. He was aware that she would marry again, but not on the very day of their marriage. Her sentence had been more severe than his own. But then, that was the way of life in the Middle East.

"I am sorry, my son," continued the Sheikh, gently. "Please do not judge me harshly. It is God's will."

Parker again nodded his assent.

"But first," continued the Sheikh, "it is necessary that you become a Muslim." His voice was nonchalant, as if it were a matter on little import.

Parker took his cue and quietly intoned the passage, "There is no God but the God, and Mohammed is his messenger." He had become a Muslim.

"When will the wedding take place?" asked Parker, not really wanting to know.

"Why," exclaimed the Sheikh, "we will do it now. Everything is in place. Zahra awaits in the next room, and three of the world's most learned men of religion have arrived to witness the ceremony."

*   *   *   *

And witness they did. Zahra, proud to the end, entered the room in a simple robe that hid everything and promised more. Parker declared that he had taken her as his wife in front of the esteemed witnesses and she had assented. Tea was served, and in an equally simple ceremony, he divorced her. "I divorce thee. I divorce thee. I divorce thee." Three times the words were repeated in front of witnesses, and that was that. Technically, the divorce would not be final for three months, Islamic law allowing a cooling off period for husbands to come to their senses. But such details are easily waved in the case of remarriage.

Zahra had seemed strangely at ease, almost ethereal. They hadn't spoken, but in a fleeting moment he had read her lips. "I love you. You will always be my husband." Romantic rubbish or a threat?

"You have been very gracious, Dr. Parker," smiled Sheikh Yassin. "Zahra has been cleansed and the Brotherhood spared embarrassment. I can see no reason why our rapprochement with the Embassy should not evolve smoothly." As an afterthought, he added, "The Brotherhood will not harm you. We shall do our best to keep others from doing so. Fortunately, your mission in Cairo is coming to an end. You have served your country well."

Parker believed the Sheikh. It would be unseemly of him to kill an Embassy spy on the eve of their new arrangement. How fortunate that the Sheikh and Jake saw eye to eye on just about everything. They agreed on the need to destroy the jihadists and they shared a passionate desire to overthrow the Minister of Interior. They also agreed that Honest Ali was the right man to do the job.

As he turned the corner surrounded by the Sheikh's bodyguards, Parker caught a glimpse of a large delegation entering the Mosque. It was headed by an elegant gentleman thirty years Zahra's senior surrounded by a phalanx of bodyguards. The Sheikh had wasted no time. A public ceremony would occur later, but Zahra would be a married woman before he had reached Galal Street. The giant seemed almost sympathetic, but said nothing.

The Sheikh, too, had been surprised by Zahra's gracious ease during the triple ceremony. Indeed, she had been almost too at ease. He knew his granddaughter well and said a silent prayer for the soul of Ali. For the moment, however, all was well. The newlyweds would be on their way to Monte Carlo for an extended honeymoon. If Parker were wise, he would be gone before their return. Ali was a jealous man.

*   *   *   *

Parker felt no remorse. The pain of his loss was eased by a sense of relief and the sure knowledge that he had saved Zahra from disgrace if not worse. The link between the Embassy and Brotherhood remained on track and, hopefully, he had saved his own life. True, he had acknowledged that there was but one God and that Mohammed was his Prophet, but was that a sin? He had not disavowed his belief in Christ as the son of God, but merely acknowledged that God had many prophets. He was the one God: the God of the Jews, the God of the Christians, and God of the Muslims. Christ was the Son of God. Mohammed was a prophet just as Moses, Noah, and Abraham were prophets. Where was the problem? None were on par with the holy trilogy.

Neither was Parker troubled by his temporary bigamy other than the fact that it had ended before it was consummated. Contracts forged under duress are not binding. The same was true of his forced conversion to Islam. If he went to hell it would be for fornication, not bigamy.

To banish whatever pangs of conscience existed, he vowed to confess his bigamy to both his wife and Mandy. He knew that neither would believe him and neither did. His wife accused him of poor taste and suggested that he grow up. The session with Mandy was more painful, the pretty one accusing him of belittling the institution of marriage at the very time that they were shaping their future together. Perhaps, he thought in half seriousness, it would have been better if they had believed him.

Chapter 28

Eve of the March

It was early evening as the throngs began gathering in the courtyard of Sheikh Yassin's mosque in Boulaq. The green neon lights that adorned the minaret flickered on and loudspeakers called the faithful to the early evening prayer, the fourth of the five mandatory prayers required of Muslims.

As a rule, the evening prayer was poorly attended, the faithful preferring to spread their prayer rugs wherever chance found them. But tonight was different. The Sheikh's special message was to be delivered at the end of the prayer. They came from Boulaq and they came from the four corners of Cairo. Of all of the banned sermons that were passed surreptitiously from hand to hand, Sheikh Yassin's were the most sought after. The mosque was soon filled to capacity as were the courtyards and alleys beyond. The circus had begun.

The Sheikh spoke to his congregation with a fervor of one who has been divinely guided. They had heard much of the speech before, but they listened as one listened to a saint, hanging on every word in the hope of finding the secret to redemption. Most of all, they listened for news of Zahra, his granddaughter. She had disappeared completely. Had she been sent abroad or had she been…? They dare not ask, for that would bring bad luck.

"Ah, my friends," he intoned softly, "we have another election before us. Ho, hum, another fraudulent election. Vain hopes that Islam can defeat the forces of evil in honest elections. What chance does faith have in the face of fraud and force? We preach patience and more patience, but to what avail? Has your lot improved? Has hope for a better future soared? Has morality increased? Are your children educated? Are you free from the yoke of repression and foreign domination? No! No! A thousand times no. Then why do we persist with this silly charade?"

"We persist," he continued with a slight increase of cadence, "because the Glorious Koran, the word of God revealed to the Prophet Mohammed, has ordered us to be patient. Be patient with your troubles and trust in God. The jihadists did not obey God's commandments and what have they wrought? Muslims are killing Muslims by the hundreds of thousands. The world weeps at the death of a single Israeli, but who weeps at the death of the hundreds of thousands of Muslims killed by the jihadists? Oh, how the Americans play us for fools. They encouraged the jihadists to attack the United States in order to blacken the name of Islam. The Americans were waiting for an excuse to occupy our lands and steal our oil, and the jihadists have given them that excuse. Did the jihadists really believe that the destruction of a few buildings would topple the American government? How ridiculous. America is not ruled by plots and coups. It is ruled by laws and institutions just as the world of Islam was ruled by the law of God during the glorious days of the Prophet Mohammed and his successors. Even if the jihadist bombs had caused consternation in the US, were the jihadists poised to attack and take over the country? How could they? The jihadists have no army. They are mosquitoes. They bite and run, hoping their poisonous venom will destroy their foe. But their venom destroys only Muslims, my friends, hundreds of thousands of God fearing Muslims."

"There was no consternation in the United States, my friends. The jihadists' strike angered the Americans and they called us barbarians. 'Kill Muslims,' they shouted. 'Launch a new crusade. Give their lands to the Israelis.' That is what the jihadists wrought. They played into the hands of the Americans and the Israelis by perverting God's message of peace and development. That is what they wrought."

"And where are these heroes now? Our home grown jihadists have sold their souls to the Minister of Interior to escape prison. The government and the jihadists are two peas in a pod. A few stragglers kill an American here and a Brit there, but most of all they kill Muslims. How convenient for the Americans and the Israelis."

"Why, my friends, do the Minister of Interior and the jihadists cooperate? They cooperate because they fear the Brotherhood. The jihadists fear the enlightened message of the Brotherhood. They would have us return to an era of backwardness. The Prophet Mohammed was not the end of God's work, my friends.

He was its beginning. It was God who inspired Muslims to take the lead in developing modern science. Do you think that God wants you to live in these hideous slums? Do you think that God wants Egypt to be ruled by the Americans and the Israelis? Why would he want that? Do you think that God wants Muslims to slaughter Muslims as our jihadist brothers have done? No, my friends. Arabs are his chosen people. He revealed his word in the Arabic language and chose an Arab to be his final prophet. God wants the Arabs to rule in his name."

"Why, then, do we suffer humiliation and sorrow? Are you really in doubt? We suffer because we defied God by placing greed above morality. Science was not used to glorify God, but to deny religion. We have defied God's will and we have suffered the consequences. Muslims slaughtered Muslims while Christians and Jews conquered the world."

"Praise be to heaven, my friends, the door remains open. Repent and build an Islamic state that praises God and honors his commandments. Not a replica of the past unable to survive in the world of the 21st century, but a modern Islamic paradise that unites Muslims and spreads the message of God to all humanity. Keep your hearts pure so that you may enter the kingdom heaven. Embrace technology so that Islam can rule the world."

"Will the Americans allow it? Do they not rule the world? Ah, my friends, the Americans have no choice. We all bow to God. The Americans have defied God and lost the way. All their weapons and technology could not subdue the Iraqis or the Afghans or the Iranians or the Palestinians. Their power has peaked and they are in decline. Why? Because they have defied God."

"Now is our opportunity to please God, my friends. Not by closing our eyes to the world, but by conquering it through faith and progress. Seize the technological wonders developed by the Americans and use them to serve God. Build upon what God has inspired and he will reward you with the splendors of the universe and the heavens beyond. That, my friends, is the message of the Glorious Koran and the traditions of the Prophet. The Prophet Mohammed did not look to the past. He looked to the future and Muslims ruled the world. Do you really want to live under the rule of crazed maniacs who burn hospitals in the name of God?"

"But let us return to the Americans, my friends. They are very clever, these *kawagas*. They fear the power of Islam and they have lost faith in the puppet governments that they have created to suppress us. How could they not lose faith in governments who make deals with the very jihadists who were responsible for attacking the United States?"

"What, then, is the alternative? In reality, my friends, they have but two choices: democracy or a military coup. We will win fair elections and they know that we will win fair elections. They can have a military coup at the drop of a hat. Oh, how our generals line up to attend the special parties of the American Ambassador. There are even those in the government who incline in that direction. But what good will a military coup do for the Americans? We know these generals. They are the same old wine in new bottles. No my friends, the only choice available to the Americans is the Brotherhood! Your patience will be rewarded."

"You see, my friends, I have learned a secret. The Americans are preparing to abandon the government. It is merely a matter of time. At this very moment, a debate is raging within the Embassy between the advocates of a military coup and the advocates of a peaceful transition to Islamic rule. We offer the Americans peace, development and morality. A military coup offers only anger, violence and ultimate defeat. Which will the Americans choose? It is their decision, but I don't think that they really want more violence. Haven't they had their fill? Do they want to occupy Egypt as they occupied Vietnam and Iraq?"

"Our duty is to force America's hand by embarrassing the ruling party in tomorrow's elections. Listen carefully, my friends. I did not say that we must win the elections, for how can one expect the forces of evil to conduct a fair election. I said embarrass the government in the elections. Show the world that the soul of Egypt is an Islamic soul. Force the Minister of Interior to suppress us with clubs. Do not back away from the security guards, but do not fight. Let the world see how the thugs who rule us beat unarmed citizens. Let the Americans see that the government has lost control and can no longer rule. Prison, do not worry. You will not be there for long."

"Will our rise to power be immediate? Of course not. Why would we want to sweep the country into chaos? No, my friends, but you will see Brothers and Sisters gradually moving into key positions. We don't want to alarm the *kawagas*, do we?" The crowd breaks into laughter.

"Has the Brotherhood negotiated a deal with the Americans? No! Why would we negotiate a deal with the *kawagas* when we are on the threshold of victory? They have heard the beat my friends. They have heard the throbbing pulse of Islam reborn."

"Will the Minister of Interior surrender power without a fight? No, my friends, he will not. He has prepared the most vicious of traps to divert our attention from the elections. A trap you say! What trap? An ingenious trap my friends, a trap worthy of the devil himself. The Minister of Interior has arranged for the feminists to march on election day. He assumed that the march would detract us from our duty. Alas, his agents informed him that we would not be swayed by his silly parade. What do we care if ladies want to march? And so my friends, he invited Israeli feminists to join in the march. Not just Israeli feminists, my friends, but Israeli gays. Yes, my friends, the Minister of Interior has conspired with the Israelis to send feminists and gays to disrupt the elections." Gasps are heard throughout the crowd.

"Ah, but we will not fall into this trap. We will not be tricked into defying God by disrupting this infamous march. It is the test of our faith. God is watching. We must not fail! We will deal with the Israeli pederasts when the time comes. Be patient with your troubles."

"A wonderful story you say, but how did you learn of this evil plot? I will tell you how I learned of the evil plot. I will tell you how I know. The *kawagas* sent a spy to infiltrate our ranks, but they failed. God informed us of their evil intent and showed us the way to turn this spy against his masters. The American spy became a double agent who converted to Islam. It was he who informed us that the Americans had lost faith in the government and it was he who informed us of the heinous plot hatched by the Minister of Interior and the Israelis."

"How did we turn this spy against his masters? I will tell you how? God sent us an angel to befuddle and confuse the American spy. Not an ordinary person, but a princess of rare beauty. The Americans are clever. Nothing else would do. The American sent to deceive us was the devil himself. Yet, even he was overwhelmed by her beauty. He begged for her favors. He opened his heart to her and revealed the secrets of the Embassy, all but the most secret of secrets. He demanded marriage as the price of his ultimate treason, but how could she marry a non-Muslim. He converted, my friends. He converted to Islam and they were married. Then, of course, she divorced him. Will these *kawaga* never learn?"

Some of the crowd laughs with the other break into "*Allah Akbar.*

The Sheikh continues, "I am pleased to report, my friends, that God has rewarded her with marriage to one of the most prominent men in Egypt. I cannot reveal the name, but you shall read it in the papers. They are now on their honeymoon. Observe how God rewards those who serve him."

"What shall we do to this devil that was sent to destroy us? What shall we do with him?"

Shouts of, "Kill him! Kill him! Kill all Americans!" erupt in the crowd.

"No, my friends. No. No. No. When will you ever learn? Kill Americans and they will have an excuse to destroy Cairo the way they destroyed Baghdad. Use your heads, my friends. Use your heads and bide your time."

"Besides, we cannot kill the *kawaga* spy. He has become a Muslim. We cannot kill Muslims. Our enemies want us to kill Muslims, just as they want the jihadists to kill Muslims and the Minister of Interior to kill Muslims. Kill Muslims! Save us the trouble. Kill Muslims so Christians and Jews can rule the world and destroy the message of the Prophet Mohammed. Kill Muslims. Oh, how they deceive us into killing Muslims. God will punish the *kawaga* spy just as he will punish all Muslims who betray him. He will relegate the *kawaga* to the most heinous of hells. Words defy me, my friends. I cannot describe the agonies that the *kawaga* will suffer. But the right to judge is God's alone. Woe to he who usurps the power of God. Woe to he who is distracted from the election. *Allah Akbar.*"

Recordings of Sheikh Yassin's message were passed from hand to hand. They were played in small groups and shouted from the loudspeakers of the Brotherhood's mosques. They accompanied the Brotherhood's poll watchers and their local organizers. Both would be targets of police brutality and attacks by thugs in the pay of local notables. But still they came, taking their place in the dark that preceded the dawn prayer. And with them came Western reporters and photographers, their identities disguised by native robes.

* * * *

The Minister of Interior played the tape several times before ripping it from the machine and smashing it against the wall. The Sheikh had declared war, but why now? There was but one answer. Jake had conspired with the Brotherhood to destroy him.

The Minister of Interior's one hope was that Jake would be recalled to Washington. The Secretary of State had said as much to the Egyptian ambassador in Washington. It was known in diplomatic circles that he feared Jake. But first he, the Minister of Interior, had to prove to Washington that he was still in control. Let the Brotherhood do their best. He would refresh their memory about how democracy works in the Middle East. Washington would be pleased.

* * * *

Sheikh Hassan, the leader of the jihadists, also listened to Sheikh Yassin's speech with care. He reached the same conclusion as the Minister of Interior. "My friend Yassin has cut a deal with the Americans," he grumbled to his adjutant. "The truce is over."

"Pity," glowered the adjutant. "We could have used a few more months."

"Or more," responded Hassan. "Praise God for the time that we have had. Tell the units to go into the crisis mode. Even if the Minister of Interior survives, he will be forced by the Americans to tear us from our hovels and the tunnels beneath them. Blood will pour."

"But he won't survive," said the adjutant. "The President will sacrifice him to the Americans in order to save his soul. It will be a new general that leads the attack."

"So be it," sighed Sheikh Hassan. He then closed his eyes and prayed for word that the jihadist leaders in Europe were ready to strike. If only the promised global attack would come soon.

* * * *

Mizjaji listened to the speech in the shadows of the Mosque, his bodyguards ever alert for an attack by Sheikh Yassin's men. The giant and his men, however, were nowhere to be seen. "No doubt," Mizjaji smiled to himself, "they were taking up positions for the election. A good sign, indeed. He would have the march to himself." So great was his joy that he found it difficult to constrain his *Allah Akbar*s. But it was more than that. He had a mystical feeling that Sheikh Yassin was talking to him personally, that he was encouraging him to rape and pillage.

* * * *

The Mosad and the CIA, too, had analyzed the speech. The Mosad agent was concerned and signaled warnings to Tel Aviv, but it was too late. Gloria and her entourage were already in Cairo. Extra security guards were demanded by the Israeli Embassy, but the Minister of Interior could offer no help. His forces were already deployed at the election sites.

The CIA agent, by contrast, found the speech comforting. It promised destruction of the jihadists and it forbade attacks on Americans. There were a few de rigueur references to US colonialism, but that was to be expected. Something was in the works, and he gave Mandy a knowing wink as he handed her a translated copy of the speech. He wanted to do more than wink, but she was bonkers for the American spy.

* * * *

Mandy read the transcript of the speech with alarm. Her heart froze and tears welled from her eyes. Parker was telling the truth about his bigamy! And yet, how could she complain. This most romantic of actors had played his role to perfection. The Muslim Brotherhood was on board with no trace of a deal. The Sheikh had said so himself. Perfect diplomacy. Was Washington subtle enough to appreciate what had been done? She would explain it to Jake once her emotions were under control. In her heart of hearts, she knew that it wasn't his bigamy that had moved her to tears. It was the reality that Parker's mission was over. There would be no summer extension. He had become a liability. How much time did he have? The Sheikh had given him a reprieve, but for how long? Days? Hours?

Smith read the speech and patted her on the shoulder in compassion. "You haven't lost him," he whispered. "He will divorce his wife and you will have a different post next year. Believe me, you are not the kind of woman that men forget. I will handle the details."

She squeezed his hand in appreciation, but said nothing.

Jake was too delighted for words. The more he listened to Mandy, the more he knew that he had the winning hand. The Minister of Interior was dead money. The Secretary of State was dead money. There would be a coup. Washington couldn't allow Muslims to rule the most important country in the Arab world whatever their bullshit about peace and harmony. Honest Ali would be in charge.

* * * *

Gloria had pointedly avoided the Israeli Embassy and was unaware of the speech. It was hard enough to manage her Israeli contingent without having to deal with the Cultural Attaché and Mosad agent. The gays were proving uncooperative and Parker's wife seemed diffident, preoccupied. The more Gloria focused on last minute details, the more Parker's wife assaulted her with prattle about marriage and children. When Gloria told her to "grow up," she had burst into tears and fled. "Good riddance," said Gloria to herself. "She was getting in the way. Everything is in order and we will have the church to ourselves."

Chapter 29

Let the March Begin

A small convey of armored Chevy SUV's approached the parade route and parked in a side street. The haze of dawn had given way to a cloudless sky. It would be a perfect day for the march. Mandy sat in the middle car and peered out nervously. They were early. The march would not begin for at least an hour; probably two hours or more if things ran true to form. Time in Cairo was relative.

Ominous figures moved in the shadows, and she saw her security guard unleash his pistol, a mammoth weapon that could stop an elephant in its tracks. The marines in the lead and trail cars did the same, but then relaxed as two children tumbled from the shadows, pushing and shoving as they scrambled for a ball. Mandy cringed. "Why is it that Americans find Arab children so frightening?" she asked herself half audibly.

"Because they carry bombs," responded her Marine security guard, dryly. His face bore the shrapnel wounds of duty in Iraq and he felt the danger of the march more keenly than she. How many peaceful marches in Iraq had exploded in carnage, mutilated bodies littering the streets, many of them American soldiers? His job was to protect her and he intended to do so.

Other shadows moved and the security guard again fingered his cannon. Those who had experienced Iraq shot first and asked question later.

"Please put the gun away," Mandy pleaded. "We are on a diplomatic mission. Gunfire will destroy everything."

"I have my orders, Ma'am," responded the guard. It would be a long day.

* * * *

The busses picked up Gloria at the church and stopped at the designated hostels en-route to the march. Her nerves were on edge as she studied the vehicles that had begun to crowd Cairo's streets. She had expected more police and was suddenly seized by the fear that most Israelis feel when they find themselves alone in Egypt. "We crave acceptance," she whispered to herself, "but oh how we are hated." A sudden swerve of the bus tore her from her thoughts, and she looked up to see a convoy of armed SUV's go flying by. Sirens screamed and the diplomatic flag of the US Ambassador furled in the wind. The Ambassador, ensconced in an armored Cadillac limousine with tinted windows, was on his way to the airport. Or, was he?

Parker struggled to catch a glimpse of the parade route as his convoy sped by. His wife looked straight ahead, still stunned by the frantic hammering on their apartment door as Smith shouted, "Open up! You are on your way to the airport." He was surrounded by marine guards, ready to break the door down if necessary. There had been no telephone warning.

"Too risky," Smith had explained as he pushed them into the Ambassador's limousine. "Your phone is tapped and we had warnings of an assassination attempt. Your things will follow." Parker prayed that the results of the project would be among them.

The convoy sped directly to the runway, and the door of a delayed Air France jet closed as they entered. The pyramids faded into the background and Parker reclined in his first class seat and closed his eyes. Smith had done them well.

* * * *

The Israeli busses came to a halt a block from Mandy's convoy, but Gloria was unaware of its presence. She had expected the streets to be lined with uniforms, but only an occasional traffic motorcycle wound its way through milling crowd. Parker's wife had promised to attend, but she was no where to be seen. Gloria was worried by her absence, for the presence of Constance Parker would have assured that the Embassy was watching. Had something gone wrong, or was Constance pouting because Gloria had snapped at her in a moment of anger? Gloria rebuked herself for her impatience, but there was no time for recriminations.

Bus loads of Egyptian feminists were arriving, but not as many as she had expected. Nor, were there signs of the plump ladies. The Israelis, proudly wearing the symbols of their faith, would be easily recognized. Most of the swarming crowd were shabby onlookers, curious for a diversion from their drab existence. They seemed peaceful enough, most laughing and buying roasted corn or other snacks from the ubiquitous vendors. It was all very disorganized, all very Egyptian. Even the organizers seemed confused about precisely how to start.

* * * *

Mizjaji's men were in place, lurking in the shadows where the children played. He restrained them with difficulty. "Not here," he commanded in a soothing voice that oozed confidence. "The road is too broad. Wait until the street narrows and there is no place to run. Then we will strike. Strike the Israelis and avoid Egyptians. Once the panic erupts, make your way to the targets. That's where the best goods are. We should have at least two hours to take God's bounty. Even then, there will be so many looters that we will go unnoticed."

They waited, but when the signal came they cared little whom or where they struck. Three squads wielding flaming butagaz canisters seared their way through the crowd like crazed animals. Others stabbed indiscriminately, grabbing purses and stripping their victims of their jewels as they fell. Egyptians and Israelis alike, the wretched of Boulaq wrecking their revenge on the rich in the name of God. Feminism was a rich lady's sport. A crazed man wielding a Uzi charged Mandy's convoy but was stopped in his tracks by the shrapnel scarred Marine, the sulfurous fumes of his cannon dwarfed by the stench of burning flesh. Mandy fainted. He puked. It was so much like Iraq.

It was a bad scene and it was all on film. It was on Israeli film, Brotherhood film, and the film of the international media. Most reporters were covering the elections, but the chosen few were following the march. All provided graphic pictures of Mizjaji, his scraggly beard and tattered robe personifying the image of the crazed jihadist. Captured on film, too, were the virulent jihadist slogans scrawled on the buildings that lined the parade route. Sheikh Yassin had left nothing to chance. Scenes of election brutality paled by comparison.

In retrospect, Mizjaji had underestimated his opportunity for pillage. Carnage reigned for most of the day. The morning sun had been an illusion and the predicted sandstorm descended with the unleashing of the gas canisters. The gusts came slowly at first, triggering mini-tornados in the dust as shrieking marchers trampled each other in a frantic effort to find safety. But where to run? Flames were coming from all directions as madmen, their knives gleaming in the last rays of the morning sun, slashed whoever crossed their path.

Panic seized Cairo as looters poured from streets of the march into the adjoining neighborhoods and those beyond in an ever cascading circle of violence. Egyptian troops surrounded the Embassy as tank formations, alerted by the President, crawled toward Cairo. They served only to ignite fears of a coup. It was clear to all that the Minister of Interior had lost control of the situation.

Mizjaji surveyed the carnage with a glee that comes only to those who are truly insane. It was his moment of glory. He was, indeed, the angel of death. But his bride! Where was his bride? Ignoring his bodyguards, he staggered through the carnage in search of Zahra. He would have her or no one would have her. Flames seared his dangling arm, but he felt nothing. A knife plunged in his back and he fell senseless to the ground, his mouth twisted in a hideous grin. His assailant smiled with quiet satisfaction as he ripped Mizjaji's holy cloak from his body. It was now he who would be prince of the believers.

The number of dead and wounded remained a mystery. How was one to count bodies in the blinding sand? It was for the best, for no one wanted to count. Sirens screamed, but to no avail. Headlights were useless against the sand; the roads choked as the rich feminists fled the chaos. Little matter, most ambulances were carrying wounded from the polling places. Caught unawares, the Egyptian President informed reporters that criminals had wounded a handful of marchers intent on disrupting the elections. "Obviously," he noted "it was the work of foreign infiltrators." If the Israelis knew, they didn't say. A diplomatic crisis was at hand, and tensions with Egypt were already at the breaking point. The American Embassy remained mum.

Chapter 30

The Morning After the Night Before

Dawn brought a terse announcement from the Egyptian President that order had been restored. He thanked the army for their prompt action and acknowledged that the elections had been marred by irregularities. New elections, he promised, would be held during the coming year. No results were announced. He closed by accepting the resignation of the Minister of Interior.

The Brotherhood proclaimed that it had won the elections and demanded that the results be made public. Negotiations took place behind the scenes and Honest Ali was appointed Minister of Interior. Other opposition politicians were appointed to minor posts, but the ruling party was allowed to save face.

Honest Ali issued a brief statement by satellite praising the Egyptian President for his fairness and thanking his former colleagues in the military for their vote of confidence. He reiterated the Egyptian's President promise of fair elections once the situation had stabilized and vowed to declare war on those who used violence to pervert the true meaning of Islam. The truce with the jihadists was at an end.

*   *   *   *

"It all happened so fast," Jake lamented to Smith.

"It always does," replied Smith dryly, "and we are always surprised." He was no longer afraid of Jake. He knew the drill. Those in charge had to go. Then, in a moment of prudent reflection, he softened his tone and congratulated Jake for shattering the truce between the government and the jihadists. Who could predict the future? Jake could well become the next Secretary of State.

Jake, as Smith had predicted, was recalled to Washington for consultations. His friend, the President, received him at the White House with full honors and awarded him the nation's highest medal for distinguished service to the United States by a civilian. There were allusions to a very senior position once the President was re-elected. Jake understood the message. The senior position would be consummate with the funds that he raised for the coming campaign.

Jake wore the medal with pride. He had gone all in and won. He had kicked ass. True, there hadn't been a coup per se, but the truce was shattered and his man was in power. He didn't know much about foreign policy, but he knew a great deal about raising money for presidential elections.

Smith and Mandy received the credit they deserved and were duly rewarded. Smith was named DCM in Jordan shortly after Jake's departure. Mandy was posted in Jerusalem following her convalescence from the march. She had been unharmed, but had spent three hours in various states of consciousness as the carnage swirled around her stranded convoy. Revulsion was eased by thoughts of marriage to Parker and her curious attraction to the Marine guard, his face scarred by shrapnel in Iraq.

Sheikh Yassin strolled past the headquarters of Sheikh Hassan and found it deserted, "Everything has its purpose," he whispered to himself. "The right to judge is God's alone. *Allah Akbar.*"

Gloria Goldensickle was unrepentant. She abhorred violence, but the gruesome pictures of jihadists slaughtering innocent females had captured the attention of the world. Perhaps now the women of the world would unite in the name of sanity. There would be no more grants from the Israeli government, but she would find a way. Perhaps she would visit rural Nebraska.

Parker and his wife sat in silence as their plane landed in Chicago. He followed the news on the Internet as best he could and guessed the rest. He, too, had won. He could write his own ticket. Everywhere, that is, except Egypt. "Perhaps," he mused, "he would spend some time in Jerusalem. Oh, how this most holy of cities dazzled." For the moment, however, he needed time to decompress.

Constance Parker read the Bible and thanked God for their deliverance from evil. She loved Parker, but knew that the Christian struggle against evil would be a long one. Perhaps his promised month in rural Nebraska would help.

978-0-595-47538-4
0-595-47538-8

Printed in the United States
99372LV00006B/70/A